FREEDOM
of the SOUL

FREEDOM of the SOUL

TRACEY BATEMAN

BARBOUR
PUBLISHING

© 2006 by Tracey Bateman

ISBN 978-1-59789-221-6

All scripture quotations are taken from the King James Version of the Bible.

This book is a work of fiction. Names, characters, places, and incidents are either products of the author's imagination or used fictitiously. Any similarity to actual people, organizations, and/or events is purely coincidental.

For more information about Tracey Bateman, please access the author's Web site at the following Internet address: www.traceybateman.com

Cover design by Müllerhaus Publishing Group (mullerhaus.net)
Cover photography by Gloria Roundtree

Published by Barbour Publishing, Inc., P.O. Box 719, Uhrichsville, OH 44683, www.barbourbooks.com

Our mission is to publish and distribute inspirational products offering exceptional value and biblical encouragement to the masses.

ecpa Member of the
Evangelical Christian
Publishers Association

Printed in the United States of America
5 4 3 2 1

~ Dedication ~

To Chris Lynxwiler—sister of my heart and forever friend.
It's a pleasure to be in the trenches with you.
This year has been challenging for us both,
but God's grace is sufficient.

~ Acknowledgments ~

Jesus—You make all things possible.

My husband and kids—Rusty, Cat, Mike, Stevan, and Will.
Your love and support, smiles and hugs
give me wings and courage to carry on.
There is no family on earth I would choose other than ours.

Frances Devine (Mom) and Vivian Bateman (Mom-in-law)—
thank you for taking care of so much for me
while I worked to turn this book in.

Pinkies—my prayer support and closest friends.
I'd be lost without you.

To the folks at Barbour Publishing, especially Becky Germany—
it's been a tough year for me, and you graciously showed me
the love and support I needed to get this book finished.

Last but definitely not least—Kathy Ide, my copyeditor, who
worked side by side with me to turn in the best manuscript possible.
I truly would not have been able to do this without you.
You are top-notch.

Dear Readers,

My family history tells of a young man, my great-great-great-grandfather's brother, who fell ill and was sent by his father to be nursed in the slave quarters. While recovering, he fell in love with the young slave girl who cared for him. After he was well again, he took her to Mexico and married her.

That story of deep, abiding love has always struck a chord in my heart, and I knew, while writing a series that explores racial tension and racial relationships, that I'd have to include that scenario. This book is a work of fiction. All I know about that true-life love story is what I told you in the first paragraph of this letter. I imagined what they might have been like. But I can never know for sure.

One thing I've learned in researching and writing The Penbrook Diaries is that real love in all of its forms (familial, romantic, friendship) transcends race. In this series, I worked to show the hearts of the individuals represented so that, hopefully, each reader was able to remove the image of color and see the relationships as they existed in spite of racial boundaries. I loved each of these characters. Each story. And I thank you for coming alongside me and enjoying the stories, as well.

Until we meet again, may God bless you richly and shine His light on you.

Tracey Bateman

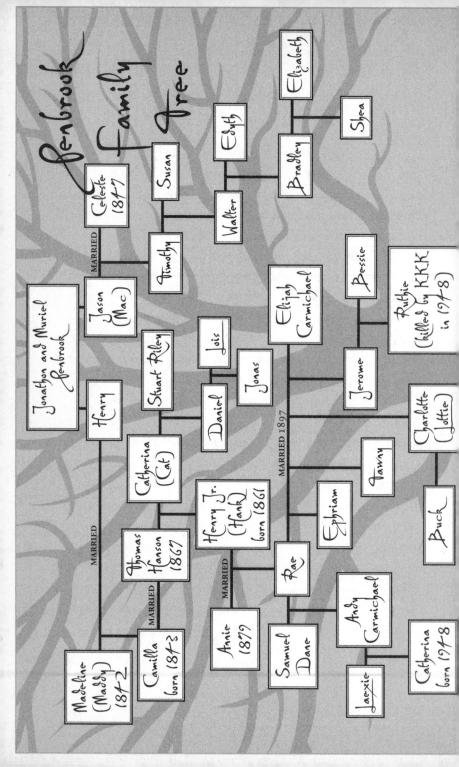

CHAPTER ONE
OREGON 1949

Shea hated drizzle. She preferred the sky to remain still or open up and pound the earth with the force of its fury. Something about all-or-nothing appealed to her. Today, as she walked away from Granddad's gravesite, she wished it would just pour. If the sky would weep, it might make up for her own lack of emotion. Perhaps then Granddad would be mourned. Shea didn't have the capacity to grieve. Not now. At this moment she could only wonder how on earth she was going to survive.

The old man's death had been no surprise. A weak heart, made weaker by influenza, had finally given out, and he'd slipped away without much of a fight. Of course, he never was much of a fighter. Shea's daddy had been the fighter in the family. And he was just as dead as Granddad.

With a shuddering breath, she tossed a handful of dirt onto the casket. "Good-bye, Granddad," she whispered. Tears burned her eyes as she slipped the preacher a few dollars.

A sense of dread filled her at the thought of returning to the empty house. Without her grandfather to take care of night and day, she didn't know what she'd do with her time. And with no job, or any prospects for one, she couldn't imagine how she'd pay all the bills.

The only other mourner in attendance intercepted Shea as she walked back to Granddad's beat-up Ford truck—well, she supposed it belonged to her now. "Miss Shea. I'm awfully sorry for your loss." The hired man twisted his raggedy old hat between his hands and shifted from one foot to the other.

Touched that he'd bothered to come at all, Shea allowed a tight smile. "Thank you, Ernie."

"I wanted to ask. . ." He averted his gaze and cleared his throat. "I. . .uh. . .well, it's. . .it's about my wages."

Ah. So that was it. Now his presence made sense. "Drop by the house in the morning. I'll have your week's pay."

And that would just about deplete her funds. Now all she had left was the house and the ten acres on which it sat. How would she be able to keep up with repairs, taxes, and all the things that Granddad had somehow made sure were always taken care of? To say nothing of putting food on the table.

"Thank you, Miss Shea. I hate to—"

She placed a silencing hand on his arm. "It's all right. We all have to make a living. I owe it to you."

He clapped his hat back on his greasy head and nodded, then walked away. Shea couldn't blame him. It wasn't his fault Granddad didn't have anyone but her to care about him at the end of his life. Granddad. . .slovenly, a man of little integrity. . .no one to be proud of. Still, she loved him. He'd taken care of her all her life. The only family she knew. And she would miss him.

By the time the sky decided to get serious about things, Shea had driven the five miles back to the home place. She stood in the yard, rain soaking the one dress she owned that didn't have a hole in it. She stared up at the rickety old house—the only thing she had to call her own. It wasn't much.

Despair, black as midnight, swept over her.

Maybe if she stood very still, a slice of lightning would cut her down and end her miserable existence. She could join Granddad—wherever he was. Even if he hadn't been much of a human being, she'd never doubted his love for her. And she'd rather have him in her life than be all alone.

The sound of a car engine mingled with the pellets of rain on the house's tin roof, pulling her from her maudlin thoughts. She turned.

"Jackson Sable." The whisper of his name on her lips forced bile to her throat. The despicable man couldn't even wait until Granddad was cold in his grave. She'd been expecting a confrontation with him. Just not this soon.

He slid his fancy new car to a stop, slinging mud across the yard. His audacity ignited a hot fire in Shea's belly. She turned with a jerk of her chin and, in spite of the mud squishing under her feet, stomped to the house with flare.

"Shea Penbrook!" His biting tone angered her even more. Her heart hammered in her chest as she heard his breathing bearing down on her from behind. She quickened her pace, hoping to make it to the door before he caught up to her.

The bruising grip of his fingers cutting into the soft flesh of her upper arms ended that hope. She spun around to face the sixty-something rancher. His brown eyes sparked with fury. "When I call you, you'd best stop. Do you hear me?"

Fear galloped through her. Last time he'd been here, Granddad had chased him off with a shotgun. Where was that thing? Jackson was a dangerous man. Her despair had caused her to forget that fact. She'd been reckless. It wouldn't happen again.

"What do you want, Mr. Sable?"

"You know full well what I want. I hear your grandfather

passed on. Surely you know you can't keep this place together by yourself. A pretty girl like you should go live in the city. Marry some young man and have babies."

The sword twisted deep. Everyone in these parts knew why she wasn't married. She'd only had two chances. Her fiancé, Jeremy, had died in the Pacific. And Jackson himself had torn his son, Colin, from Shea's life. The man had no heart.

Drawing herself up to her full height—all five feet of it—Shea drudged up a haughty look and tone. "Thank you for your concern, Mr. Sable. But I think I'll try to make it right here on Penbrook land." Land that had been in the family for one hundred years.

"What's left of it, you mean."

"All the more reason for me to hang on to what's mine." Although she had no idea how she'd manage to do it.

Anger mottled his face. "Don't push me, girl. This last ten acres splits my land, and I mean to have it. Now, I'm willing to pay you twice what I offered last month, but the deal is only good for forty-eight hours."

Shea tried not to let her jaw drop. Double was enough for her to. . .to go to secretarial school. Live in Chicago. Or New York. Because despite her brave announcement, she longed for change. A fresh start where the name of Penbrook wasn't a cause for shame.

Without giving her a chance to speak, he twisted his lips into that smug sneer she'd come to despise over the years as Granddad sold off the land a few acres at a time. "I'll be back in forty-eight hours with a bank draft." He turned to leave without bothering to say good-bye.

Anger shot through her again. This man deserved to be boiled in oil, drawn and quartered, all manner of ancient torture she'd read about in her great-great-grandfather's books. Still. . .

"Mr. Sable, wait!" The rain beat down on her as she hopped off the porch and stood before him, legs planted defiantly, hands on her hips. "I don't need forty-eight hours. I've already made up my mind."

"Indeed?" His face grew red. "And I suppose you're going to be difficult?"

"The land and the house are yours, but I need a week to pack up and move."

Never had she seen a man's expression change as quickly as Mr. Sable's. Smug satisfaction shifted through her. For once, she had the upper hand.

He recovered his composure with barely a beat. "A wise choice." His eyes raked her figure. Shea fought the urge to gag. "I'll be back tomorrow. I will expect to be given the deed at that time."

"I'll give you the deed when I see cash money. And I told you one week. Not tomorrow. Not the next day. One week from today. If you show yourself on Penbrook land before that time, I might just change my mind."

Mr. Sable sized her up for a moment. Then, apparently unwilling to call her bluff, he pursed his lips. "Cash it is. One week to get out before I take over—lock, stock, and barrel. And don't worry about cleaning the house; it won't be here for long."

"You're tearing it down?" Memories flooded Shea. She'd spent every day of her life after the age of five in this house. Twenty-two years. A lifetime of memories. Some good, some not good. But the thought of her entire existence being reduced to a pile of rubble cramped her stomach.

A sneer curled Jackson's lips. "Do you think my wife would

live in this hovel?" His mockery stung like a yellow jacket. "Surely you know I want the land for my cattle."

"Of course." Shea stuffed down her second thoughts and squared her shoulders. She lifted her chin. "I don't care what you do with it."

But she did care. If her house was gone, she had no home.

Shea climbed the pull-down ladder leading to the attic. The musty smell acted as a tonic, filling her with a sense of satisfied nostalgia. The attic had always been her sanctuary—her port in a troubled sea when the grown-ups downstairs started yelling. Her hiding place when her daddy came staggering home after a night at the roadhouse.

How long had it been since she'd hoisted herself through the square opening and enjoyed the solitude the attic afforded? Three years? Four? At any rate, too long.

She stood, hands on hips, looking around the dusty, cramped space. Despite the wretchedness of the past couple of days, she felt more at peace at this moment than she had in a long time. There was something soothing about being up here in the dust, wearing a pair of Granddad's trousers and suspenders and an old button-down shirt, her hair pulled back with a kerchief.

Boxes of books lined the floor of the attic. Shea had wondered more than once how on earth the half-rotted planks held up under the weight of the boxes—or why Granddad had kept them in the first place. It wasn't as though he ever bothered to bring the books down and read them. But as a girl, Shea had spent hours becoming lost in the pages. *Little Women*, Charles Dickens, Mark Twain, the poetry of Lord Byron. . .oh, what a time she'd had. All alone in a world of make-believe.

She shook her head at the irony. Was it any wonder she couldn't fathom the reality of living in this house alone? That she'd just agreed to sell off the last of her great-great-granddad's legacy? She'd never really lived in this world. Couldn't have borne it.

There wasn't much she could take with her anyway. Or that she wanted, for that matter. The rickety wooden furniture wasn't good for much besides firewood. Anything of value had long since been sold. Even Great-Great-Grandmother Celeste's grand-father clock. The day Jackson's men took that out of the house, Shea, at ten years old, had wept for the loss of heritage. Oh, how she hated Jackson Sable. The devil himself had more kindness.

And here she was giving him exactly what he wanted—the last of Jason McCourt Penbrook's land. Her great-great-grandfather, Mac as he was called, would likely roll over in his grave. The gravesite where Sable cattle would be grazing by this time next year.

Helpless fury swept over her in waves. She reared back and gave the nearest crate a hard kick.

The rotted wood gave way and moved with her foot. A startled cry tore from Shea's throat as splinters gouged into her calf, forcing her to the ground. Reaching forward, she deftly peeled back the broken pieces until she finally pulled her leg free. Luckily Granddad's trousers took the brunt of the sharp edges.

A shrug lifted her shoulders as she studied the destroyed wooden box. She supposed this crate was as good as any to begin with. She intended to look through every single one and examine each book. The furniture she couldn't take; the books she wouldn't leave behind. Not the special ones. Her childhood friends.

She reached inside the dusty box and pulled out an old

volume. A frown marred her freckled brow. She'd never seen this one before.

She opened the cover and pressed her hand to her chest as she read the name sprawled across the inside cover: *Jason McCourt Penbrook*.

> *January 1892*
>
> *Robert Sable came sniffing around again, making another offer on the south pasture. I gave him a good view down the barrel of my shotgun. I've never seen the man so angry, and I admit I got a chuckle out of the whole thing. There's bound to be repercussions. But I'd rather lose the place than sell that evil man one blasted acre.*

Shea gasped. Her stomach flipped over and sank. This must be a sign that she wasn't meant to sell that dirty snake Jackson one more single solitary blade of grass of Penbrook land.

The no-good Sable family had always wanted this land, and her great-great-grandfather Penbrook hadn't felt any better about selling than Granddad. Only Granddad hadn't held out under the pressure. He'd sold off the first field only a month after the land passed to him.

The stinging cuts on her calf were reduced to a mere annoyance in the face of her extraordinary find. Shea hastened to open the crate from the top. Many diaries filled up the space. On a whim, Shea opened more crates. She nearly squealed with glee at the wealth of diaries. Her hands shook as she lifted one at a time and checked the dates. Her heritage, written on yellowed, dusty pages.

She spent the better part of the afternoon arranging the

diaries in order. Tomorrow, when Ernie came for his pay, she would ask him to do one final job for her—bring the crates downstairs. For tonight, she took the first three diaries and carried them carefully down the ladder.

The lonely ache in her chest lifted sometime over the next few hours, although Shea couldn't pinpoint when. All she knew was that after a light meal of leftover beans and cornbread, she was ready to settle into bed with the journals. Hope, foreign and wonderful, swelled in her breast as she carried the journals and the oil lamp to her bedroom, dressed in her threadbare nightgown, and settled into bed with the earliest diary.

> *I must record in as much detail as possible the last month while I have been incapacitated. I have never fully believed Mother's words that God works in mysterious ways, but I can only attribute the events that have brought love into my life to the hand of the Almighty. . . .*

GEORGIA 1847

Mac hurt all over. His muscles, his bones, his insides.

"Try to sit up, Mastuh Penbrook."

The soft words flowed over Mac in lyrical waves, but his eyes hurt too much to open them and see where the voice came from.

"Take some water. It'll soothe your throat."

A firm arm slipped beneath his shoulders. He cried out in pain.

"I's sorry, suh."

Did he detect fear in the gentle voice?

"I'll soak a rag fo' you to suck on."

Fighting against the pain, Mac opened his eyes a slit. He saw a slender, curvaceous young woman. She poured water from a pitcher into a basin and dipped a rag into the clear liquid.

Dizziness swept over him, and he closed his eyes once more. In the next instant, he felt the cool cloth at his dry, cracked lips. He grabbed it and pressed it hard against his parched tongue, sucking like a newborn babe until the sweet liquid trickled down his throat, soothing him like the balm of Gilead.

"Thank you," he whispered once he was no longer able to draw another drop of water from the rag.

"Is that a smile, Mastuh?"

He couldn't answer. But he *felt* a smile.

He awakened again to soft singing and a warm fire. The aroma of cooking meat filled the little cabin.

The young slave girl turned as he opened his eyes. A quick intake of breath filled the cramped room. "Mastuh, you awake again?"

Mac nodded and cast a glance around the dingy shack. "What am I doing here?"

"You don't remember?"

Mac shook his head. "I have no idea."

"You took sick wif de fever. Old Mastuh sent you down here to be nussed."

"I suppose my father was afraid I'd pass along my sickness to Henry. And we couldn't risk getting my brother ill, could we?" Sarcasm thickened his throat.

She averted her gaze to the cloth in her hands as she walked closer and pressed it against his forehead. "I guess so, Mastuh."

Slowly, he began remembering things. Going to bed before

supper, feeling miserable. Waking to muffled voices and violent chills. "How long has it been?"

"Ten days." She took the rag from his head and dipped it in the basin to cool it again.

Mac took hold of her wrist and forced her to look him in the eye. "How do you feel?"

"I's fine, Mastuh. Jus' a little tired." Her eyes widened at the admission. "I's fine," she repeated.

Surveying the dark circles under her eyes, Mac felt a twinge of guilt. "You've been caring for me round the clock, I take it?"

She nodded.

"Alone?"

"Old Mastuh say he din' want more dan me catchin' it if you wuz givin' the sickness out."

He sighed. He'd never forgive himself if this sweet, young slave girl became ill and perished because of him.

He sat up with difficulty. The blood rushed to his head and he closed his eyes, taking deep breaths to steady himself.

"Please, Mastuh Mac, suh. You best go on and lay back down. I believe you's over the wust of it, but you is far from well. And you is still all yellow."

"I'm fine. I want you to give me that water and that rag, then you should go rest." He glanced around the room again as the words left his lips. "I'm in your bed?"

Her light brown skin reddened. She nodded.

Mac scowled. "Where have you been sleeping the past ten days?"

She hesitantly lifted a shoulder. Mac reached out and raised her chin until her eyes were level with his. "Tell me."

"Over there," she said with a sigh and a jerk of her head toward the floor in front of the fireplace.

"Have you been comfortable? Warm enough?"

"Yessuh."

He didn't believe her. But she was right. He wasn't well enough to be up. With a groan, he lowered his body back to the mattress and rested his head on the pillow. "Well, you can't sleep here again until the bedding has been replaced."

His stomach gave a loud protest against the last few days of neglect combined with the heavenly aroma that filled the room.

She gave him an indulgent smile. "I'll fix you a bowl of stew, Mastuh."

"I'd be grateful."

"I's glad you's doin' so much better, Mastuh Penbrook."

He gave a short laugh. "You're ready to get me out of your cabin, I suppose."

"You ain't been no trouble at all."

Of course he had been. But she wouldn't admit it.

She filled a bowl and carried it across the room. Gracefully, she lowered herself to his bedside, her slight weight barely making a dent in the straw mattress. She scooped a spoonful of stew and raised it to his lips.

"What's your name?" he asked before accepting the bite. He watched her expression as he chewed the wonderful chunks of meat, potatoes, and vegetables.

"Celeste, Mastuh." She kept her gaze averted as she lifted another bite for him.

"That's a lovely name."

She dipped her head and fed him the bite. "Thank you."

He waved her hand away as the food in his stomach filled up the emptiness much quicker than before his illness. She set the bowl aside and started to rise.

Mac reached out a restraining hand. "Wait. Talk to me for a few minutes."

She dropped back to the bed. "Yes, Mastuh."

"Do you live here alone, Celeste?"

She shook her head. "No, suh. My ma and sistuh lives here, too."

"Where are they staying while I take over your quarters?"

"My ma's staying wif Mammy Jasmine."

"And your sister?"

Her nimble fingers worked at a loose thread in his blanket. "Old Mastuh Penbrook took Esther into the big house fo' yo' ma."

"That's good news for Esther."

For the first time, she allowed her gaze to sweep upward.

Her large hazel eyes, framed with long, bristly lashes, told a story of pain that brought a lump to his throat. "Isn't it good news?" Mac reached out and took Celeste's hand. "Or would you prefer having your sister work in the fields?"

Panic lit her eyes. She reminded him of a cornered calf. Her hand inside of his felt rough from exposure to the sun and the telltale sign of hard labor—calluses.

"It's all right, Celeste," he said. "You can tell me your true thoughts. I won't use them against you."

Her eyes narrowed. Why should she believe him?

"As God is my witness." He smiled, though he was losing strength fast. This young slave woman intrigued him. She wasn't lovely in a Southern belle sort of way, or even in the exotic manner that so many of the mulatto or quadroon slave women had about them. This woman wasn't beautiful at all, really, except for those large, expressive eyes. But something in her manner drew him. Intrigued him. "Would you prefer for Esther to work in the fields?"

Her shoulders rose and fell. "Don't figger it makes much difference, Mastuh."

Mac turned her palm over and ran his thumb from the tip of her index finger to the soft skin of her wrist. Sensing her discomfiture, he fought the urge to press his lips to each callus. "I guess that depends on how you look at it."

She shivered and pulled her hand away. She stared at him, her striking gaze capturing his. "I guess it do at that."

CHAPTER TWO
OREGON 1949

Shea awoke after a fitful night's sleep. A dream-laden sleep filled with images from the past. A young slave girl, a handsome young master sent to the slave quarters to be nursed back from yellow fever. It was like a wonderful, romantic dream. Or a beautiful novel. At times she forgot she was reading the words of her ancestor.

This slave girl had the same name as her great-great-grandmother: Celeste. That was too much to be coincidence. But if Great-Great-Grandmother Celeste had been a slave, that would make Shea. . .

This wasn't the first time she'd thought of it during the long night of reading, dreaming, and wondering. She held out her bare arm and stared at the freckled skin. Skin that was about as far from Negro as a person's could be. But then, Mac never specified the color of Celeste's skin except to say it was light brown. And that could mean anything. Perhaps she had been light enough to pass for white. Had he taken her from his father's plantation, married her, and passed her off as a white woman?

Surely not. Such a secret couldn't have been kept by the entire family all these years.

Shea climbed out of bed, then yanked the covers over the straw mattress in frustration, making little attempt to straighten out the wrinkles. She grabbed the diary and headed downstairs to the kitchen. If only she'd found the diaries before Granddad died. He would have known the truth about his grandmother.

Halfway down the steps, a soft gasp left her throat at the memory of the framed photograph on the mantel over the fireplace. She took the last three stairs in one leap and fairly flew into the living room. She snatched the photograph from its perch.

She studied the photograph. Great-Great-Grandmother Celeste sat, unsmiling, in a wooden chair. Despite the grim line of lips, Shea had always taken note of the slight twinkle in her eyes. That twinkle had held her captive since childhood. She'd always known her ancestor was a happy woman. Great-Great-Grandfather stood behind her, his hand on her shoulder. Great-Granddad Timothy Penbrook stood behind Susan, his wife, who sat at his mother's side.

Shea's granddad stood next to his mother. No more than ten years old, his eyes already reflected that insolent, lazy attitude with which he'd conducted himself all his life. Or at least the part of his life Shea had any recollection of. He had been the only child of an only child, and his parents had died when he was too young to remember. Mac and Celeste had raised him.

Walking into the kitchen with the diary in one hand and the picture frame in the other, Shea studied the images carefully. Every man and woman in the photograph appeared to be white. She peered more closely at Celeste and for the first time noticed the thickness of her lips. The wideness of her forehead.

Mac's assessment had been correct. There was nothing remarkable about Celeste's appearance, except perhaps the gentle peace written across her face. Though she had obviously passed for a white woman, an astute observer could easily note the presence of African blood in her features and the darkness of her skin next to the pale complexions of her husband, son, and grandson.

Shea sat hard in a kitchen chair. Amazing that she'd never noticed before. Never knew that African blood flowed through her own veins. Her stomach flip-flopped at the new information working its way through her mind.

She'd always been a little nervous in the presence of anyone from the Negro community. Granddad had often warned her to stay away from the shantytown. Fear of murder—or worse, rape—had kept her close to home and most likely kept her out of trouble on more than one occasion.

There had been no question how Granddad felt about the race as a whole. He had not allowed a colored man or woman to work around the place. Nor had he ever "met a colored man worth the dirt the Almighty used to make him." Had he known the truth? Was that why he'd held such hatred in his heart toward anyone with dark skin?

Shea fixed her breakfast and glanced out the kitchen door, noting the blackness of the sky. Let it rain. What good would the sun do her anyway? The only thing she had to look forward to was the diaries in the attic.

GEORGIA 1949

"Now, Judge McNabb, you know as well as the prosecution here that there ain't going to be any evidence to convict my client. I move to dismiss this mockery of a trial before wasting any more of these good taxpayers' hard-earned dollars."

To his credit, the old judge shook an arthritic finger at the attorney. "Mr. Boone, this isn't a hearing. It's a trial. Either give your opening remarks or forfeit the floor to the prosecution to call its first witness."

From the balcony, Andy Carmichael listened to the opening statements from the sweating, rotund defense attorney. The defendant, Sam Dane Jr., son of the renowned Georgia senator, stood accused of murder for ordering a hanging by the local Klan. Truth be told, he'd caused two deaths that night last year—not only a white man but also a black girl. Lovers, desperate to be together at any cost. But when the charges came down from the grand jury against Sam, they were for Rafe's murder alone.

Somehow, the sleepy town of Oak Junction, Georgia, had forgotten that there had been two people yanked from an old Ford truck that night. Justice for a colored girl would have to be attached to the man she loved, but no one would ever pay for her death. Outrage shocked the Negro community at the revelation, but no one spoke out.

But on this first day of the trial, anger boiled below the surface. The balcony was so packed, Andy worried it might not hold up under the strain. Ruthie deserved to be vindicated, but protesting wouldn't do any good. Just cause more unrest. Maybe even more killing. And Lord knew they didn't need any more killing.

White hoods and fiery torches filled the dreams of colored men and women throughout Floyd County. Folks desperate to keep their children safe and homes protected stayed in at night and didn't draw attention to themselves during the day. Survival was the first priority.

As a transplanted newspaperman, Andy had certainly had his share of nightmares lately. Chicago wasn't the friendliest place to be if you were a black man, but it was nothing like living in Georgia. At least in Chicago he'd never been dragged from his bed at night by men in white robes and hoods as he had here in Georgia one terrifying night last year. He shuddered. He'd never forget the terror.

He stared down at the overcrowded courtroom. Standing room only in both the main floor and the balcony, where the blacks were allowed to view the proceedings.

His eyes lighted on a well-dressed businessman. A clean-shaven face, full head of gray hair. Sam Dane's father, the senator. Slowly, the man lifted his gaze to the balcony. Andy swallowed hard. For the first time, he stared into the eyes of the man he'd only recently learned was his own father.

Even now, when his life was on the line, Sam Dane couldn't hold his father's attention. He blazed at the senator through hate-filled eyes, while the aging man kept his focus on the balcony. On Andy. The Negro son of his father and a black mistress.

If Sam could have had his way, Andy Carmichael would have joined the two young lovers who'd hung that night. Then the Dane family name would be purged from such a filthy abomination. And perhaps his father would be free of the spell of the black witch who, even in death, held his heart captive.

Only a little bit of regret had entered Sam at the thought of ordering the killings. There had been nothing wrong with Rafe—nothing he could help anyway. He was a good sort. A man to be pitied, really, having fallen for the seductions of a black woman.

Too bad Andy hadn't been with them that night. Sam cut

his glance once more to the man who should never have been born. Fresh rage penetrated his soul. He clenched his fist. Once he got out of this mess, Sam vowed, he'd do what he should have done last year.

OREGON 1949

The sun broke through lingering clouds around noon. Shea heard the rattle of a wagon outside and smiled. Miss Nell Carter refused to give up her horse and wagon, despite being the last of the county folk who still used the avenue of travel on a regular basis. The old woman had been like a grandmother to Shea—would have liked to have been her grandmother, she always thought. If only Granddad had taken the many hints over the years.

Stepping onto the porch to greet her, Shea dropped her smile at the sight of the anger mottling Miss Nell's lined face.

"Girl, what were you thinking?" She grabbed her chest with one hand and her knotted wooden cane with the other as she stomped up to the house.

"Miss Nell! Remember your heart."

"You let me worry about my heart and you worry about yours."

Whatever had the old lady up in arms, Shea could see she wasn't going to be appeased by soft words and health concerns. "Come inside out of the sun. I have some fresh lemonade."

"Lemonade!" She spat, holding her ground. "You didn't tell me you were burying Mr. Penbrook. I had to find out from that gossip Hattie Long, and you know how I feel about learning anything from that woman. I thought I was like kin to you, and this is the way you treat me?"

Shea met Miss Nell at the bottom of the steps and reached

out to take her arm, but the old woman jerked away. "I can get into the house without the help of someone who doesn't care enough to invite me to the funeral of the man I loved."

Ah, so there was the admission. "I'm sorry, Miss Nell. You know I love you, but I was afraid for your heart."

"My heart is my business," she snapped.

"What would I have done if I'd had to bury you both?"

The old woman's expression softened, and she extended her elbow. "Help me up these confounded steps."

When she was a little girl, Shea had figured out that Miss Nell was thunder without lightning. A lot of noise, but no threat. She took the woman's arm and steadied her as they moved up the stairs and into the house.

"Miss Nell," Shea said after settling the old woman into a seat at the kitchen table and pouring them each a glass of lemonade, "what do you know about my family's past?"

The woman shot her gaze to Shea's. "What do you want to know?"

"I've been cleaning out the attic and found some old diaries from my great-great-grandfather Jason—everyone called him Mac." Shea drew a deep breath. "You've lived here all your life. Have you ever heard any rumors about my family?"

Miss Nell cackled, showing an incomplete set of half-rotted teeth. "You know full well folks have been talking about the Penbrooks as long as I can remember. And why wouldn't they? Your daddy ended up in prison for murder, your granddad had his own share of troubles, and your great-granddaddy was killed in a brawl over another man's wife. The Penbrooks have not had the best reputations in this part of the country. Why do you care?"

Shea pushed the diary across the table. "Mac Penbrook's diary. Celeste, his wife, was a slave." She said the words without emotion—easier to gauge Miss Nell's reaction that way.

The woman lifted her sweating glass of lemonade to her brow. "Sure is a hot day," she said, smacking her lips.

"Yes, ma'am. Would you like a fan?"

"Naw. Those things make my arm tired."

"I could fan you."

The old lady looked at her askance. "I'm not that old."

Why wouldn't the woman just address the matter at hand? "Miss Nell. . ."

"Don't rush me," came the testy reply.

Shea waited, not patiently, while Miss Nell took a sip from the glass.

Finally, the old woman set the glass back on the table and leveled a narrowed gaze at Shea. "You want to hear what I know about Celeste Penbrook?"

"Please. Anything you remember."

"I figure I'm just about the only one in these parts who still does remember old Miz Penbrook."

Shea's heart picked up a few beats. "What about her being a slave?"

"Your great-great-grandma was a decent, Christian woman. She held that lot of selfish, lazy men together with her strength. But things weren't easy after Mac Penbrook died. She took in washing and did cleaning—even worked for old Miz Sable."

The news nearly tossed Shea from her seat. Why did the Sables always have to win over the Penbrooks? For as long as she could remember, Jackson Sable had lorded it over them. Only his son, Colin, had ever been kind to her. And Jackson had put a halt to any kind of childhood friendship or teenage romance that might have happened between the two of them.

"If Mac hadn't passed on at such a young age, I believe your family would have a much different story. But once Celeste started doing washing and cleaning houses, people started commenting on the darkness of her skin. I suppose someone finally put two and two together and figured out that she wasn't all white."

Shea blew out a pent-up breath. "So she and her son were ostracized?"

"Not so much. No one was ever able to fully prove she was part colored, and most folks didn't want to believe they could have been fooled for that many years. But the speculation was enough to do damage, even without proof, among folks who were willing to believe."

Leaning back, Shea stretched her legs out in front of her beneath the table. She folded her arms across her chest and rested on her tailbone like a young person ten years her junior. Rebellion beat a furious rhythm in her chest. She wanted to rail against the injustice of her family's plight.

"Your great-great-grandma refused every Sable offer to buy the land. She wouldn't sell one single acre to that family. She'd scrub their floors, but she wasn't about to let them have any of Mac's land. They eventually fired her and made it very difficult for her to make a living."

"How did she survive?"

Miss Nell smiled. "Mac had a few friends who hired her to clean. Her son, Timothy, went to college with money Mac and Celeste had put away to send him. He turned into a fancy lawyer and sent money home, so for a while Celeste didn't have so many struggles—not financial anyway. A few years after he married Susan and established a good practice, he and his wife decided to go to England. They left their son—your granddad—with Celeste. While in London, your great-grandfather had an indiscretion with the wife of a lord or duke or some such nonsense those British think are so important. He was in a pub, and the lady's husband shot and killed him in a fit of rage."

"What happened to my great-grandmother?"

"Far as I know, Celeste and your granddad never heard from Susan again. The house Timothy had lived in was mortgaged to the hilt. There was nothing left to do but auction everything of value to pay his debts. When everything was settled, Celeste was sixty years old and once again starting over with a young boy to raise."

"Why didn't you ever tell me any of this before?"

The old woman stared back at her without a bit of remorse. "Wasn't my place."

"Then why didn't Granddad ever tell me?"

She shrugged. "I guess he had his reasons. Could be he wanted to spare you from knowing about the blood flowing through your veins."

"Maybe he was ashamed of the blood that flowed through *his* veins," Shea shot back.

"Perhaps. Do you blame him? You think your life was difficult just from being a Penbrook? What do you think it might have been like if folks knew your ancestor was a slave?"

"If there was speculation anyway, how come no one ever made an issue out of it?"

"I figure once Celeste passed on and your granddad stayed out of trouble, people forgot about the Negro blood."

Shea gave a bitter laugh. "So the Penbrooks were merely white trash. I suppose in society's way of thinking that's a step up from being black."

The old lady jutted her chin. "You don't have to like the way things are. But no Penbrook is ever going to get any respect in these parts. Your great-granddaddy saw to that with his philandering, and your granddad surely didn't help matters with his laziness. And then there's your pa, who most folks thought was crazy as a loon. Ain't nothing you can do about it, so you might as well accept things as they are."

"I don't have to accept anything. I'll be leaving this town for good in a week."

Miss Nell slapped her hand on the table. "What are you talking about, young lady?"

"All my relatives are gone. Why should I stay someplace that only brought my family pain?"

"Where are you planning to go?"

"I don't know. Jackson Sable offered me twice what the land is worth. I'd be a fool not to take it."

"So you're selling out to them Sables, are you? Making a mockery of everything your family has stood for. Letting them win once and for all."

"I don't care if they win or not. What are they winning anyway? The last ten acres of a farm that hasn't produced enough to make ends meet for fifty years. A broken-down farmhouse that should have been torn down ten years ago. I don't know why the Sables and the Penbrooks never got along in the first place, but the Sables beat the Penbrooks a long time ago. They have all the money in the county and we have nothing. So whatever the rivalry between the two families, the Sables don't have anything left to prove. And neither do I."

Pressing her palms flat against the table, Miss Nell braced herself and rose to her feet. She slid the diary back across the table with enough force that Shea had to catch it before it sailed off the other end. "Read it," Miss Nell commanded. "I'd lay odds all the answers about the Sables and Penbrooks are right there in those diaries."

Shea stared at the book in her hands. Did it really explain the reason for the rivalry between the Sables and the Penbrooks?

"I best be going," Miss Nell announced. "But you mind what I said. You're the last Penbrook in these parts. Stay here and try to make your name strong. Something to be respected."

"I thought you said no Penbrook would ever get any respect around here."

A scowl scrunched the old lady's face. "Well, not if you run off like a scared rabbit."

"Oh, Miss Nell. Maybe it's just better to go away and make a new start. Don't I deserve that?"

She gave a snort. "Only you can answer that." But the look on her face spoke loudly of Miss Nell's opinion on the subject.

Shea helped the elderly woman out of the house, then into her wagon. "I'm sorry to disappoint you, Miss Nell. But I'm twenty-seven years old and have nothing to show for my life. I want to go somewhere and make a new start. Can you understand that?"

A nod moved the gray head as Miss Nell gripped the reins. "Go ahead and sell the land if that's what you need to do. But read the diaries first. Try to understand your past."

"How is it you know so much about my family?"

"I paid attention. My heart was invested."

Poor Miss Nell. She truly had loved Granddad.

Shea watched as she rode away in the wagon, the horse moving so slowly Shea figured Miss Nell probably could have made it home faster if she'd walked.

❧

Pride shot through Jackson Sable as he sat at the head of his table and waited for his family's response to his announcement.

"Well?" he prodded when no congratulations were forthcoming.

"What will Shea do, Father?"

Irritation combined with pride and brought a frown to Jackson's brow. "What difference does that make?"

Colin averted his gaze. "None. I just wonder where she plans to live."

Jackson narrowed his eyes and stared at his son. "Perhaps you should concentrate on your wife and stop concerning yourself with Miss Penbrook."

As Jackson had intended, his son's face grew red. "I wasn't concerning myself with Miss Penbrook, Father. Simply curious as to her plans."

"Really, Colin. Your father is right." Melinda, Colin's wife, gave her husband a tight smile. "Perhaps you should stop worrying about that white-trash girl."

Anger mottled Colin's face. "Don't ever call her that again." His chair scraped against the wood floor as he pushed back from the table and shot to his feet. Jackson watched him stalk away.

"Well, then." Melinda's face went ashen. She looked down at her plate and picked up her fork.

Disgust slithered through Jackson. If his rotund daughter-in-law would stop stuffing her face and lose some of that blubber, maybe Colin would give her some attention. At least enough to provide an heir.

GEORGIA 1847

Sometimes Mac felt anxious as a squirrel to leave the slave quarters. Other times, like now, he could stay here forever. The muted light of dawn was just beginning to push back the darkness inside the four walls as he awakened to soft singing, ham frying, and biscuits baking.

"Mmm. Smells good."

Celeste whipped around, her hand pressed to her cheek. "Mastuh. I din' know you was awake."

"Who could sleep with breakfast smelling so good?"

Her eyes widened and she scurried to the fire, grabbing the skillet with the hem of her apron. "I's sorry, suh. You go on back to sleep. I'll just take this off the fire until you wakes up."

"Celeste. Put the pan back on. It's all right. I don't mind waking up this early. I've slept enough over the last few weeks." He pushed himself to a sitting position. "As a matter of fact, I believe I'll have a bath today and get dressed. I'm beginning to offend myself. I can only imagine how grateful you'll be if I scrub off the dirt." He'd meant it as a joke and was rewarded with a half smile from her. That smile caused his heart to soar.

She cast a sideways glance in his direction. "You thinkin' you might be goin' back to the big house soon?" Her hand trembled slightly as she settled the pan back over the flame.

Trying to gauge the emotions of a carefully guarded woman was difficult in the best of circumstances. When the woman was also a slave, trained to mask her feelings, it was a nearly impossible feat.

But Mac had lived with this woman for a month. Granted, the first ten days he was unconscious, but since then, he'd studied her. Had learned that when she touched her face with the slightest brush of her fingertips, she'd been taken off guard and felt shy. And the past couple of days he'd noticed her doing that often.

Like right now as she stood over the skillet longer than necessary.

"Are you ready for me to go back to the big house, Celeste?" Mac knew it wasn't a fair question, given their positions, but for the life of him, he couldn't resist asking.

Her chin jerked slightly, the only sign that the question's impropriety bothered her. "It ain't my place to be ready for you to do nothin', suh."

"Maybe I care what you think."

Her gaze captured his as she walked forward, his plate of food perched between long fingers.

Mac scanned the woman from head to foot. Her hair was tucked beneath a blue rag, and her shapely form spilled into a dress that was too thin and too tight. Nice for a man to look at, but he could see her discomfort as his eyes returned to hers and her face darkened with embarrassment. Her arms tucked into her body in an attempt to hide her figure without being obvious about it. But Mac wasn't fooled. Nor did he wish to make her feel more uncomfortable.

He cleared his throat. "I thought it was about time I got out of your hair."

A hint of a frown creased her brow. "Is you sure you feel well 'nuff to do that, suh?"

"I think so." He was anxious to return to his position teaching at the local school. His father had sneered at his choice of profession. Wasn't the eldest son responsible for taking over the family land? But his younger brother, Henry, was as passionate about building the empire as was their father, so at least he had one son who hadn't disappointed him.

Celeste put the breakfast tray on his lap. "I is glad yo' better."

"I *am* glad."

"Suh?"

"You said, 'I is glad.' It's correct to say, 'I *am* glad.'"

Her brow rose, and Mac feared he'd offended her. But she took a deep breath. "I am glad yo' better."

"And I am glad that you are such an exquisite cook. Mother should put you in the kitchen. You're wasted in the fields."

Immediately her wall of deference rose, and Mac could have kicked himself.

"Would you like me to talk to Mother on your behalf?"

As she lifted her gaze, her hazel eyes, large and expressive, flashed with interest. But her tone remained carefully guarded. "I reckon you is gonna do whatever you wants, suh."

That was the closest she'd come to revealing her desires.

He smiled. "I reckon I am."

CHAPTER THREE
GEORGIA 1949

Andy had never experienced the kind of mental exhaustion he felt each day after sitting in the courtroom balcony, listening to testimony. The trial had only been in session for two days, and already he felt as tired as if he hadn't slept in months.

He waited for the lower floor to empty out, then trudged down the balcony steps after the crowd.

He missed his wife and baby girl. It had been difficult to leave them behind in Chicago and come down to Georgia alone. But tensions were too high right now in Oak Junction for him to risk their safety. The atmosphere too volatile. Last year, he'd been a target of the Klan under Sam Dane Jr.'s leadership, and he had no doubt that once they figured out he was here covering the story for his adopted family's newspaper in Chicago, he would be a target again.

He kept up his guard as he walked the two miles back to the boardinghouse owned by his younger sister, Lottie, and her husband, Buck. Every car that passed clenched his gut. Mainly, he wanted to get back before dusk settled over the sleepy Southern town. After dark, the fires blazed, the white hoods appeared. Andy shivered and quickened his pace.

Two blocks from the boardinghouse, a car approached from behind and crawled alongside him. Andy's heart hammered in his throat. He kept walking, trying to ignore the vehicle. But after a few moments, curiosity got the better of him. He turned. The car inched along beside him. Andy fought the urge to run. Memories of being tied to Sam's truck, coming close to being dragged along the dusty road, shot to his mind, bringing with them the terror of the actual moment. If not for Rafe—the man Sam Dane and his hooded cowards had murdered—Andy would have been killed that day. Rafe had come upon them, talked them out of their plans, and saved his life.

"Excuse me."

Andy swallowed his fear and turned toward the shiny black car. The driver's window was rolled down, but Andy could see Senator Dane sitting in the backseat—he caught a glimpse of his face for a split second. "What can I do for you?" Andy asked the driver.

The man reached out and handed him a slip of paper. As soon as it touched Andy's hand, the car drove away.

Andy stared at the paper. He read the request for a meeting. Andy couldn't decide. Was he ready or even willing to meet with the man who had fathered him? Why should Samuel Dane want to see Andy at a time like this? Didn't he understand what the ramifications might be for them both?

OREGON 1949

Shea woke up two days after Granddad's funeral with one thought on her mind: How could she possibly sell the place now that she was getting to know the ancestors who'd originally settled this land? But what would Jackson Sable do to her if she backed out?

Shuddering at the thought, she pushed back the covers and swung her legs over the side of the bed.

There wasn't much to pack. A few mementoes. Clothes—not many. And books, most of which she would leave at Miss Nell's until she could send for them from wherever she was going. Boxes of books cluttered the living room floor. She had all of Mac Penbrook's diaries in order and had been reading slowly from the faded yellowed pages.

A knock at the door pulled her from the morning ritual of dressing and straightening the room. She finished buttoning her dress and hurried down the stairs.

"Ernie?" What could he be doing here? She'd paid him the day before after he'd carried the boxes down from the attic. She thought she'd made it clear there would be no more work for him to do.

The former hired hand stood on her sagging front porch, hat in hand, looking as nervous as a cat. "Pardon me for bothering you, Miss Penbrook."

"No bother at all." She stepped out onto the porch.

He shuffled his feet. "I was wonderin'. . . . Well, rumor has it you're selling the place to Mr. Sable."

There were no secrets in Prudence, Oregon. "That's right."

He lifted his gaze across the yard. "I wonder if you'd allow me to pull down the barn for use of the wood. I couldn't pay ya much, but possibly I could help move your things from the house to wherever you'd like them to go."

Shea smiled at the man with the grizzled hair. Ernie never would amount to much by society's standards, any more than she would, but he certainly had a kind soul, and he had worked the land faithfully for as long as Shea could remember. "The barn is yours. And I'd appreciate any help you could give hauling crates of books over to Miss Nell's."

His lips, drawn from years of living without teeth, lifted into a smile. "Thank ya kindly, miss. Iffen you don't mind my askin', where ya plannin' on goin'?"

Her chest rose and fell. "I really don't know."

But somewhere in the back of her mind, the thought of Mac Penbrook's family in Georgia rifled through, taunting her with the possibilities.

GEORGIA 1847

How could I have ever thought she wasn't beautiful?

Mac stood in the doorway of the sprawling kitchen of the main house and watched, mesmerized, as Celeste moved gracefully from one task to the next, taking his breath away with each step.

His mother had not been keen on the idea of adding the girl to the house. "She's always been a field hand, son. I fear she is too old to learn the necessary graces of a house servant."

That had been a month ago. And she had recently recanted her original assessment. "The girl is graceful as a cat. She moves in and out of the room so quietly, it's as if the food appears and empty plates disappear by magic. I am so pleased that you suggested bringing her to the house."

So was Mac. He'd barely had the opportunity to speak more than two words at a time with her since his recovery and her subsequent move into the house. Not what he'd originally had in mind. In having Mother bring her into the kitchen, he'd hoped to lighten her workload as well as have the opportunity to spend time with her.

The heat of the kitchen caused perspiration to glisten on her neck and forehead. Steam rose from a large pot on the stove.

He took a step forward, finally catching Celeste's attention.

Her eyes grew wide. "Mastuh," she said in a breath.

He smiled as she brushed her fingertips against her cheek and averted her gaze to the stone floor. "How are you, Celeste?"

"Fine, suh."

Deep inside he felt a strong desire to pull her away from the kitchen and walk with her outside in the cool of the evening. Hand in hand.

"Girl, that pot's biling over!" Cookie Mary breezed by, scowling at them both.

A gasp shot from Celeste. "I's—I mean, I am sorry, Cookie. I'll clean that up."

"Just stay out of the way. Go set the dining room table with the good china. Mastuh and Missus are havin' guests. And don' let me catch you droppin' so much as a single napkin."

Mac stared helplessly, feeling guilty for having caused Celeste to be reprimanded. "I'll help you carry dishes."

Cookie scowled once more. "Why you want to go and do that, Mastuh Mac? You still ain't got all yo' strength back."

He sent her a dry grin. "I'm strong enough to carry a few plates into the dining room."

The rail-thin cook shrugged her bony shoulders and shook her head with an "Uh, uh, uh." Cookie always had to get the last word. No matter that she was a slave. She owned this family and everyone knew it. "Don't drop yo' mama's good dishes," she commanded before turning her back and leaning over the fire.

"Yes, ma'am." Mac winked at Celeste behind Cookie's back. He was rewarded with a tremor of a smile as she walked past him with a stack of plates. "Can I take some of those?"

"Get the silverware." Cookie's brusque voice shot through

the room, reminding them that her eyes and ears were seeing and listening.

In the dining room, Celeste moved from one setting to the next at the elegant cherrywood table. She deftly set each place. Mac tried to imagine her seated at his side with the family, but the thought was absurd.

Why did he feel so tongue-tied around this woman? He'd had his share of slave girls over the years. No one who hadn't been willing. But this wasn't the same.

She turned to him. "Mastuh?"

He stepped closer to her.

Her eyes widened. "I—I need to place the silverware."

Her hand shook, and Mac knew she felt the same attraction he did. He took hold of her fingers.

"Please, Mastuh Mac, I can't. . .I don' want to. . ."

"This isn't like that, Celeste."

Her gaze swept upward, eyes sparking in disbelief. "Then. . . whut?"

Dropping her hand, he shoved his hands into his pockets and shrugged. "I don't know what there is for us. But I know I feel something for you."

"Celeste!" Cookie's voice pierced the atmosphere. By the stormy look on her face, Mac knew she'd heard every word.

"Yes, Cookie. I'm 'bout done."

"I's gonna finish here. You dish up that sweet potato casserole and greens."

Celeste nodded and headed toward the exit. Mac drew a breath to speak, but Cookie interrupted. She cut her sharp eyes to Mac. "You best go on and change into yo' good clothes. Dat Janette and her ma and pa be a-comin' any second." Her knowing glance to Celeste induced a blush on the girl's cheeks.

Celeste paused without turning around, then disappeared through the door.

"Wait, Celeste."

"Mastuh," Cookie hissed, "leave her alone."

He turned on the elderly slave. "You forget your place, Cookie. I will speak with whomever I choose."

"And whut good you gonna do that gal when you marry Miss Janette and start raisin' babies? Den where she gonna be? You gonna take her to be yo' cook?"

Mac scowled. She had a point. Even tonight's supper was a shameless attempt on his parents' part to marry him off to Janette Blythe. Janette was a beautiful, talented young woman, and any man would have been honored to marry her. But Celeste was in his blood. Had been from the moment he'd awakened in her shack to her singing softly in the dark.

Without another word to the outspoken cook, Mac followed Celeste. He caught up to her just before she entered the kitchen door. "Celeste, wait. . . ."

Carefully guarded, her face was arranged into an expression of deference. "Yes?"

"Meet me after dinner. In the garden."

"Yes, Mastuh."

He wrapped his fingers around her arm and demanded her gaze. "Are you coming because you want to?"

"It don' matter whut I want."

"I'm saying it does." Mac dropped her arm. "Look at me."

She did.

"Do you know how I feel about you?"

"No, suh."

"I want to spend time with you."

From the hesitance in her eyes, Mac could tell he had a lot

of convincing to do before she would believe that his feelings for her went much deeper than physical attraction. "Will you meet me?"

She nodded. "In the garden, suh."

"There you are."

Celeste jumped, and Mac turned at the sound of his mother's voice.

"Mac, you aren't dressed. The Blythes will be here any minute. Please run along and dress yourself properly for our guests." She turned and smiled fondly at Celeste. "Everything smells heavenly. Remember to serve from the left."

"Yes, ma'am." With a curtsy, Celeste disappeared behind the kitchen door.

"I am so glad you suggested bringing her into the kitchen. I must say, though, her sister isn't much of a maid. I'm about to send her back to the fields."

Mac's heart went out to his mother. It was no secret why Father had brought Celeste's pretty younger sister into the house. And Mother didn't have the power to send her back until Father tired of her. Bending, he planted a kiss on his mother's cheek. "I'll go dress."

"Don't be late. Janette is coming to see you, after all." She placed a hand on his arm. "Son, leave Celeste alone. Please."

Tempted to deny her words, Mac looked into his mother's knowing eyes. "It's not what you think."

"That is the only thing it can be. You know it can go no further than your bed." Her face reddened at her bold words and Mac felt his own cheeks warm. "I'm sorry to be so indelicate, darling," his mother said. "But I saw the look on your face. You can't fall in love with a slave. Nothing can come of it."

Mac remained silent. She took his arm. "You do know that, right?"

"Yes, Mother. I know what's expected of me."

OREGON 1949

With great reluctance, Shea set aside the diary, donned work clothes—trousers, a button-down shirt, and a scarf to cover her head—and headed out to the barn. Granddad had left tools and other personal items there, and she wanted to go through things before Ernie and his six sons started tearing down the barn one board at a time.

The work was dusty, tedious, and mostly unproductive. The rusty tools were not worth the time it would take to clean them up and find someone to buy them.

By the time she climbed into the loft, two and a half hours had passed. She was anxious to clean herself up, eat some lunch, and dive back into the diaries.

She carefully stepped across the half-rotted planks. "Oh, Granddad," she called into the empty air when her foot slipped slightly on a crooked board. "Why didn't you ever take care of things? I could kill myself up here and no one would know until Ernie found my stiff body under the rubble."

Smiling ruefully at her nonsense, Shea moved to one corner of the loft, where she intended to go through crates, much like she had two days before in the attic. Part of her looked forward to the task. Maybe she'd find treasures, such as the ones she'd discovered in the attic.

But at the end of the day, she'd found very little of interest— a few handmade items from her childhood and a locket with a broken chain, which had hung around her mother's neck until her death when Shea was seven.

The sound of a wagon rattling up the drive made her decide there was nothing more to gain in the barn. Let Ernie tear it to the ground. Everything in it could be turned to kindling for all she cared.

She climbed down and left the barn to greet Miss Nell.

The old woman's face lit with amusement. "Girl, you look like you've been playin' in the dirt."

Shea emitted a chuckle and slapped her palms against her thighs, raising a cloud of dust. "I guess I have. I've been going through the junk Granddad had stored in the barn."

"Find anything interesting?"

"Not really." Arm in arm the two women headed toward the house. "What brings you this way again so soon? Could it be that you're going to miss me when I'm gone?"

"You know I will."

Silenced by the woman's uncommon show of affection, Shea helped Miss Nell into the kitchen and set a kettle on the stove.

"That should only take a few minutes to start boiling, then we'll have some tea."

Miss Nell nodded, the lines of her face etched into a serious pattern without the slightest hint of humor. "I wish I could offer you a place to live with me. Then you wouldn't have to leave."

A smile twitched the corners of Shea's lips. Miss Nell's home was a two-room shack without electricity or running water. The woman barely had enough room for herself, let alone a house-guest. "I understand, Miss Nell. Really I do."

Miss Nell's eyes filled with pleading hope. "With Sable's money, why not buy yourself a little house nearby? Or you could find a job and rent a little apartment."

Shea sighed. "I couldn't bear to live around here knowing

that my home doesn't belong to me anymore."

The elderly woman patted her hand. "Where you figuring on heading?"

"I don't know." Shea shrugged. "A city, maybe. Chicago or even New York."

"Now, what do they have in the city that you can't find right here?"

The teakettle whistled and Shea stood, smiling at Miss Nell's question.

"Well?" the old woman asked. "What is it you're lookin' fer, child?"

She poured tea into two cups. "Dignity. A chance to make something of myself."

"Rubbish. You already are somebody."

"You're the only one around here who thinks anyone with the name Penbrook has any value."

Miss Nell's eyes flashed. "Don't you talk that way. Your granddad wasn't trash and neither are you, young lady."

"Tell that to the likes of Jackson Sable."

"Pshaw. What do you care what folks like him think?"

Shea dumped a spoonful of sugar into her tea and stirred longer than necessary. "I care because they're the decent folk around here. Supposedly. Their opinion carries weight. As long as they think I'm trash, the rest of the people around here believe it, too." Except Colin. He'd known better. But he hadn't had the backbone to fight for her.

Miss Nell patted her hand. "I understand." She reached into her bosom and pulled a newspaper clipping from her undergarment.

"What's that?"

"Here. Take it."

Confused, Shea unfolded the newspaper and stared at a photograph of an old woman. She read the text beneath it.

C. Penbrook passed away with no living heirs and has therefore willed her estate to close friends in Chicago. Mr. Daniel Riley, owner and operator of The Chicago Observer, *has full ownership of the mansion and lands with the exception of acres the deceased left to certain sharecroppers.*

Shea looked up from the article. "What are you trying to tell me?"

"Look where the estate is."

"Oak Junction, Georgia." Memory shot through her. The diaries. Mac Penbrook's home was in Oak Junction. A gasp hit her throat. "Do you think. . . ?"

"I'd say this C. Penbrook had an heir after all."

The thought slowly wound through Shea's mind like a snake around a branch. It was a fantastic idea that she might actually be the heir to Mac Penbrook's original home in Georgia. "Do you really think it's possible?"

"You never know. Your granddad thought that article might come in handy. That's why he gave it to me for safekeeping."

"Granddad knew about this?"

"He always read his newspaper. This C. Penbrook was a famous author. I suppose that's why her name ended up in the *Prudence News*."

"Why didn't Granddad go after the inheritance? He would have been the rightful heir before me and more closely related to Miss Penbrook."

"He just wanted to live out the rest of his days in peace.

Your granddad wasn't greedy."

"That's for sure."

"So, what are you going to do now?"

Shea stared at the black-and-white photo of the woman who was more than likely a distant relative. If the old woman had known Shea existed, would she still have given the Penbrook estate to this man in Chicago?

Butterflies formed in Shea's stomach as she stared into Miss Nell's smiling face. "I guess I know where I'm going when Mr. Sable pays me for this place."

CHAPTER FOUR
GEORGIA 1949

A knock at his door pulled Andy from an early-evening doze. He'd come upstairs to clean up after the hot day in the courtroom and to rest awhile before his sister put dinner on the table.

"Coming, Lottie," he called.

"I know I'm pretty like a dame," a male voice called back through the door. "But I'm not Lottie."

Andy grinned and opened the door. He stuck out his hand at the sight of his adopted brother. "Jonas! What are you doing in Georgia?"

A shrug lifted his shoulders. "I decided to get away from the city for a while and relax."

Andy laughed and pounded his friend affectionately on the back. "I'm not sure how much relaxation you're going to get in a town with a Klan-related trial going on."

A dubious grin played at the corners of Jonas's lips. "You're probably right. The real reason I came was to look after you, anyway."

"Are you planning to stay at Penbrook House?"

Jonas walked across the room and sat in a straight-back chair against the wall. He held his hat on his lap, fingering the brim. "The thought of staying in that old house seems kind of creepy to me. Think your sister might have a room I could rent for a few nights?"

"Scared?" Andy taunted without trying to hide a grin.

"Naw, it's just odd, that's all. I know Miss Penbrook was close to my grandfather, but to leave us all of this? Seems strange to me. I'd rather stay in town with you."

"You'd stick out like a sore thumb, stayin' at a black family's house. You really want to risk it with the trial going on? Might not be the best idea. For you or for Buck and Lottie." Or anyone else.

Jonas stroked his chin thoughtfully. "I hadn't thought of it that way."

But he needed to think of it. He wasn't in Chicago where racial issues, though definitely present, weren't as volatile as in Georgia. Especially during a race-related trial. "Tempers are hot right now. Rafe spent a lot of time here with Ruthie and the rest of the family. People are watching to see if there's any race mixing going on."

"You think I might make it harder on your sister if I stay here?"

Never one to mince words, Andy nodded. "You could."

"All right, then, I'll go to Penbrook House after dinner." He paused. "Unless you think I shouldn't stay for dinner either."

Andy grinned, buttoning his shirt over a white undershirt. "Only a fool would pass up Lottie's fried chicken and collard greens."

"Is that what smells so delicious?"

"It is indeed." Andy sat at the edge of his bed and slipped on his brown wing tips.

Jonas crossed an ankle over his knee. "How are Ruthie's

parents holding up?" Andy's brother and sister-in-law felt their daughter's death with every bang of the judge's gavel. They were in court every day without fail.

"The trial's been rough on Bessie and Jerome, knowing their daughter won't be avenged. Even if Sam's found guilty, he'll only be punished for Rafe's death, not Ruthie's."

"Are the police still investigating?"

"Of course not," Andy sneered, not even trying to hide his disgust. "Rumor has it that Rafe's dad, Sheriff John, went to Sam Jr.'s house that night to confront Sam about Rafe's death. When the sheriff found his son swinging from a tree, he went crazy. Sam claims the sheriff broke into the house and aimed the gun at him. He says he shot the sheriff in self-defense. Naturally, his father backed him up."

"Do you believe him?"

"No. But no one around here is going to challenge the word of a respected senator."

"Even if his son stands accused of murdering another man's son?"

"That's just not the way things are down here."

Jonas gave a low whistle.

Andy shoved his hands into his pockets and felt for the paper the senator's driver had given him. The note had requested a meeting with the senator out on the road where Rafe and Ruthie had been ambushed and dragged from Rafe's truck. Andy's insides quivered at the thought of complying with the request. Was it nothing more than a trap? The very real possibility had to be considered. When he thought about his wife and baby girl, he vowed not to go anywhere near that road after dark.

But curiosity made him wonder if he should meet with the senator. He wanted to know the white man his mother had loved, the man who had fathered him, and to hear what he had to say. Surely a man who had loved his mother wouldn't kill their son in cold blood. Unless, of course, he was worried that the truth about him might come out now that Sam was being tried for murder. Was he afraid that Andy's coverage of the trial might somehow disclose the true nature of his relationship to Sam and the senator? He should know better. Andy didn't want their association known any more than those two men did.

"You're thinking too much." Jonas's words broke through Andy's thoughts. He tossed Andy his hat.

Andy caught it easily and set it on his bed. "You don't think enough."

"I think plenty. I just don't wear my heart on my sleeve the way you do."

"Touché."

The two men had been raised in the same bedroom in Chicago. When Andy's mother sent him north to get him out of reach of his abusive stepfather, Jonas's father, Daniel, had taken him in. Andy had been ten years old at the time. It wasn't until last year that he'd discovered that Daniel, the man he knew as more of a benefactor than a relative, was his uncle—a couple of times removed, but family nonetheless. A white man not on his father's side, but his mother's. Amazing. For the first thirty-five years of his life, he hadn't known about his white relatives. But for the last year he'd known he not only had a white father but also white extended relatives on his mother's side. The revelation had come as a shock but finally explained why his skin was so light.

Jonas still didn't know about his relationship to Andy. Daniel hadn't chosen to tell him yet. And Andy didn't feel he should be the one to share the news.

Daniel's mother, Catherina, had grown up a slave in the Penbrook household. Though one-eighth of her blood was African, her skin was as white as any Southern belle. Throughout the Civil War years and beyond, during the rebuilding of the nation, her presence was taken for granted. But eventually, she was the only one left to claim the Penbrook house and lands.

She hadn't held any legal claim to the property. But that didn't matter. There were no Penbrooks left to dispute the validity of her leaving the house and part of the land to her son, Daniel Riley.

Andy was glad she'd done right by Jerome and Bessie, who still lived on the land where he had spent his first ten years. She'd discreetly given each member of his black family a sum of money or a bit of land. No one seemed to mind that she hadn't willed any of them the house or a substantial portion of the acreage. The ramifications of a black family moving into the historic house would have caused a Klan frenzy.

Andy's head swam trying to keep straight his family connections he now knew existed. The man who'd raised him—Daniel Riley, a white newspaperman in Chicago—was his uncle. His great-grandmother, Catherina "Cat" Penbrook, whom he'd always assumed was a white woman—a writer and an icon of Southern literature—was one-eighth black. Through marriage over two generations, African blood had entered the line. Andy's mother was dark and beautiful.

His natural father—the white senator, Samuel Dane—and Andy's half brother, Sam Jr., lived here in the South. Neither of them would claim him. Nor would he claim them if he knew what was good for him.

Andy wanted nothing more than to get back to his wife and daughter. To forget the twisted familial lines and live in peace.

But Daniel Riley had sent him here to cover the trial for *The Chicago Observer*. Andy had planned to take time off and be with his brothers and sisters and their families anyway. Covering the trial helped pay the bills at home while he was gone.

He glanced at the clock. Six o'clock. Lottie would be expecting them downstairs any second.

"You're thinking too much again." As though sensing Andy's need to be pulled out of his deep thoughts, Jonas broke through.

"You're right." He started thinking past supper to his meeting with Senator Dane.

His palms dampened at the thought.

OREGON 1949

Shea glanced around the bare room. All the photographs and knickknacks were packed away in boxes and had been taken to Miss Nell's barn for storage. The things that were left, she'd deliberately decided not to keep. School records, broken dishes, letters from Colin. . . She stared down at the bundle in her hands, disbelieving that she'd actually kept them. Love letters written by a man who wouldn't fight for her. A man who was only willing to love her from afar.

Shea no longer cared for him that way, but the experience had convinced her of one thing. She would find a man who would be willing to fight for her, or she would never marry. And at twenty-seven years old, it was beginning to look like the latter might be the more likely of the two choices.

Disgusted with herself for allowing thoughts of romance to enter her mind, she tossed the pile of letters into a tin garbage can, then padded across the wooden floor to her bed. She curled up on the soft mattress and tucked her bare feet under the quilt. Lifting Great-Great-Grandfather Mac's diary, she pushed aside her sentimental thoughts and once more allowed herself to escape into the past. . . .

GEORGIA 1847

If this woman didn't cease her incessant prattling, giggling, and eye-batting, Mac feared he might be forced into rudeness for the sake of his sanity.

She squeezed his arm, tightening her already blood-stopping grip. "Oh, Mr. Penbrook, the garden is wonderful. The roses are beautiful."

"I'm glad you're enjoying the view, Miss Blythe." Ignoramus didn't know the difference between honeysuckle and roses. He could never marry such a fool.

Cutting a coy glance up toward his face, she tilted the corner of her lips in a studied half smile. "I don't enjoy the view nearly so much as the company."

"I'm flattered you should say so." His responses came as naturally as taking a sip of sweet tea when it was set before him. They meant nothing. Less than nothing. But to be honest and tell her how repulsed he was by her presence would dishonor the girl's parents and strain his father's business and personal relationship with Mr. Blythe.

From the corners of his eyes he kept watch for Celeste. This walk in the garden should have been with her. He resented Janette, not only for her irritating presence, but because she wasn't the woman he would have chosen to be with this evening. In the unlikely event that Celeste found her way to their meeting place, he didn't want her to get the wrong impression about his intentions.

"Mr. Penbrook." Janette's high-pitched voice brought him back to the present. "I'm afraid you are not listening to a word I say."

"I apologize, Miss Blythe. I was distracted by your beauty."

Her fingertips fluttered to the low neckline of her ridiculously wide-hooped, pink satin gown.

By instinct his eyes followed her fingers, and he couldn't help but appreciate the contours of her bosom. He caught himself, but not before eliciting an expression of victory from the young woman.

She tapped his arm with her fan. "You know, our families are quite sure of a union between us."

Outrage shot through Mac's breast. Of all the brazen—

Apparently she caught his indignation, for a wail broke from her throat. "Oh, I've misspoken." Janette's voice cracked as though she were on the verge of tears. She whipped away from him and hurried a few steps down the dirt path.

Mac suspected her escape was merely a game to win his sympathy, but he did have an obligation to his parents. And that included making sure this simpleton didn't feel slighted. "Miss Blythe, wait. Please."

She stopped before a mimosa tree but didn't turn around. A sigh caught in Mac's throat at the obvious tactical move—and frustration that his nature and upbringing as a gentleman forced him to respond to it as she expected. "I'm sorry if I insulted you. I was just surprised that you would bring it up."

That was honest. Probably too honest for a gentleman, but it was the best he could do.

"Oh, Mac." She turned and fluttered her lashes up at him. "May I call you Mac?"

"You may call me whatever you like." He forced a smile.

"Mac, then. I am mortified to be the one to bring up our parents' wishes in regards to our future. But you see, I am going abroad in a couple of months and will not return for two years."

Now, that was the best news Mac had heard all evening. "I'm sure we shall count the days until your return."

She leaned toward him, pressing her ample bosom against him. "Will you truly miss me?"

Discomfited by the impropriety of her actions, he grasped her upper arms, intent on forcing her to step back. Misinterpreting his move, she pressed closer, wrapping her arms about his waist. In a horrific, nightmarish second, she raised up on her toes and took his lips with hers. She tasted of garlic and greens.

Before Mac could react, he heard a loud gasp in the bushes a few feet from where he stood with this despicable girl in his arms. He pushed her away just in time to see Celeste running through the garden toward the slave quarters. "Celeste. Wait!"

"Why, Mac!" Janette's incredulous voice shot through the evening air. She grabbed his arm. "Whatever are you doing?"

"Forgive me, Miss Blythe. Please see yourself into the house. There is someone I must speak to."

Her blue eyes flashed. "Surely not that darky girl." Her face, twisted with rage, demanded his attention. "You will not leave me in a strange garden to run off after a Negress." She stamped her foot. "I will not allow it."

Frustration slammed through him. She was right, of course. Even the commonest of decency demanded he remain with his guest.

With a furtive glance at Celeste's shadowy form retreating through the brush, he reluctantly turned back to Janette and offered her his arm. "I apologize for my rudeness, Miss Blythe. May I see you back to the house?"

Her carefully arranged smile returned. "Do you mean to say you're ready to return inside already?" Her eyes smoldered with seduction. He knew she was offering him more kisses. Never had he been less tempted by a beautiful woman.

"Your father may come after me with a shotgun if I don't get you back before twilight ends and the moon comes up fully."

"And would that be so bad?"

He couldn't resist a smile, sardonic though it may have been. "When I marry, it will be the woman of *my* choosing. Not her father's."

Her eyes widened, accompanied by a sharp intake of breath. "Do you mean to say you would refuse to marry a girl if you compromised her?"

"I would never allow that to happen. But if it did, I would try to do the right thing."

"Well, we'll just keep that little kiss between us." She squeezed his arm. "There are plenty more where that one came from." Turning, she stepped toward the house.

She stopped short just after entering through the backdoor. Mac nearly collided with her.

"There you two are."

Mac had never been more relieved to see his mother in his life.

"We've just had the most wonderful stroll in the garden," Janette replied breathlessly.

Mac's mother and Mrs. Blythe walked through the foyer toward the two of them. He said nothing. No matter what his mother asked of him, that was the last time he would be alone with this girl. He would suffer her presence for coffee and dessert with their parents, and then he would find Celeste and tell her how much he loved her. He would beg her to. . .to what? Marry him?

"Are you coming, Mac?" Janette's voice smacked of ownership.

Mac looked up to see his mother and Mrs. Blythe exchange

knowing smiles. They were in for quite a shock when he revealed the identity of the woman he truly loved.

OREGON 1949

Only Shea's rumbling stomach had the power to draw her away from Mac's love story with Celeste. Although she knew he would eventually win the slave girl's heart, the telling of it, from the man himself, filled her with a sense of understanding about her history. It also led her to acknowledge her own loneliness.

At twenty-seven years old, she'd only had two prospects for a husband: five years ago, a young private in the army who had fallen in love with her while on shore leave in Seattle—and then there had been Colin Sable.

Shea had truly cared for Jeremy, and he'd been crazy in love with her. She would have been happy, she thought, married to him. If he hadn't died in the Pacific. But he did. And that was that.

If she stayed here, she'd never find a man. Everyone knew she was a Penbrook, and no mother wanted her son marrying into the likes of this family. The humiliating memory of her one-time almost-romance with Colin swam across her memory. They'd snuck out to see a movie together, but Jackson had discovered Colin's secret and came after them. Made a scene during *Gone with the Wind* and forced them to leave the theater before Scarlett could throw the vase at Rhett.

Shea never heard from Colin again. Three years later he'd married Melinda Ames. No great loss. But definitely the stuff great tragedies are made of—if the young man in question were endowed with half a spine. Which Colin, obviously, was not.

Shea carefully marked her place and laid the book on her nightstand. She'd spent more time in her bedroom reading over the last three days than in her entire life. But she was reading with a purpose. Urgency, really. To find out who she was. To recognize something of herself in these ancestors. Too bad Celeste hadn't written diaries. How wonderful it would be to read her account of the love between herself and Mac.

In the kitchen, Shea pulled out eggs and lit the stove. A nice egg salad would hit the spot. She had just set the eggs to boil when a knock at the door startled her. She had four more days before the agreed-upon day for her transaction with Mr. Sable, so it wouldn't be him. Miss Nell always visited the library on Wednesday.

On the porch, Ernie greeted her. Unable to hide her surprise, she stepped outside. "What can I do for you?"

"I just wanted to give you—well, here." Red-faced, he shoved a few bills into her hands.

"What's this for?"

"The wood of the barn. I sold it for a good sum." He inclined his head toward the bills in her hand. "That there money is half what I sold it for. 'Lessen you figure I ought to give you more."

"No. Of course half is fair—but not at all necessary. I gave you the barn."

"Well, then. Good-bye." He tipped his battered hat and shuffled down the steps to his beat-up truck.

The wheels of Shea's mind began to spin as she headed back inside to her boiling eggs.

This was more than enough to get a bus ticket to Georgia. What if. . .what if she didn't have to sell her property to Mr. Sable just yet? She wanted to know what the land had meant to her great-great-granddad Mac. Why did the Sables want to wash the Penbrooks from the county? Why had they fought against each other so hard?

Maybe the only way she could keep Mac and Celeste's legacy alive was to have herself proclaimed as the legal heir to the Penbrook estate in Georgia. She hated to take it away from Mr. Riley. But after all, the man owned his own newspaper in Chicago. Surely he didn't need the inheritance the way she did. Even if he did, she was a Penbrook. Not him. And apparently being a Penbrook in Georgia didn't hold the same disgrace that it did in Oregon.

CHAPTER FIVE
GEORGIA 1949

Something was up with Andy, and Jonas didn't like it one bit. Andy wasn't behaving like himself. And that meant he was hiding something. Since they were ten years old, the two of them had shared just about everything, with only the rarest of secrets.

But then, Jonas had a few secrets of his own these days. For instance, the old lady who'd left the house to his father had been Jonas's grandmother. Mind-boggling information that Jonas himself was still trying to figure out.

Father had given him the news just last week, and for Jonas, coming to grips with his heritage was less difficult than accepting the reality that no one had allowed him to have a relationship with the woman. At least not a familial one. Questions fluttered through him. A sense of wanting to know about the old lady and yet, for some reason, nervous to find out. After all, if she hadn't wanted him to know her in life, why would she have wanted it to happen after her death?

Except for the fact that she'd had some sort of epiphany in her last days and had apparently decided honesty was the best policy, he might never have known the truth. She'd commissioned Andy to write her memoirs and provided him with the information to accomplish the feat. Only it never happened. According to Andy, the things he'd learned would more than expose her; they would also expose other people. People still living, who could be hurt by the information leaking out.

People like Jonas? Some of what Andy had learned must surely have included Jonas and the Riley family. For instance, his grandfather's affair with the writer—and the product of that affair, Daniel, Jonas's father, who had been raised by Jonas's grandfather and his wife.

Staring about the dinner table, he watched the faces of his black friend and his family. He felt alone. But then, when didn't he feel alone? The bachelor son of a newspaper mogul. Andy was the star. The one who took after Jonas's father.

He didn't blame Andy. Truthfully, having Andy fulfill all of Father's dreams for his son took some pressure off Jonas. Left him free to be second-rate without much expected of him.

OREGON, 1949

"Shea, wait!"

Shea clutched the handle of her suitcase and halted just before stepping onto the bus. She turned to face the man calling her name.

"Colin." The word rushed out with a cool breath.

"You're seriously leaving?" He took her arm and pulled her out of the line of passengers waiting to board. "Then my father was right."

She'd have to tread carefully. She'd hoped for at least a couple of days' leeway before Jackson discovered she was gone. "Yes, I'm leaving."

The expression on Colin's face was one of misery and regret. "I should have taken you away from here ten years ago."

Compassion rose up in Shea. "It would have been a disaster, Colin. Believe me. Your father did us both a favor by stopping the romance between us."

His face reddened. "Do you really mean that?" He gripped her arm tighter as passion flared in his eyes. "Not a day goes by that I don't regret letting my father tear us apart. I look at Melinda and despise her because she isn't you."

The bus driver exited the station and started loading the bags sitting on the ground. "You comin', lady?"

"Yes. Hang on just a second."

"Look, I ain't got all day. This bus is pulling out in five minutes, with or without you. You want that bag underneath?"

Shea nodded and walked back to the bus. She handed the driver her suitcase. Colin followed her. "Listen, I didn't mean to make you uncomfortable. I just wanted you to know how sorry I am about. . .everything."

"Listen, Colin. I've had ten years to move on with my life. Please try to forget about what might have been and learn to love your wife."

"For ten cents I'd hop that bus and follow you wherever you go." His impassioned words caused Shea to draw away from him. She hadn't allowed herself moments alone with him since the day his engagement to Melinda was announced, and she certainly wasn't tempted now. But neither did she want to insult him.

"I wouldn't allow it, my friend."

A car flashed by and Colin stepped back quickly. Shea couldn't hold back a smile. He'd hop the bus and follow her wherever she went, huh? Same old Colin. Afraid of being caught talking to the girl from the wrong side of town. Just as well. For his sake.

"Good-bye, Colin. Please try not to think about me anymore. And please don't say anything to your father about seeing me here." She hesitated. "I haven't spoken with him in a few days.

A frown furrowed his brow and then was immediately replaced by a smile of understanding. "You mean you aren't selling the last of the land to him?" He said it with such a sense of glee that Shea wasn't sure how to respond. The truth seemed the best way.

"Not until I return. But he wasn't supposed to get the deed for a few more days. I'd appreciate the time to get far enough away that he won't come after me. You know how he is when his mind is set on something."

Colin inclined his head. "I understand. He won't hear it from me."

Reaching out, Shea pressed her palm to his arm. She would have pulled back immediately, but Collin covered her hand with his. "Take care of yourself, Shea. You deserve the best."

Tears sprang to her eyes. Apparently misunderstanding the reason behind her tears, Colin tried to pull her close. But Shea shifted away. "Thank you for your kindness, Colin. I hope you find the courage to be truly happy."

Climbing the steps of the bus, she left him staring after her.

GEORGIA 1949

"I need a favor," Andy said to Jonas as they walked toward Jonas's Ford.

"You're not driving my car. I know how you drive."

Andy gave a cursory laugh. "It's not that."

Jonas's face clouded as they climbed into the car. "You need cash or something?"

"No. I want you to come with me to meet someone."

"Who?" Jonas turned the key in the ignition and the car roared to life.

"I need to meet Senator Dane."

A low whistle left Jonas's puckered lips. "You start at the top. What makes you think the senator is going to give a black man an interview about his son?"

"He asked to see me. But I don't want to go alone."

"Should I be worried?" He checked his mirror and pulled away from the curb.

"I hope not. He wants to meet me on the same road where Ruthie and Rafe were hung."

Jonas gripped the steering wheel and turned his attention from the road. His brow creased in a frown. "Forget it. It's a trap."

"I thought that, too." Andy shrugged. "As a matter of fact, I still think it's a possibility."

"Then you're an idiot to even consider going. I think we should tell the sheriff."

"The new sheriff is Rafe's brother, Gabe."

"So he might be on our side."

"No white man is ever on a black man's side down here. Rafe was a rare exception."

Gabe had probably been with Sam the night his brother was murdered. He was part of Sam's little entourage, after all. Definitely a member of the Klan.

Andy remembered the night he'd been dragged by that group of white-hooded cowards outside of Lottie's boarding-house to witness a burning cross. He also remembered the bullwhip. His back still bore the jagged scars, just like so many of his ancestors.

"I'm not taking you into a trap."

"I'm going to meet the senator. With or without you."

"Why would you do something so crazy just to get a big story?"

"This has nothing to do with a story." Andy's heart lurched as they neared the fork in the road that would lead past the hanging tree and on to Penbrook House.

"Which way?" Jonas groused.

Andy pointed right. Jonas took the left fork.

"I have no intention of letting you risk your life. Mother would never forgive me."

Andy remained silent until the senator's black car came into view, driving toward them from the opposite direction.

Jonas turned to Andy and scowled. "You're a liar."

"Maybe so. But it worked."

"Well, I'm not stopping."

"Then I'll have to jump out of a moving car. What do you think your mother will say about that?"

Jonas slapped his palm against the steering wheel. "All right. But I'm coming with you. And I'll do the talking."

Andy chuckled. "No, you won't. But you can come with me."

Jonas parked the car at the side of the road, no more than ten yards from where the senator's car had stopped. He bolted out of the vehicle. Andy joined him quickly, before he went off half-cocked and got them both into trouble. That was the problem with born-and-bred Yankees like Jonas. They had no idea how things worked down here.

Andy touched his friend's arm. "Before we go any farther, I need to tell you something."

"What? That you've sustained a head injury since I last saw you?" Jonas clapped him on the shoulder.

Andy shook his head. "Senator Dane is my father."

Jonas's jaw dropped. Then a slow grin spread across his face. "Oh, boy. You really do have brain damage."

"Fine, don't believe me. But in a few minutes, the senator

will confirm my biology. And then you'll feel bad for calling me a liar twice in one night."

"We'll see."

The car parked on the opposite side of the road killed its motor, and the back door opened. Andy's throat went dry as he recognized Samuel Dane. It was one thing to find out his father's identity through the pages of his great-grandmother's diaries. But meeting him face-to-face filled Andy with foreboding.

They were almost close enough to speak when the sheriff's car zoomed down the road and skidded to a halt in the middle of the street. Sheriff Gabe exited, carrying a shotgun. Jonas leaped forward, shielding Andy's body with his own.

GEORGIA 1847

It seemed to Mac as though an eternity passed before the house grew quiet and everyone, from servants to guests, settled down for the night. Mac looked out across the field from his bedroom window, wondering if Celeste was with her mother in the slave quarters. Celeste slept in a room off the kitchen with Cookie Mary. But he hadn't seen her return to the house after she'd seen his embrace with Janette, so Mac assumed she was visiting her mother.

Was she confiding in her mother right now about her love for him? Or perhaps crying over catching him with Janette? He needed to see her, to explain that the harlot had kissed him before he could stop her. Revulsion shuddered through him at the memory of the odor of garlic and turnip greens.

He saw a shadowy female form walk through the garden. Stepping out onto the balcony, Mac made his way to the end of the platform and to a flight of outside steps. He made as little noise as possible as he descended. Once he reached the garden, he called in a loud whisper. "Where are you? It's Mac."

"I'm here."

Mac's heart stopped as Janette stepped out of the shadows.

"Oh, I'm sorry," he said. "There's been a—" He was going to say "mistake," but she gave him no chance. In a flash, she wrapped her arms around his neck and pressed against him. "I knew you'd come." Her shawl dropped from her shoulders and slid to the ground.

He curled his fingers around her wrists and pulled her arms from his neck. "I'm truly sorry, Miss Blythe, but I thought you were someone else."

"Someone else? What do you mean?"

Mac's heart nearly stopped when he realized she was clad in her white dressing gown. He turned his gaze away from the silhouette of her legs through the thin fabric. "Why are you out here in your nightclothes?"

Her slender shoulders lifted. "I thought you might like to see what you'll be getting after we marry."

"That's a pretty bold statement."

Her lower lip pushed out in a studied pout. "And now you must think so little of me."

Expelling a weary breath, Mac lifted her shawl from the ground and placed it around her shoulders. "To tell you the truth, Janette, I don't think of you one way or another. I'm in love with someone else."

Janette's eyes grew wide, and the light of the moon caught a glint of tears. "Surely not that slave girl you called after earlier."

"I don't mean to be rude, but I must ask you not to delve into matters that are not your affair."

"Not my affair!" The carefully sweet demeanor vanished as she glared at him. "We've been practically promised to each other since I was six years old and you were twelve. How can you possibly say it's none of my affair?"

The woman was delusional. "We are not promised. Nor have we ever been. It is true, our parents have expressed a desire for a union between us. But I have made it perfectly clear to mine that when I marry, it will be a woman of my own choosing."

She jerked her shawl close to her body and sneered. "Like the little Negress?"

"I'll thank you not to speak uncivilly. It isn't becoming."

"I'll not speak to you at all." She gathered her dressing gown between her hands and lifted it slightly so she could walk with ease. "You disgust me."

The feeling was mutual, but he chose to stay true to his upbringing and not allow his anger to take over his tongue.

Mac watched her flounce to the house, then he turned toward the back entrance into the kitchen. Perhaps Celeste had returned while the family ate dessert. He'd assumed, since Cookie had served them in the parlor, that Celeste hadn't returned yet. But perhaps. . .

He heard voices coming from the little room. Celeste and Cookie must still be awake. Hesitating, he wondered if he should bother them so late.

"No, Mastuh Henry. Please." Celeste's terrified voice penetrated the closed door.

"Stop fighting me, girl. What else do you think you were brought into the house for? My brother isn't the only one who gets a turn with you."

Mac's head spun as he realized what was happening. He pushed through the door. "Henry, stop!"

Henry jumped off the bed, yanking on his trousers.

Mac flew at his brother and they tumbled to the ground. Somewhere in his mind he registered Celeste's scream as he pounded Henry. Blood sprayed the room. But Mac's rage rendered him powerless to stop.

Finally, he felt himself being lifted off his brother and to his feet.

"What is going on here?" Their father's voice boomed through the air.

Jerking free of the two slave men who held him, one on each side, Mac fought for breath. "He was raping her!"

"Rape?" Henry said through a lip already beginning to swell. His tone remained cocky despite the broken nose and battered face. "You can't rape a slave. They're too willing. She should be flattered I gave her a second look."

Mac lunged for his brother again, but a whimper from the bed stopped him. He turned. Celeste sat huddled against the wall, clutching her torn gown, trying to cover her exposed flesh. "Only a fool would think she was willing." Mac went to her, but she looked away. He grabbed her thin blanket and covered her.

"You just want her for yourself," Henry sneered. "I don't mind sharing. Why can't you?"

Anger and outrage boiled Mac's blood. "You're a fool. How can you want any other women when you have a wife like Maddy?"

"Leave my wife out of it. This has nothing to do with her."

"Both of you shut up before you awaken our guests or your mother," their father growled. He turned to the two slave men. "Kindly help my son off the floor." He turned to Mac. "I will see you in my study directly after breakfast in the morning."

"Yes, Father."

Bent over from the waist and assisted by the slave men, Henry followed their father from the room.

Cookie flew from her cot to Celeste's. Startled, Mac gave her an incredulous stare. "You were here the whole time she was being brutalized? Why didn't you do anything?"

The old woman wrapped Celeste in her arms and turned to him. "Whut you think an old slave woman can do to stop the young mastuh?"

Watching tears flow down Celeste's face filled Mac with helpless fury. "I guess you couldn't have done anything."

Celeste remained huddled against the wall on her cot. Purple bruises darkened the soft flesh of her neck and shoulders.

Anger surged through Mac's veins. What kind of a man groped a woman so tightly that he left bruises to remind her of his brutality? "Celeste, look at me."

Reluctantly she turned her face toward him.

"Did he hit you?"

She shook her head.

He hunkered down in front of her cot until he was eye to eye with her. "Celeste, did he. . .did he hurt you?"

A sob caught in her throat. She nodded, obviously understanding that he was asking if she'd been raped.

Mac felt like he'd been kicked in the gut. As though something precious had been taken from him. "I'm sorry, honey."

Sobs wracked her body. Cookie pulled her gently into old, comforting arms. Celeste wilted against her.

Suddenly feeling like an intruder, Mac stood. He wanted to tell her how sorry he was that he hadn't arrived sooner. That he would have done anything to take this pain from her. But he knew in his heart that the last thing she wanted was for him to stay in that room.

"Lock the door after me, Cookie."

"Dere ain't no lock on dat door."

"I'll put one on tomorrow. Is there anything you can set against the door for tonight?"

"Mastuh, yo' brother ain't in no shape to come back here tonight. Thanks to you. Don' you worry none. You go on and let me take care of our gal here."

With one last look at Celeste, he left the room.

WYOMING 1949

The bus carrying Shea east toward Georgia rattled down a pockmarked rural road. This was her second day aboard the stifling vehicle, but she scarcely noticed the discomfort, so enthralled was she with the diaries of Mac Penbrook. She had left the deed to her property with Miss Nell and locked the house up tight—not that the rusty old locks would keep anyone out who truly wanted to get in.

She could only imagine Jackson Sable's fury when he discovered she had left town without selling him the ten acres to complete his empire. Hopefully Colin had kept his word. So far, though she'd looked over her shoulder practically the whole way, Jackson hadn't followed her to insist she complete the sale.

But just in case he became destructive, she had packed most of the diaries in a trunk along with her meager clothing. They now sat with the other passengers' luggage.

She had no real plan of action for when she arrived in Oak Junction, Georgia. She'd never been farther east than Oregon City, so she had no idea what to expect.

But she was no shrinking violet. She would face whatever she had to face—head on. This was the beginning of a new life for Shea Penbrook. If everything went her way, she'd inherit this elusive Penbrook home in Georgia. Then maybe. . .she'd find a reason to hold her head up when her name was spoken.

Was it possible there would actually be a day when shame didn't follow her?

CHAPTER SIX
GEORGIA 1949

Andy's stomach quivered at the sight of Gabe and his double-barreled, sawed-off shotgun. The young sheriff made an imposing figure sauntering toward him, silhouetted against the red sky of the Georgia sunset.

"Let me take care of this," Jonas growled next to him.

Alarm seized Andy's gut. "Keep your mouth shut unless you want to see me swinging from that tree over there."

"Look who came back to Georgia." Gabe fingered the trigger. "I thought you was smarter than that."

"I'm not here to cause trouble." Andy tried not to show his fear. He wasn't a coward, but only a fool would look down the barrel of a gun and not feel anxiety.

"You sure about that?"

"Absolutely."

Gabe turned to the senator, who so far had remained silent. "This boy giving you any trouble, sir?"

Gratified to see the senator flinch at the use of the word *boy*, Andy watched as the senator's chest rose and fell in indignation. "This *man* has consented to meet me at my request, Sheriff."

"Your request?" Gabe lifted his foot and rested it on the

fender of the senator's car. "You feeling the need to find the redemption that only comes with repentance?"

Andy felt the senator's alarm as keenly as his own. Did Gabe know Andy was Samuel Dane's son? If so, how safe were they standing out here on a country road at dusk, miles from town? "What redemption are you talking about, Sheriff?" he said before the senator could respond.

"That's Sheriff *Sir* to the likes of you, boy."

Jonas bristled.

"Easy," Andy said under his breath.

"Excuse me, Sheriff *Sir*." Samuel Dane's steely voice penetrated the growing darkness. "If there's nothing more, I have business to discuss with Mr. Carmichael."

Gabe nodded grudgingly and pointed a fat finger at the senator. "If you're gonna apologize to anybody, it better be me."

"I don't recall mentioning an apology to anyone." Senator Dane took a step forward. "However, is there something you'd like to say to me?"

"We both know that son of yours ought to be on trial for two murders."

A small measure of hope surged in Andy. Was Gabe actually going to implicate Sam in Ruthie's death as well as Rafe's? Perhaps losing his brother had changed him for the better, despite his recent belligerence.

"What are you getting at, son?" Senator Dane asked.

"I think Sam killed my pa and you're covering it up."

Disappointment clutched at Andy. He should have known better.

"Your father's death was an unfortunate tragedy, Gabe." The senator's voice took on a conciliatory tone that Andy didn't quite believe. He watched his father closely. The man knew more than he was pretending.

Gabe wasn't buying his act either. "Murder usually is a tragedy, Senator."

"Now, Gabe. Your father was my good friend. You know that. I mourn the loss of him every day."

Gabe's freckled face twisted with sardonic anger. "Well, your *friend* is dead. And you know who killed him. But you ain't sayin'."

"Of course I know who killed him. I've admitted to seeing my son kill him. . .in self-defense."

Rage thundered across Gabe's face. "It wasn't self-defense. You know it and so does everyone else in this town. If you weren't a big, powerful senator, no one would have even pretended to believe your cockamamy story."

"I'm sorry you feel that way, son. If I could bring your pa back, I would."

"If you call me 'son' one more time, I'll put a bullet through your head."

Andy stepped forward. "Whoa, Gabe. You don't want to toss threats like that around."

"Shut up, nigger."

Jonas stepped forward. "Watch how you speak to my friend. I don't care if you're the sheriff or not, I'll flatten your nose if you call him that vile name one more time."

Gabe whipped his attention from Andy to Jonas. He gave Jonas a once-over and sneered. "We don't like strangers around here. Especially strangers who hang around with coloreds."

Jonas clenched his fists and spoke through gritted teeth. "Put down that gun and I'll teach you all about us Yankees."

"Oh, yeah?" Gabe leaned the shotgun against the senator's car. "What kind of teachin' you thinkin' on, *Yankee*?"

"How to be a decent human being is probably a little too ambitious for your first lesson, so how about we start with shutting your mouth?"

"All right. That's enough. Both of you."

Jonas and Gabe fell silent at the senator's stern voice.

"Look, I have business with Mr. Carmichael, and I am sure, Sheriff, that you have other law-related duties to attend to. After all, isn't that what we citizens pay you for?"

Andy held his breath, praying the situation would defuse itself with the senator's words. It wouldn't do for Jonas to get into a fight with the local law. Being a Yankee was pretty much on an even keel with being a black man. He wouldn't have a chance if Gabe got it into his head to arrest him for battering an officer of the law.

Gabe grabbed his shotgun. Jonas tensed, but Andy knew Gabe wouldn't kill a white man in cold blood. At least not without a white hood to hide his cowardly face.

"Watch yourself while you're here," he said, pointing first at Jonas, then at Andy. "I don't want any trouble out of either of you."

"Don't worry, Sheriff," Andy interjected before Jonas could egg him on any further. "You won't even know we're in town."

"Make sure I don't."

He turned on his booted heels and sauntered to his car. Andy, Jonas, and Senator Dane turned away from the dust as he spun his tires and sped away.

Andy turned to his father. "What's this about, Senator?"

Samuel cast a furtive glance at Jonas. "I thought you'd be alone."

"Never can be too careful when you're a black man in the South."

A nod raised the senator's chin. "I suppose that's so. Although I must admit I'm a little sad at the thought that you felt you needed protection from me."

"The truth is, Senator, I don't really know you, do I? You might be my father, but you didn't exactly tuck me in at night."

The man gave a nervous cough and cut his gaze to Jonas. Good grief. Even now, he couldn't admit to their relationship.

"I already know you're Andy's father, so you can stop acting like you're trying to hide something." Disdain thickened Jonas's words. "But I'm getting eaten alive by these mammoth Southern mosquitoes, so I'd appreciate it if you'd get to the point."

"Let me introduce the two of you." Andy's nerves were taut, and for the first time in a long time, he felt unsure of himself. "Senator, this is Jonas Riley. I was raised by his parents in Chicago. You remember why I had to leave, don't you?"

A look of honest pain shone on the senator's face, discernable even in the waning twilight. "Your stepfather's beatings. I'm so sorry."

But Andy didn't want to hear apologies. What excuse did a man have for turning his back on his child while another man harmed him?

"I wish—"

Andy cut off the senator's words. "Jonas and I were raised like brothers. So anything you have to say to me, you can say in his presence."

Stepping toward Jonas, the senator extended his hand. "It was good of your parents to take Andy in."

Jonas leveled a hard gaze at the senator. Andy had seen the look many times. His foster brother was trying to decide if this man was on the level or not. Did Samuel Dane deserve a handshake of friendship?

Slowly, Jonas reached out, though he didn't seem convinced. "He was easy to love. Too bad you never gave it a try."

"Jonas." Andy clapped him on the shoulder. "Leave it alone. You don't understand how things are."

An awkward silence filled the space between the three men. Finally Jonas cleared his throat. "Well, now that I can see you aren't about to be lynched, I guess I'll give you two some privacy." Jonas fixed the senator with a sharp gaze. "But I'll be watching." He spun on his heel and stalked off toward his Ford.

The senator turned to Andy. "Would you care to sit in my car?"

Unease tightened his gut, but Andy pushed it aside. There was no danger. That much was certain. "I don't have much time."

The senator stepped aside and gestured for Andy to precede him into the car. Andy slid across the black leather seat, smelling the newness and richness of his father's life. The same richness Andy had grown up with in Daniel Riley's home. Except that this man had accumulated his wealth in a class system where the Negro race was treated like dirt. The only time his people mattered was when their votes were counted. And still nothing changed to better the black man's cause. Their lips were too thick to drink from a white water fountain, their hair too nappy to be cut by a white barber, their backsides too black to sit in the main section of a theatre or courthouse or even the pew of a church where the pastor was a white man.

The senator had never done a thing for Andy or his mother. And he never would.

As the man slid into the car and closed the door, his driver exited.

Andy watched the chauffeur swat his neck. "He's just going to stand out there with the mosquitoes while we take shelter?"

"He's amply paid for his trouble." The senator gave a half smile—the first sign of humor Andy had detected in him. "Will your friend Jonas be staying in Oak Junction?"

"We haven't had much of a chance to talk about it. I'm the one who suggested he make use of Penbrook House. Since his father, who inherited it, is living in Chicago, it's just been sitting there empty. I'm sure Daniel would be pleased to let him have the house if he wants to live in Georgia indefinitely. It's kind of large for one person, though."

The senator heaved a sigh. "I had rather hoped Miss Penbrook would will the house to you. It's every bit as much yours as Daniel's."

His comment caught Andy by surprise. "You knew she was my great-grandmother?"

He nodded. "I kept her secret. And she kept mine."

"How convenient for you both."

"You know how things are, son. Perhaps someday a man and woman can love each other regardless of the color of their skin. But not today. Not for a long, long time, I suspect."

"If you understand that, then you also know folks around these parts would never have let me and my family move into Penbrook House."

Andy's father chuckled. "Imagine if they knew Miss Penbrook's true heritage. Weren't you hired to write her memoirs before she died?"

"Yes. But that was mostly a ruse so she could tell me about my heritage."

"Including my contribution?"

Andy's jaw clenched. "Yes." His collar seemed to tighten around his neck. He wanted nothing more than to leave this man's presence. "What do you want from me, sir?"

The songs of tree frogs and cicadas filled the air from the trees beyond the road. Andy wished he could get lost in the music and push aside the complications of his troubled life. Why had he ever agreed to this meeting?

"I wonder if you might allow me to contribute to your child's education."

Andy gulped. "How did you know about my child?"

"Your sister told me."

What right did this man have to weasel information from Lottie? If he really wanted to know about Andy, why hadn't he bothered to contact him? "You'd better be careful hobnobbing with so many black folk, Senator. People are going to talk."

Rather than being offended, Senator Dane smiled and nodded. "You're right. Three women from the ladies auxiliary saw me talking to your sister outside the library six months ago and sent their husbands to find out if I had formed an attachment to a colored woman."

Considering that the senator had formed an intimate attachment to Andy's colored mother, Andy found the story less than amusing. Indeed, he considered it downright offensive and didn't bother trying to hide his feelings. "It will be a long time before my daughter is of age to worry about her education. But my uncle Daniel has set up a trust fund for her. So although I appreciate the offer, it's not necessary."

The senator winced as though he'd been kicked. "Is there anything you'll allow me to do for my granddaughter?"

For a second, Andy almost relented. Instead, he pushed aside the sudden and unexpected compassion. This man had never done a thing for him. Why should Andy let him off the hook now? He put his hand on the car door. "You can do for her what you did for me. . .absolutely nothing." He pulled the handle and opened the door. "Good-bye, Senator. I hope my half brother gets exactly what he deserves."

OREGON 1949

Jackson Sable knew as soon as he pulled up to the dilapidated Penbrook home that something wasn't right. There were no signs of life. The house seemed empty. His stomach churned as he made his way to the porch and knocked. Knocked again. Waited for five minutes with no answer. Fury burned through him. Where could she be? After he had made plans for the land, boasted to his colleagues about finally ousting the Penbrooks from the area—as his great-grandfather before him had intended to do. If the girl had made a fool of him, he would teach her a lesson she'd never forget.

Movement at the side of the house caught his attention. Jackson turned. The only employee on the place was still here. That gave Jackson reason to hope.

Ernie inclined his head. "You lookin' for Miss Penbrook?"

"Yes. Will she be back soon?"

The farmhand removed his hat, scratched his greasy head, and crammed the hat back onto his head. "Well, now, she never said. But I got the feeling she might be gone for quite awhile. Took all her important papers and books over to Miss Nell Carter's house."

Barely able to contain his rage, Jackson spun around and stalked to the car. He cranked the motor, revved the engine, and slung dirt behind him as he turned the car toward Miss Nell's shack.

KENTUCKY 1949

Shea wasn't sure how much more of the jostling, stifling, stink-ing bus she could take. If she'd have been smart, she would have driven Granddad's pickup as far as the rattletrap would have taken her and caught a bus in the town closest to where the old Ford quit. Then she wouldn't have had to ride the bus as far. Fortunately, her current seatmate was a pleasant young woman with a sweet baby boy.

"My name's Tina," she had said with a shy smile as she plopped into the seat beside Shea four hours earlier. "We're goin' to Atlanta. You?"

"Oak Junction."

Her eyes had brightened with recognition. "Why, that's just a hop, skip, and a jump from where I live." She dimpled. "This is Charley. He's six months old."

"Pleased to meet you." Shea chucked the baby's chin and re-ceived a captivating giggle. She couldn't suppress a laugh. "You, my dear lad, are a charmer."

"I can tell by your accent that you aren't from around here. Where are you from?"

"Oregon."

Tina's face brightened. "I've always wanted to go west. What's it like in Oregon?"

"Lush and green and not as sweltering as down here."

"Sounds just as wonderful as I always imagined."

"Is someone waiting for you in Atlanta?"

Tina nodded. "My folks. My husband's parents are from Kentucky, so that's where we lived until. . ." She clutched the baby tighter to her breast. "He died a couple of months ago."

Shea reached over and pressed what she hoped was a com-forting hand to the young woman's arm. "I'm so sorry. It's a horrible thing for a woman to—lose the man she loves."

As though she hadn't heard, the young widow rubbed her palm lovingly over Charley's nearly bald head. "It was so sudden. He just collapsed one day on the farm. The doctor said his heart gave out." She turned to Shea with a frown. "Have you ever heard of a twenty-four-year-old man up and dropping like that?"

Shea shook her head. "Never. I guess it was just his time."

"Maybe." Tina's silky brows pushed together in a frown, and her eyes filled with questions. "Why do you think God would take Paul when he was so young and had a son to raise?"

Shea pulled back. She was the last person anyone should ask about God, but she didn't have the heart to express that to Tina. "Sometimes bad things happen to good people. That's the nature of life. Maybe God didn't have anything to do with it."

"I was raised with the notion that God is sovereign." Tina gave a shuddering little sigh and pressed Charley to her chest as the sway of the bus lulled the little fellow to sleep. "It would be easier, I think, if I could believe that God didn't have anything to do with it. That life—and death—just happen. But I like the notion that God is directing things."

"Maybe His sovereignty means that He set everything in place and watches the world He created take care of itself. That makes a lot of sense to me."

Tina lifted her head and looked into Shea's eyes as though trying to read her soul. "You don't go to church, do you?"

Shea gave a rueful smile. "Sorry."

"Oh, it's okay." But a frown creased her brow. "We believe what we're brought up to believe, I guess."

"I guess."

Tina's expression remained troubled as she closed her eyes

and drifted off to sleep, with Charley clutched protectively against her, leaving Shea to reflect on their conversation. For the next hour, as she listened to the steady breathing of mother and child, Shea remained lost in thought. If good things happened to bad people and bad things happened to good people, then God either wasn't sovereign or didn't care.

Pondering Celeste's life—her slavery and her rape by Mac's brother, Henry—Shea had to wonder. What kind of a God allowed an entire race to be enslaved and abused?

She'd never really thought about slavery from the individual's perspective before. Oh, sure, she'd read *Gone with the Wind* and had seen part of the movie, but Mac's account of the slaves at Penbrook was vastly different from those happy-go-lucky, mostly dimwitted servants in Margaret Mitchell's epic tale.

As the sun rose above the Kentucky-Tennessee border, she pulled out Mac's diary and began to read again.

GEORGIA 1847

Mac hesitated a moment in front of his father's study before rapping his knuckles against the gleaming oak door. His father beckoned, and he entered, knowing he was about to be pleaded with, yelled at, threatened, and dismissed.

"Sit down, son." His father didn't even bother looking up from the account books. Mac crossed the room, his boots clacking on the hardwood floor—the only sound in the room. Taking the seat in front of his father's desk, Mac sat silently, resenting feeling as if he were ten years old and being intimidated by the headmaster of the Academy for Young Men he and Henry had both attended through primary school.

Just as he was about to speak, his father expelled a heavy breath and pushed aside the books. He raised his head, laced his fingers atop the desk, and met Mac's gaze head on. Eye to eye. Father to son.

"Thank you for being prompt." Such was Father's tactic. Always begin on a pleasant note. Put the person about to be chastised at ease. Gain his trust.

"You said directly after breakfast," Mac said. "And as I recall, my promptness was never a matter of choice."

Father gave a curt nod, and the pleasant expression drifted from his face. "Very well. Let's get to the matter at hand."

Knowing that once his father began his well-planned rebuke, he wouldn't have the opportunity to bring up his own concerns, Mac broke in first. "I'm glad you called this meeting, Father. There is something I would like to discuss with you, as well."

His father's expression lifted in surprise. "Has it anything to do with last night's events?"

"It has everything to do with that."

"Then you may proceed."

This was it. His chance to defend the defenseless. He only hoped he had the wherewithal to do them justice. "I don't approve of Henry raping the young slave girls."

"Rape?" Father scowled. "Isn't that a bit crude?"

"Yes, it is. Unfortunately, the despicable act is much worse than the mentioning of it. Henry must be stopped."

Father slammed his palm down on his desk. "Do not presume to tell me what must occur in my own household." He stood and leaned over the desk. "Your actions last night were an embarrassment. Our guests informed me they are leaving tomorrow morning—a full day early. And don't look so relieved. They are considering withdrawing their willingness for you to wed Janette. Apparently, before the events with the slave girl and Henry, something happened between you and Janette that left her feeling you insulted her. I hope you're happy."

He was. But he didn't say so. "Father, the most embarrassing actions of last night came from Henry, not me. He raped Celeste."

"Stop overreacting," Father snapped. "The girl belongs to this family. He can use her as he sees fit. And you can, too, for that matter."

Mac very much doubted theirs was the only household where the men felt entitled to the slave women, and he was ashamed to think about his own encounters with their slaves, but he'd never sunk so low as to rape anyone. Besides, things were different now. His heart had become involved with Celeste. He didn't know why. And the emotions raging through him defied explanation. All he knew was the way he felt. He didn't care to reason it out.

His love for Celeste emboldened him, and he looked his father in the eye without flinching. "I care about her, Father. She isn't like the others."

His father's eyes narrowed and he stroked his moustache, his expression thoughtful. "Fine. You can keep her. I'll instruct Henry to stay away from her from now on. But you still must find a wife." He seemed pleased with his concession.

As though that settled the matter, he dropped into his chair and took a sip of brandy, then regained eye contract with Mac. "Now, you must make this up to Kendall Blythe and his daughter. Perhaps it's not too late for a union."

"Father, Janette is a fine young woman, I'm sure," Mac said, nearly choking on the lie but knowing better than to reveal his true thoughts. "I will not, however, ask for her hand. I don't love her. Nor shall I ever."

With an impatient wave, Mac's father shook his head. "Love is unimportant. You can take the kitchen girl with you if you want affection. But marry Janette. She'll be a proper mistress for Penbrook when I'm gone."

Repulsed, Mac tried to remain calm. "Father, I am not interested in Janette becoming mistress of Penbrook."

"Ridiculous. The girl hasn't been able to keep her eyes off you since she arrived."

"That's her misfortune, sir. I, on the other hand, have barely been able to look at her without disgust. And I do not intend to make her my bride."

Anger snapped in his father's eyes. "You'll do as you're told, or perhaps I will leave Penbrook to Henry. Is that what you want? To see your inheritance pass to your younger brother? He's already given us one grandchild—even if it was a girl—and Maddy is going to have another baby in a few months. I will not bequeath this land to a childless son. I refuse to take a chance that everything my father and I worked for might leave Penbrook hands."

More threats. More manipulation. If only his father could understand what Mac truly valued. But he never would. The land on which Penbrook House stood meant everything to the older man. Mac had no doubt if given a choice between his children or his land, he'd let his children go. "Father, I've told you many times, I won't hold it against you if you decide to leave the plantation to Henry. He clearly has the same love of the land that you do. I would most likely mismanage it and lose everything you've worked so hard for."

Jerking his head up, Mac's father expelled a frustrated breath. "Don't be a fool. I won't disinherit you. The plantation will go to you. Perhaps you can offer Henry compensation in exchange for managing your affairs."

Gratified that he'd called his father's bluff and won, Mac

gave a small concession. "I never thought to do otherwise."

"But you must find a wife, and soon."

Mac gathered a deep, cold breath. "I am in love with Celeste. She's the only woman I can think about."

His father's eyes widened as though full understanding of Mac's words had finally dawned. "Are you saying you want to live with her as husband and wife?"

"Yes."

Lines of anger and horror etched his face as he shot from his chair. "Are you mad? No Negress will be mistress of Penbrook. Not only is it an abomination, it's against the law."

A short, humorless laugh escaped Mac's throat. "It's an abomination to marry her but not an abomination to use her for pleasure? It's against the law to marry her but not against the law to violate her, even though any man who violates a white woman is hung?"

"Stop being so dramatic." Father turned away and stared out the window behind his desk. "I don't make the law."

Mac stood, unable to stand his father's presence any longer. "Yes, you do. We all do. That's what democracy is about."

"You listen to me, son." His father shot around the desk and came nose to nose with Mac. "You will not spout this drivel outside this room. Is that understood? You're as bad as the abolitionists. I will sell that kitchen maid if you go near her again."

Alarm squeezed Mac's chest. "You can't sell her. That would be too cruel. Her mother and sister live at Penbrook."

His father stroked his chin. "I am not an unreasonable man. If you give me your word that you will stay away from her, I won't sell her. I'll merely send her back to the fields."

Sending her to the fields was no more acceptable than selling her away from her mother and sister. "It's not fair to punish her because I fell in love with her."

"Stop saying that!" His face was so red, Mac feared he might collapse before the conversation ended. Clearly, Father was through negotiating. "She goes back to the fields tomorrow or I sell her. It's up to you."

Arguing about Celeste was getting them nowhere. Mac could see that the best course of action was compliance, for the moment. He'd find a way to change his father's mind later, when the man wasn't so upset. "All right. But she was injured last night when Henry. . ." Her battered image once more came to mind.

His father waved aside the rest of the sentence. "Of course, of course. She can recover first. If I have your word that you will not see her again."

His heart tightened within his chest. "Yes, Father. You have my word."

Chapter Seven
Georgia 1949

Jonas stepped out of the car and stared up at the antebellum building. Towering columns, a wrap-around porch, a full balcony. He'd lived in a beautiful home all his life, but nothing had prepared him for the grandeur of Penbrook House.

"Wow."

"Pretty amazing, huh? This place often has that effect on people," Andy said with a chuckle. "Buck let Miss Delta know you'd be coming, so she's opened things up and prepared the house for you."

"Miss Delta?"

"Buck's aunt. She was Miss Penbrook's housekeeper for fifty years. She's been living with her brother in a cramped shack in a rough section of town since the old lady passed on. But if you're going to be here, you might offer her the use of her old room. She'd probably appreciate the opportunity to take care of the place, even if it's just for a little while."

Good old Andy. Thoughtful to the core. Jonas preferred to be alone, but he supposed it wouldn't hurt to let the old lady take care of the place. As long as she stayed out of his hair.

"If she's Buck's aunt, why isn't she staying with him?"

Andy shrugged. "They offered her a room, but Delta said her brother Ronald was a pathetic old bachelor and he needed her more. Personally, I think Buck's kids get on her nerves. She devoted herself to Miss Penbrook and never got married or had children of her own. So not much tolerance."

The front door was locked, so they rang the bell. In moments, an elderly black woman answered. Her stern expression was replaced with a wide, white smile at the sight of Andy. "Get in here, boy, and let me take a look at you. My, my, my, you look tired. And thin. What's Lottie been feeding you over there? Nothing?"

Andy bent and kissed the weathered old cheek. "She's been feeding me like a king."

"Well, you don't look it."

Jonas smiled at the two and stepped forward, extending his hand. "I'm Jonas Riley. Thank you for coming out and getting the place ready."

Delta turned shrewd eyes on him, sizing him up like one would a prize horse before a sale. Jonas wasn't sure he measured up. "No need to thank me, boy. I been tending this house longer than you've been alive."

"Yes, ma'am. But thank you all the same. It smells fresh and clean. I like that. Reminds me of my grandma."

Delta gave a humph, though Jonas could tell the praise pleased her. "I ain't no grandma. Just used a bit of vinegar and elbow grease." She grabbed his bag. "Come on, I'll show you to your room."

Jonas laughed and took the bag from her. "I'll carry that."

"Suit yourself. If you want to lug it up all these stairs when you got a perfectly able housekeeper to do it for you, that's up to you."

Andy lifted his hand in a wave. "You two get acquainted. I'm headed back to town."

Jonas turned in surprise. "Don't you want to stay here with me?"

"I'd rather stay at Buck's. Besides, I still need to go over some notes from today's testimony."

Delta humphed again. "Mock trial if you ask me." She wagged her plump finger at them both. "You mark my words. That boy is going to go free to kill again."

Jonas heard the disgust in her voice. The anger, the pain. He couldn't help but feel compassion. There certainly didn't seem to be a lot of justice in the South for anyone who had the wrong color skin.

He dipped into his pocket and pulled out his keys, handing them to Andy. "Take my car."

"I'm not sure that's a good idea."

"Well, you're not walking. And it would be dumb for me to drive you to Buck's and then come all the way back here. Besides, Miss Delta has my room all made up and smelling nice, and all I want to do is get some shut-eye. Come get me before you go to the courthouse tomorrow."

Andy's face showed reluctance, but he took the keys.

"It ain't a good idea." Delta apparently wasn't the type to keep her opinion to herself. Jonas had a premonition that the two of them might clash. But he supposed he could handle a seventy-year-old woman.

"It'll be all right, Miss Delta," Andy said, sending the old woman a reassuring smile that seemed to appease her.

"You be careful, Andy."

"I will."

When he closed the door behind him, Delta glared at Jonas

and started up the steps without a word.

"What was that look for?" Jonas asked. He gripped the rail and started to follow her.

The old woman stopped midway to the top and turned on him. "Givin' a black man the keys to your car." She shook her head. "You don't know nothin'."

"What's there to know? Did you want him to walk all the way to town after dark?"

"A black man driving a new car upsets white folks in the South. If that no-good sheriff catches Andy drivin' it, there's gonna be trouble."

Unease gnawed Jonas's gut. That sort of scenario hadn't occurred to him. "Bad trouble?"

"Bad enough to put a black man behind bars and leave him there for ten years."

Jonas sprinted down the steps and flung open the door in time to see the car lights heading away. "Andy!" he called as the vehicle continued down the oak-lined lane.

"Ain't no point. He can't hear ya." Delta's tone gentled. "We just gots to trust the Lord now."

A ball of sweat trickled down Jonas's back. He couldn't hide his frustration. "Why didn't you tell me what kind of trouble he could get in before I let him go?"

"It ain't my place."

The old woman didn't seem to have a problem with her "place" any other time. "Where's the telephone?" Jonas headed back into the house without waiting for an answer. He assumed she'd follow. And he was right.

She caught up to him, her eyebrows raised. "Whut you gonna do?"

"Call the sheriff and let him know to leave Andy alone."

Miss Delta scowled and shook her head.

The look of wizened disapproval on her face stopped Jonas in his tracks. "What? You don't think I should?"

"It ain't my place to tell you whut you should or shouldn't do. But if you tell that no-account Gabe that Andy's out there all by himself in a white Yankee's car, there's gonna be trouble. Better to hope Andy makes it to Buck's without Gabe being any wiser. If he takes the back roads into town and don't look other drivers in the eye as he drives past, he should make it fine."

The woman made sense, but Jonas couldn't shake the fore-boding tightening his chest. "You're likely right. But I need to call Buck. At least he'll know to be on the lookout for Andy and can let us know when he arrives."

Delta nodded. "Telephone's over here."

Jonas dialed the number, mentally kicking himself for not thinking ahead. He had a rudimentary knowledge of the way things were in the South, but he hadn't taken time to consider. . .

"Dear God," he whispered, although he rarely prayed. "Please don't let Andy be hurt because of me."

GEORGIA 1949
Andy had known that borrowing Jonas's car was a mistake the second Jonas offered him the keys, but the stubborn side of him wouldn't allow him to acknowledge his fear. Now it appeared his pride may have gotten him into serious trouble. When the squad car flashed its lights behind him, he could only do one thing: pray for God to take care of his wife and baby.

GEORGIA 1949
A jarring pain at the side of her head woke Shea. She opened her eyes, rubbing the side of her head where it had hit against

the window. Still on the bus. Her stomach fluttered. Today she would arrive in Oak Junction.

"They don't seem to worry about being too gentle, do they?"

Shea turned to the sound of Tina's voice and smiled at the baby on her lap. "I guess not. When's the next stop?"

"The driver just called out a few minutes ago. We'll be pulling into Atlanta soon."

"That's where I change buses."

Tina's face clouded. "That's where I get off."

"Won't you be relieved? If I never see another bus it will be too soon."

She shrugged and seemed a little hurt. "It's not the bus I've enjoyed. It's our talks. Haven't you been glad to have someone to talk to the last two days?"

It was impossible to dislike this genuinely kind young woman. But personally, Shea would have preferred be left alone to her diaries and her strategies. She still had no idea how she was going to go about claiming her inheritance.

Regardless of her inward struggle, she smiled and nodded. "Of course I'm glad. Who wouldn't be happy to sit next to such a gorgeous little baby?" She held out her arms to Charley, and he launched himself toward her. Shea laughed and glanced at Tina. "Do you mind?"

"Not at all. I welcome the relief. My arms positively ache."

For the first time, Shea noticed the dark smudges under the young mother's eyes. "Oh, Tina, you should have said something sooner. I would have been happy to take turns holding him."

Shea reached out and Tina handed him over.

"I didn't want to be a bother."

"I wouldn't have considered it a bother at all. I just assumed you were being protective." She smiled at the baby and received a toothless grin in return.

"Do you have children?" Tina's words cut like a knife inside Shea's gut.

"I've never been married."

Tina's eyes widened, but she had enough tact to keep her curiosity to herself. "I'm sorry. I didn't mean to pry."

"It's okay. I was engaged once, but my fiancé was killed in the Pacific during the war."

"Pearl Harbor?"

"No. He didn't die until a few months before the war ended. He almost made it home." It only ached when she thought of it that way. How different her life would have been if he'd lived. They'd have married, moved to Seattle. He had wanted a big family, and Shea had, too. Now, at almost thirty years old, she figured her ship had pretty much passed her by.

"I'm sure God has another man for you, Shea. It's hard to know why things happen."

"Sovereignty?"

Tina blushed at Shea's teasing tone, and Shea immediately regretted mocking her.

"I'm sorry. It's just that I've decided to be content without a husband and children."

"But you're so good with Charley. And I can tell you'd like to have one of your own."

Shea felt the knife twist. "Perhaps. But I can't wait around for happiness to find me. I'm all alone in the world, and it's time to make something of my life. Without a man, apparently."

"What do you intend to do?"

Shea wasn't sure how it happened, but somehow, on a hot, stinking bus surrounded by strangers, she found herself confiding in her new friend, opening up about her reason for going to Georgia. She told about the newspaper article reporting Miss Penbrook's death and the subsequent reading of the will. About the diaries she'd found, chronicling the past of Mac Penbrook, her own ancestor.

Tina listened intently, as though she were personally invested in the outcome of Shea's quest. "So you think you're Miss Penbrook's rightful heir?"

"It's almost too much to be coincidence, don't you think?"

"I sure do. It makes me want to come to Oak Junction with you and help you fight."

Shea was tempted to beg her to come. But she knew this was something she had to do on her own. "I just wish I knew what I should do first."

"My daddy is county clerk in Atlanta. I know he'd tell you to go to the courthouse and look up birth and death records. Now, a lot of buildings were burnt during the war, but Oak Junction was headquarters for the Yankees after occupation. Not many homes in the area were burned and none of the town buildings."

Funny how she said "the war," as though there hadn't been two world wars since the War Between the States. Shea knew from history books and literature that true Southerners still hadn't surrendered. And most likely never would.

Well, maybe she had more in common with her Southern ancestors than she did with the Oregon clan. After all, she wasn't willing to accept defeat either. She would fight until she proved her rightful place as heir to the Penbrook estate. This Mr. Riley would have no choice but to relinquish his so-called rights to her land.

Her stomach churned as the bus pulled into the station in

Atlanta. When it was time to say good-bye, she hugged Tina tightly and pressed a kiss to Charley's soft head before watching them walk away. Then she boarded the final bus in her week-long journey to what might very well be her ultimate destiny.

GEORGIA 1847

After two unbearably painful days of obeying his father's orders, Mac could stand it no longer. He waited until the household was sleeping and made his way downstairs to the kitchen. He'd played the perfect son and had forced himself to play the perfect host to the Blythes, who had decided to extend their stay for another week—much to Mac's chagrin.

After a furtive glance around, he tapped gently on the door. Cookie Mary had assured him she'd be awake so that he could see for himself that Celeste was recovering well.

The old woman appeared in a beat, as though she'd been standing next to the door, waiting for him to arrive. She reached out gnarled brown fingers and pulled him inside. "Get in here befo' somebody sees ya."

Mac entered quickly and shut the door as softly as possible. "How is she?" he whispered.

"Heartsick, Mastuh." The old woman shook her head, regret wrinkling her face even more. "Jus' about as heartsick as anyone I ever saw."

Mac moved cautiously to Celeste's bed, where she lay curled under the covers, knees to chest. He was gratified to note that as bad as she looked, Henry looked a lot worse. He'd suffered a broken nose, broken ribs, and two black eyes. He'd told his wife, Maddy, the injuries occurred during a brawl while playing poker. Of course, Henry had been the hero of that particular yarn.

He would be in bed for at least another week, so Mac felt

a measure of relief that at least he wouldn't have to pass him in the hallways of the vast Penbrook House, nor would he have to face him at mealtimes. And he didn't have to worry about him violating Celeste again.

"Is she awake?"

"I's—I'm awake, suh." Celeste sat up slowly, her face twisted with pain. She pulled the covers up to her chin. Her display of modesty nearly broke Mac's heart after the ordeal she'd been through. He sat on the bed next to her, but she seemed to shrink farther against the wall behind her cot, and her breath caught in her throat.

"I'm sorry." How could be have been so stupid? Of course she wouldn't want a man sitting on her bed. He slipped to the floor and knelt beside her. "Is this better?"

Celeste averted her gaze. "I can't tell you where to sit, Mastuh."

"Mac."

"Suh?"

"Call me Mac."

Cookie clucked her tongue. "Now, Mastuh, you knows she can't do dat. Why you tryin' to put ideas in her head?"

He gave the old woman a reproving frown. "Hush, Cookie, before I send you from the room."

"I'll hush alright, but dat gal had better mind her place."

Mac ignored the last comment and focused his attention on Celeste. "How are you feeling?"

"Better."

"I'm sorry I didn't get here sooner that night. I thought you were still down at the quarters with your ma. I went out to the garden and waited, hoping to see you when you came back so we could have our talk. But you never came."

"My ma wasn't home. She done been hired out to Mr. Haverty's place. Their cook is ailin', an' they needed someone to cook fo' the family."

"So the whole time I thought you were down at the slave quarters, you were here?" Regret clutched Mac's gut. If only he'd known she was in the house that night, he would have gone to find her, and his presence would have prevented Henry's brutal attack.

She nodded miserably.

"I'm so sorry this happened to you, Celeste. I'd have my brother arrested if the law allowed."

Her eyes glistened with tears. Startling hazel eyes that bespoke her mixed blood. She reached out and gently touched her palm to his cheek. She had never touched him before except to nurse him, and Mac was unbelievably moved. "Please don' blame yourself, suh. . .Mac. You done the best you could. I felt jus' like a princess in a child's book, bein' rescued by a han'some prince."

He curled his fingers around hers and brought their clasped hands down to the bed. She didn't pull away, so Mac kept them. "You deserve to be treated like a princess. I'll see to it that you are never hurt like this again."

"That be enough." Cookie stood over him, broom in hand, ready to use it as a stick of discipline. He'd never seen her look so fierce and determined. "You get on out of here 'fore I tell yo' pa you been here."

Mac scowled. "You mean to tell me you couldn't have used that broom to stop Henry from harming Celeste, but you'd use it on me for caring about her?"

There was no relenting or apology in the old black face as Cookie continued to stare him down. "Whut yo' doin' is wuss. Fillin' her head full of nonsense an' lies."

"Loving her is worse than violating her?"

"At leas' she know what to expect from Mastuh Henry. From you. . .she always be wantin' whut she can't have."

"That's not true. I love her."

"Love." Cookie shook her head and poked the broom menacingly close to his chest. "Git up and git yo'self on out of here."

Mac looked back at Celeste. She refused to meet his gaze. "Honey, don't listen to Cookie. I love you. I'll find a way for us to be together."

"If you love her so much, how come you ain't asked her if she feel the same ways 'bout you? Hmm? Maybe she want you and yo' brother to leave her be."

An arrow of pain pierced Mac's heart. Was it possible Celeste didn't feel the same way about him? He hadn't imagined the look in her eyes when she'd pressed her warm palm to his face just moments before. Now, however, she wouldn't meet his eyes. "Celeste?"

"Please leave me alone, suh," she whispered.

Stung, Mac rose slowly to his feet. How could he have read her so wrong? "I am not my brother," he said, trying to muster all his dignity. "I don't force myself on women."

He waited for her to respond. When she finally drew a deep breath and nodded, meeting his gaze head on, he had his answer. She obviously wanted nothing more to do with him. He'd been fooling himself these months, believing she had cared for him during his illness out of a sense of affection. Instead, she'd been doing as she was forced to do. The knowledge shook Mac to the core.

"I won't bother you again." Humiliation burned his neck and face as he exited the room.

He closed the door and turned, nearly jumping out of his

skin when a shadowed figure stopped in front of him. "Well, it appears your brother isn't the only one visiting the slave girls at night."

The sound of Janette's voice turned his stomach. "What are you doing up at this hour?"

"I don't know." Her voice came closer, and the smug tone set Mac's defenses on guard. "Call it women's intuition. Or possibly I heard you walk past my door."

It took all of Mac's control not to lash out at the bold woman and tell her exactly what he thought of her meddling. "You shouldn't be here."

"Perhaps you shouldn't be here either. As a matter of fact, I'm almost certain your actions are much more clandestine than mine. And I have an insatiable curiosity."

The woman was unbearable. "There's nothing here to satisfy your curiosity, Janette. I came to check on Cookie Mary. She's been feeling poorly today. Thinks she might have a stomach ailment."

"Well, aren't you just the sweetest thing?" She moved closer to him, her voice as smooth as maple syrup. And completely unbelievable. Mac's eyes were adjusting enough to the blackened room that as she stepped closer, he could see almost clearly. Dressed in her nightgown, without a dressing gown covering it, the outline of her generous curves was apparent. He swallowed hard as his pulse quickened. It could not be denied that Janette had certain desirable qualities. His defenses began to wane.

Why was he wasting his time on a slave woman who obviously could care less about him, when this woman before him was willing to compromise herself to be with him?

Still, he wondered if the Southern belle had any idea what she was offering by being alone with him, in the dark, dressed in her nightclothes. "What are you trying to do, Janette?"

She raised her arms and slipped them around his neck. Mac was all too aware of his body's response. "I want you," she whispered. "I want to marry you and bear your children. I want to be mistress of Penbrook. And I'm desperately trying to make you fall in love with me."

"I can't do that, Janette." He knew he should push her away, but her softness felt too good against his bruised ego. His eyes drifted to her lips.

She smiled. "You can kiss me," she whispered.

A vision of Celeste's face swept over his mind. Why couldn't it be her so willing in his arms? Anguish shoved at his heart. Mac pulled Janette tighter against him and lowered his head, pressing his lips against hers. He closed his eyes and allowed himself to become lost in her willingness. But his mind saw only Celeste.

The sound of an opening door pulled him from the frenzied kissing. He opened his eyes and blinked at the wrong woman in his arms. He turned toward the door with Janette still cuddled close to him.

Celeste.

"Excuse me, Mastuh. I was jus'. . ." The break in her voice was all Mac needed to convince him she had lied. She definitely cared for him. He put Janette away from him as Celeste started to close the door.

"Celeste, wait." He shoved out his booted foot and stopped the door just before it clicked shut. "I know you care about me."

"Cookie be right, suh." Celeste shifted her gaze to Janette, who stood where he'd left her in the center of the dim kitchen. "Miss Janette'll make you a good wife. I can't be no more to you than I wuz to Mastuh Henry."

"I would never—"

"You might not hurt me in the doin' of it, but it would be the same."

Janette wrapped her arms around him from behind. "Mac, really. Stop begging the girl and come back to me."

As he turned to rebuff her, Celeste's door closed.

Removing Janette's hands from his waist, he stepped away from her. "Leave me alone, Janette. I'm sorry I led you on. This was a mistake. But it will never happen again."

She sashayed close to him again, this time staying a few inches away. "It will happen again. Trust me. You won't resist me forever."

Her candor pulled all words from Mac's mind, and he couldn't formulate a rebuttal. Just as he found his voice, she beat him to speech.

"You listen to me, Mac Penbrook. I mean to marry you. I am not opposed to your dalliance with this slave girl as long as you use discretion and do not claim any children born of the union. If you do not come to me willingly before my family leaves Penbrook, I will be forced to tell my parents about your kisses and caresses in the dark while I am clad in nothing but my nightgown."

Incredulity filtered through him. He stared at her to determine whether she could possibly be serious. "You brought this on yourself. You followed me, dressed like that, and offered your kisses. How can you claim to be compromised?"

"That's the beauty of being a lady, Mac. I can say whatever I please about the situation and no one will doubt my word."

Now he saw her objective. Janette had planned every second of the last few minutes. She had played a hand and he had folded, handing over the jackpot. Only this wasn't a friendly game of poker. This game was hers and the prize was the rest of his life. Feeling every inch the fool he was, he sneered at her. "Lady, huh?"

"Now, darling, don't be insulting. I think I'm offering you a generous arrangement. You'll have me—whom you clearly want—and you may keep your little Negress. All I ask is that you make me your wife."

Rising on her toes, she briefly pressed her lips to his once more. "Think about it, Mac. You have twenty-four hours before I go crying to my daddy, ashamed that I allowed my love for you to cause me to act against my better judgment." A smile of triumph curved her lips and she turned and walked away, leaving Mac feeling helpless fury burning through him.

CHAPTER EIGHT
GEORGIA 1949

Jonas didn't hear from Andy's brother-in-law, Buck, until daybreak. When the man finally called, Jonas picked up the phone at the first ring.

"Andy never came back to the boardinghouse last night," Buck said.

"Why didn't you call me sooner?"

"I kept waitin', hopin' he had jus' gone to Georgie's club and had too much to drink."

"You know Andy doesn't drink anymore. Something's wrong."

"I think you might be right."

"Is there a taxi service I can get to come out here and drive me into town?"

"I got a truck. I can come and get ya."

"Thanks, Buck."

Delta seemed to appear in the hallway out of nowhere. "He done got hisself in trouble, ain't he?"

"I don't know, Miss Delta. He might have." Jonas looked at the grandfather clock sitting against the wall. Eight o'clock. "Buck's on his way to get me and we're going to go look for him."

Jonas's gut tightened at the thought of what they might

find. If the sheriff was truly part of the Klan and found Andy driving a new car, Andy may have suffered the same fate as the two young lovers last year. The image sickened Jonas—horrified him. He tried to shove the thought aside.

"You find that boy. Your grandma didn't fight so hard to make sure your cousin would live just for him to come back to Georgia and get hisself kilt."

"You knew she was my grandmother?"

"I did."

"But Andy's not my cousin." Jonas shook his head. "I think you're confused, Miss Delta."

"No, I ain't."

He looked closely at the older woman. What secrets did she know? "What is it you're not telling me?"

"What I knows ain't for me to tell. I didn't tell Andy and I ain't tellin' you."

A horn beeped outside. "Buck must have flown over those roads."

Jonas went outside, where he spied a 1930 Plymouth truck that looked like it might be on its last leg. Stuffing his curiosity, Jonas made a mental note to draw more information from Miss Delta as soon as possible. For now, he had to find Andy.

"Don't just stand there," Buck hollered. "Git in and let's go."

"First stop should be the sheriff's office," Jonas said as he climbed in. "He'd better not have harmed Andy, or I'll have a lot to say about Southern justice when I write my next column for *The Observer*."

After walking for what seemed like hours, Shea came to a fork in the road. When the abrupt man at the bus station had given her directions, he hadn't mentioned a word about the road coming to a T. Which way was she was supposed to go?

She set her heavy suitcase on the ground. The man had said he'd store her trunk of books for twenty-four hours before throwing it in the garbage. Couldn't have unclaimed baggage cluttering up the place. So she'd hauled the suitcase with her on her quest to find Penbrook House. Now, merely an hour later, her arms felt as if they might fall right out of their sockets. She should have left all the diaries in the trunk instead of transferring some of them to her suitcase.

The sun bore down on the dusty little road. A combination of exhaustion, heat, and weakness from not having had much to eat over the past couple of days left her with no more energy to walk. She plunked herself down on the suitcase. Where on earth was this Penbrook House? The fellow at the bus station had claimed, "Can't miss it. Just follow the road out of town until you get there." Well, she'd followed the road, and now she had two more roads to choose from.

Relief flooded her when she heard the sound of a truck and saw dust swirling through the air in its wake. She stood in the middle of the road and waved.

The truck skidded to a stop. "What do you think you're doing, lady?"

"I'm looking for—"

"Get out of the way," the man growled. "We're in a hurry."

"But I just needed to ask—"

The man in the passenger seat flew out of the truck and stomped around to her. He swung her up in his arms and carried her toward his side of the truck.

Fear seized Shea. Flashes of Celeste's ordeal and images

of her attack shot terror through her mind. A scream tore at her throat. She kicked and wiggled until he lost his grip. Her squirming body dropped out of his arms, but he steadied her. She landed on her feet, stumbled, then regained her footing.

"Take it easy, lady. I'm just getting you out of the way." He didn't bother to spare her another glance as he hopped in the truck and the driver sped away.

So much for Southern hospitality. Shea trudged back over to her suitcase and sat on the hard edge, fighting back the tears burning her eyes. One thing was for sure, she wasn't going to walk the direction the truck came from. The two men had driven back toward town, so there was only one way left for her to go. Picking up her suitcase, she straightened her shoulders and started down the unfamiliar road.

Twenty minutes later she'd seen nothing but fields and trees and red dirt. She was about to turn around when she spotted a car at the side of the road a quarter of a mile ahead. The driver's side door was open. As she approached, she saw a body hanging out.

Fighting the urge to turn and run, Shea listened carefully. At the sound of a muffled moan, she picked up her pace.

"Hello?" she called. "Are you okay?"

She knew it was a dumb question, but nerves always made her ramble. She peeked inside, half expecting the man to jump out at her. She stopped short when she saw a black man, badly beaten, blood soaking the seat. He opened his eyes and moaned.

Compassion replaced fear. "What can I do to help?"

"D–d–drive m–me."

"To where?"

"P–p–penb–brook."

Penbrook. Maybe there was more to Tina's sovereign God

theory than Shea had given credence. "I've been looking for Penbrook for hours. Which way is it?"

He pointed weakly. Back the direction she'd just come from. "Figures," she mumbled. "I had two choices and chose the wrong road." Shea shook her head. "Do you think you can move over so I can get in?"

He nodded weakly. After tossing her suitcase into the back-seat, Shea helped him sit up, but the agony in his face spoke to the effort he exerted at each slight movement. No sooner had she helped him across to the passenger seat than he passed out, with his head leaning against the window.

She turned the key in the ignition. Shea placed her hands on the steering wheel, trying to ignore the blood there, trying to pretend it wasn't moistening her palms and soaking into her fingertips. *This stranger's blood.* Her mind conjured up numerous scenarios as to how he came to be in this position.

Was he a killer? A robber? If so, why would he have been beaten and left in this condition? Seemed like he was the victim.

Shea turned the car around, but even the snail's pace seemed too much for the barely conscious man. He groaned.

"I'm sorry," she whispered.

She inched the car forward so as to create as little pain as possible and headed down the road. When she reached the T, she went in the direction the two men had come from earlier. After what felt like forever, a mansion came into view. The front door opened before she could get out of the car. An elderly black woman ran down the steps with surprising agility. "Who are you?" she demanded.

"I found this man on the side of the road."

The woman's face darkened with worry and recognition. She flung open the car door and caught him before he fell out.

She held on to his shoulders but turned a stormy gaze to Shea. "Why didn't you take him to the hospital?"

Shea's defenses rose. After all, she could have just left him. "He asked me to bring him here."

"Well, don't just stand there. Help me get Andy in the house before he bleeds to death."

Frustration exploded in Shea's mind. After being sent on a wild-goose chase, getting manhandled by a so-called *gentleman*, and becoming her own brand of a Good Samaritan, Shea certainly didn't deserve to be treated this way. "If you don't mind, I'd prefer not to be growled at. I'm obviously the only person who stopped to help him." She spread out her palms for the woman to see. "I'm standing here with this man's blood on my hands. The least you could do is show me some respect."

The old woman sized her up and gave a grudging nod. "Okay. No more growlin'. But I still need some help gettin' him in the house."

Shea nodded. "Let me take his arms. You get his legs; they won't be as heavy." Without waiting for the woman to argue or agree, Shea reached around her and slipped her arms under the man's shoulders. She pulled. If he were conscious, the action would cause him pain. Fortunately, he remained unconscious.

It took every ounce of strength in Shea's body to half carry, half drag him up the long porch steps, into the house, and to the parlor. He gave another unconscious moan when she laid him on the wide sofa. She straightened, panting and covered in blood.

"Thank you," the elderly lady said.

"Is he your son?"

She shook her gray head. "No relation, just a good boy."

Shea looked back at the bloodied, bruised man. "Are you

going to call the hospital?"

"Andy must have his reasons for asking you to bring him here. I'll call the doctor and have him come examine him. If he thinks Andy should go to the hospital, we'll get him there no matter what the boy says."

A smile touched Shea's lips at her determined words.

"The washroom is upstairs and down the hall to the right," the elderly woman said. "I'd take you there myself, but I gots to call the doctor."

"It's all right. I can find it. I'll go get my bag so I can have a change of clothes."

When Shea returned with her suitcase, the woman was hanging up the phone. "Is the doctor coming?"

"He on his way." The woman looked her over with a frown. "Honey, you go on and take a bath. Just toss them clothes out into the hall where I can pick 'em up and get 'em clean for you. You best stay here for tonight. Andy's gonna want to thank you properly."

"I wouldn't want to impose."

"You'll stay."

"Thank you, ma'am."

The old woman inclined her head in acknowledgment and allowed her tight lips to pull into a smile. "Call me Miss Delta. Everyone does."

Shea returned her smile. "All right, Miss Delta."

"You got folks around here that you need to call, let 'em know where you be?"

Shea stared at the carpet. "No, ma'am. I just arrived in town."

"I figured as much," she said, eyeing Shea's suitcase. "You go on up now. I'll air out the guest room."

Walking up the steps, Shea couldn't help but marvel at

the turn of events. Could this all be coincidence? Or was there something to what Tina had said on the bus? Maybe someone sovereign was looking out for her after all.

GEORGIA 1949

Sam Dane Jr. looked around the crowded courthouse. Despite the jam-packed balcony filled with folks who hoped to see him swinging from the end of a rope, it seemed empty without the colored Yankee looking down at him. A smile tipped the corners of his lips. Ol' Gabe had taken good care of him, hadn't he? Had done Sam a favor by getting Andy out of the way.

Sam saw his father—the honorable senator—sitting near the wall, staring up at the balcony, obviously searching for Andy. When he didn't find him, he looked away, worry clouding his eyes.

Disgust twisted through Sam like a summer storm. He should have shot the old man when he shot Sheriff John that night. The sheriff had given him no choice. But Father. . .Father was an abomination. Claiming to love that black woman. Not finding a good way of disposing of her vermin offspring. Justice wouldn't be served until he found a way to rid the world of both men.

"The deputy told me the sheriff's still at the courthouse," Jonas said to Buck as he slid into the old truck parked in front of the jailhouse. "Let's go."

Buck glared at him from the driver's side. "Mister, I got me seven kids to raise, and I don't aim to make them orphans 'fore the day is through. If you got it in your head to hotfoot it over to that courthouse, you gonna have to do it without me."

Jonas stared back at the older man. The dark lines of Buck's face showed the hard life he'd endured; the depth of wisdom in his eyes revealed the lessons learned. The man had a point. Confronting the sheriff at the courthouse would probably just get him and Buck killed, or at the very least, arrested. He had to harness his temper if he had any chance of learning Andy's whereabouts.

"You're right. Let's check in at the boardinghouse and ask Lottie if she's heard anything."

"Now, that's the first smart thing you done said all day. I still can't believe you didn't offer that gal we saw at the side of the road a ride this mornin'. But no, you jus' picked her up and set her out of the way. Whut sort of upbringin' did you git?"

Jonas scowled at the memory of the tiny waif struggling in his arms. He'd never been much of a smooth-talking ladies' man, but he'd never manhandled anyone either. And that girl had definitely been afraid. She'd trembled like a dog in the snow.

"You didn't speak up, either."

"Now, how am I supposed to offer a white woman a ride? You is about as green as a blade of grass about the nature of things down here."

"Look, I don't need a lecture. It's over now and she's probably long gone. Looked to me like she was going somewhere anyway. Didn't you notice she had a suitcase with her?"

"No, I didn't."

"Well, I'm trained to notice everything around me and reason out things like that. It's the nature of the newspaper business."

Buck cut him a sideways glance. "Well, now, if that gal had a suitcase, I'd say it's most likely she be walkin' down the road to

Penbrook, seein' as how that's the only house out that way." He shrugged. " 'Course, I ain't no trained newspaperman."

Mocking aside, the man made sense. Still, Jonas didn't like being outwitted. Irritation slithered through him. "Well, if she's still out there waving down traffic when we get back to the T, I'll stop and offer her a ride. Happy?"

Buck pushed his thick lips together. He gripped the wheel and drove in silence until they reached his home.

Lottie ran out the door and down the steps. She waved her arms as they opened the car doors. "Don't get out!"

"What is it, woman?" Buck called around the hood. "You hear from Andy?"

She shook her head. "Aunt Delta. Andy's at Penbrook. Beat up bad. He ain't come to yet, but Delta said an angel of mercy brung him home."

Both men slammed their doors at the same time. "Let's go," Jonas said, urgency playing drums in his chest.

Shea pulled her threadbare housecoat tighter around her and opened the bedroom door slightly. "Miss Delta," she called for the tenth time, "are my clothes dry yet?"

The woman bustled into the hallway. "They be done when they be done. Blood stains ain't easy to get out of clothes. Just put on something from that suitcase of yours."

"I only have one more set of clothing, and I had hoped to save it."

"Save it for whut, child?"

"To wear when I look for a job."

That seemed to silence the housekeeper. "Well, you cain't

come out wearin' that old thing. The men be on their way here, and that ain't got enough thickness to cover anything."

Shea's cheeks warmed at her scrutiny.

"Land sakes, gal. When was the last time you put some food in that scrawny body?"

"Yesterday," Shea said frankly.

"Well, you hold on. I can whip you up a ham sandwich in no time."

"Could I have two?"

The woman gave a quick nod as she left. "Hang tight; I'll be back in a jiffy."

Shea walked over to the bed, unable to resist its allure. She sat on the edge, closing her eyes as she sank into the pillowy clouds of the feather mattress. She'd grown up on straw mattresses. She'd had no idea such luxury existed. With a deep sigh, she settled back against the pillow and closed her eyes. A week's worth of jostling, lack of sleep, and worry caught up with her. Before she knew it, she felt herself drifting off.

"What do you mean I can't go in there? It's my house, isn't it? I have a right to know who's sleeping in my room." The demanding voice outside her door startled Shea from somewhere between asleep and awake. She jerked to her feet as the door swung open.

The rude man she'd met on the road this morning barged in, all six feet of him, with broad shoulders that had barely rippled beneath her weight when he'd lifted her earlier that day.

Delta shot in behind him, carrying a tray of food. "This was the only room ready, so I gave it to the woman who likely saved Andy's life. Ain't you got no manners? No gratitude?"

Shea tried to cover herself while the man sized her up.

His chin rose. "I saw you on the road today."

"I just arrived in town this morning."

"Why don't you put something decent on?"

"Why don't you stop staring at me?"

Satisfaction grazed her belly as his ears turned pink. He slammed out of the room.

Shaking her head, Delta set the tray on the table by the bed. "I swear I ain't never seen anyone with less manners than that boy."

"He's not exactly a boy. You'd think a *man* wouldn't need to be taught to be polite."

At that moment he returned to the doorway. His blue eyes pierced hers as he tossed a man's flannel robe onto the bed. "Put this on and maybe men wouldn't stare at you."

"I suspect that was supposed to be a nice gesture. So thanks."

He gave a grudging nod and turned away while she slipped on the robe.

"I'm decent now."

He shot around and leveled a gaze at her. "That remains to be seen."

Could he not speak anything pleasant? "Someone not so *decent* might have left your friend in the road to die, you know."

He drew a long, slow breath and offered his hand. "Let's start over." Finally, a gentler tone. But not enough for Shea to drop her guard. "My name's Jonas Riley."

Riley. Must be the son or brother of Daniel Riley, the man who'd inherited Penbrook House. Shea reached out and took the hand, briefly shook it, and withdrew hers at the slight brush of his fingers. "Shea."

"Shea what?"

Unwilling to reveal her identity just yet, she glanced around, trying to think up a last name. Her eyes landed on the glass of frothy milk. "White. Shea White."

"Humph."

Jonas turned to Delta. "Did you say something?"

"I didn't say a word." The old woman shot a knowing glance at Shea.

Unable to resist the call of that thick ham sandwich, Shea took a large bite.

"Miss White," Jonas said, his voice conciliatory, almost pleasant, "thank you for everything you've done for us. Delta informs me that your clothing is in the wash. I'd consider it an honor if you'd be my guest for the night."

Good grief, he switched gears quickly. "Where'd you get those fancy manners all of a sudden?" she asked around the bite she was still trying to chew.

His eyes narrowed and his square jaw clenched. "Apparently the same place you received your table manners." His lips twisted into something of a grin. "There is plenty where that came from, Miss White. I suggest you take smaller bites before you choke."

Shea wanted to kick the obnoxious man. But he didn't seem the type to be toyed with.

A thick-necked black man appeared in the doorway. He cast her a cursory glance and turned to Jonas. "Andy's awake."

Jonas sprinted from the room.

Miss Delta stared hard at Shea, as though trying to read her soul. "Now, what kind of trouble you in that you ain't tellin' your real name, gal?"

How on earth could the woman possibly know who she was? Shea's heart raced in her chest. "I don't know what you mean."

"You made up a last name. I noticed it, even if Jonas Riley couldn't see past the end of his nose."

Never able to hold on to a lie, Shea expelled a breath. "My

first name really is Shea, but my last name isn't White."

"I know. Could tell it right off, the way you looked at that milk. For a second there I thought you was gonna say your last name was Cream."

Shea laughed out loud. "Or Butter."

The old woman grinned for the first time Shea had seen. "Or Cow." The old woman's eyes lost their twinkle and the smile faded. "What trouble you in, honey? Can't you tell old Delta?"

Tears burned in Shea's eyes. She pretended for a half second that Miss Delta was Celeste. That her great-great-grandmother was here to comfort her. But she had to let the image die. No one could know who she was. She had evidence to gather first. She couldn't reveal her true identity until everything was in place and she could prove that she, not the Rileys, deserved to be the heir to this land.

"I can't, Miss Delta. Not yet."

The elderly woman patted her hand. "That's okay. You'll tell when you is ready. Until then, we'll call you Miss White."

"Miss Delta?"

"Yes, child?"

"I have a trunk at the bus station that has to be picked up by tomorrow or the man said he'd destroy it."

She nodded. "You leave it to me. I'll have my nephew, Buck, go around and get it for you."

Relief spread through Shea at the woman's kindness. "Thank you."

"No need to thank me. Get on in that bed now and get some rest. You look about to fall over."

"Yes, ma'am."

Shea climbed into bed and closed her eyes. A sudden thought made her bolt upright. Was this room where Mac had slept?

CHAPTER NINE
GEORGIA 1949

Jonas's blood boiled at the memory of Andy's battered face, his lips so swollen he could barely explain what had happened. The sheriff had pulled Andy over, and he and two of his cronies had jumped Andy, beating him until he'd been knocked unconscious. That was the last thing Andy remembered until he woke up this morning alone in the car. He had prayed for help and soon after, Shea arrived. When Andy finished the story, Jonas couldn't contain his anger.

Amid loud protests from Andy, Miss Delta, and Buck, he'd hightailed it into town. The drive hadn't cooled him off one bit.

He barreled into the courthouse just as the spectators were filing out for the day. "Sheriff," he called, "show yourself!"

The crowded, buzzing room grew silent. The judge looked up from his bench. "What seems to be the trouble, son?"

"My trouble is with the sheriff, Your Honor."

"Then I suggest you take it outside my courtroom. I'd like to go home to my lovely wife and the nice ham she's been baking all day."

The room rumbled with polite laughter.

"I'd be happy to take it outside, Your Honor, just as soon as that redheaded coward shows his face."

"Now, there ain't no sense being insultin', is there, Yankee?"

Jonas turned at the sound of Gabe's mocking tone. The sheriff stood in the doorway, his hand on the pistol hanging below his ample gut.

"You and your so-called deputies beat up a good friend of mine. And I intend to see you pay for your crime."

Gabe's nostrils flared. "I don't commit crimes. I punish the folks who do. Besides, I was off duty last night."

"Who said it was last night?"

"Well, I was here all day today guardin' this alleged murderer. So I assumed your friend must have been beat up last night—when I was out of town."

"Out of town, huh? And I just bet you have half a dozen friends willing to perjure themselves on a witness stand to corroborate your bogus story."

"Bogus? Sounds to me like you just called me a liar." He shook his head. "You really are startin' to offend me, Yank." The sheriff waved toward the group of men starting to file in around them. "Me and a few of my buddies went into Atlanta and saw the new Danny Kaye film."

"That's right," said a tall, slow-talking fellow in a brown suit, walking forward to stand next to the sheriff. "I was with him. It was a real good film, too. Lots of laughs."

The judge cleared his throat. "Well, that ends that. Let's clear the room, folks."

No one moved. All attention turned to Jonas.

"Your Honor," Jonas said, "my friend was beaten to a state of unconsciousness, and when he woke up, he implicated this lousy excuse for an officer of the law."

Gabe's face blanched.

Jonas turned from the judge back to Gabe, fury spurring him on. "You thought by pushing his car two miles down a back road, you could leave him to die and no one would be any the wiser. You're nothing but a bloody coward. Didn't have the guts to put a bullet through his head, so you left him to bleed to death. Can't you murder without a white hood over your head?"

Gabe shot forward and stood nose to nose with Jonas, the man's foul breath nearly gagging him. "I tell you," Gabe said through gritted teeth, "I wasn't in Oak Junction last night. I didn't go nowhere near your colored friend."

"Who said he was black? For that matter, who mentioned Oak Junction?" Without waiting for an answer, Jonas took a swing and planted his fist against Gabe's left eye. Pandemonium erupted. Wild shouts accompanied pain as heavy fists and billy clubs slammed against his body.

Shea stared at Miss Delta, still not believing the woman was suggesting she bail Jonas out of jail.

"Honey, you is the only white person around these parts that Jonas knows. You gots to go to that jail and post bail for the boy."

"With what money?"

"Now, don't you worry none about that. I gots plenty saved. You just get that dress you brung for getting a job. And put on some lipstick. Gabe likes the pretty girls."

"Miss Delta! I am not going to prostitute myself for a man I don't even know." Realizing how that sounded, she quickly added, "I wouldn't do it for a man I did know, either. But I will not sashay into that courthouse and flirt with the sheriff in order to get Jonas out of jail."

Besides, Shea reasoned, with Jonas out of the way for a while, she had more time to come up with the birth and death certificates she needed. Her conscience pricked her with this last thought. "Okay, fine. I'll go. But I'm not flirting with anyone."

Thirty minutes later, Shea climbed out of Buck's old truck in front of the sheriff's office. Miss Delta had decided she'd better drive there alone so as not to exacerbate the situation should anyone see them together.

Gabe looked up with interest when she walked through the door. He leaned back in his chair and tipped his hat back from his head, eyeing her up and down until she felt her skin crawl. "Well, who have we got here?"

"Sh–Shea. Pen—White."

"Shea Penwhite? Your family from around here?"

"I don't have any family. And it's just White."

He gave her an insolent half smile. "Darlin', you're starting to confuse me. Good thing you're so pretty or I might have to arrest you."

Shea glanced at the line of three jail cells to the right of Gabe's desk. She caught her breath at the sight of Jonas lying on a cot, bruised much the same as she'd found Andy. What kind of lawman was this?

"I've come to post bail for Mr. Riley so he can be released."

The sheriff's face clouded. "I'm sorry. That ain't possible."

"What do you mean?"

"Well, I don't know how things work where you're from, but down here I'm the law. And if I say he's stayin' in jail for a month, then by golly, he stays."

The injustice ignited Shea's ire. "You can't sentence him. He's had no trial. No formal charges have been brought against him."

He let the legs of his chair drop with a thud. "Lady, you better get out of here, or I might decide to arrest you after all."

Fear slithered through her, and she had no doubt he would carry through with his threat. "I'm going." She spun on her three-inch heels and nearly tripped in the process. As she found her balance, she caught Jonas's eye. "I'll be back," she said with relish. "I'll get you out of this hellhole."

The sheriff shot from the chair and lunged toward Shea with surprising agility, given his bulk. "You come back and I'll put you in a cell with Sam. He ain't had a woman in a long time."

The man in the far cell chuckled. "I wouldn't mind taming an uppity Yankee gal. Come on, Gabe. Go ahead and arrest her."

"Not just yet," he said, never taking his eyes off of Shea. Gabe pointed two fingers at her. "Get out of here."

"I'll be back, Jonas. You take care of yourself and don't give this thug any reason to kill you." She slipped out the door and hurried to the truck before Gabe could come after her.

Back at Buck and Lottie's, she relayed the entire scene. "That boy sure did cause himself a heap of trouble."

"An angry man is a foolish man," Lottie agreed. "Jonas always finds trouble."

"The question is," Shea said, pacing the kitchen where the couple sat at the table, "how are we going to get him out of there? He should probably pay a fine or spend a night in jail for throwing a punch at the sheriff. But this revenge tactic on Gabe's part is wrong. And you should see poor Jonas. He looks about as bad as the man out at Penbrook." She glanced at Buck. "Did you tell your wife about the man I found at the side of the road?"

Buck gave a nod. "Andy be Lottie's brother."

Shea turned to the woman and saw the worry in her eyes. "Oh. I'm so sorry, Miss Lottie."

"No need to call me miss. And there's no need for you to ever be sorry for nuthin'. You saved my brother's life."

"I'm glad I was there. Truly I am." *For more reasons than one.* Saving the man's life had given her entrance into Penbrook House. "Now, what do we do about getting Jonas out of that pit?"

CHICAGO 1949

Daniel Riley was just sitting down to a nice cup of coffee, meant to get him over the hump of overtime weariness, when the phone on his desk startled him. His hot brew slopped across the scarred mahogany desk that had been his father's prized possession. He yanked up the phone. "What?" he growled.

"Well, I can see where your son gets his disposition." The woman's slightly belligerent tone raised Daniel's hackles.

"Who is this?"

"My name is Miss White. I am an acquaintance of your son Jonas."

Daniel pinched the bridge of his nose. Why did Jonas insist on getting involved with women of questionable character? "Listen here, young lady. If you intend to blackmail me, you may as well hang up right now. I will not be manipulated."

"I wouldn't take any of your money if it was handed to me on a silver platter. If you're going to insult me, you can just forget I called."

Daniel felt regret slither through him. "I apologize," he said. "I'm afraid your phone call caught me off guard. You're right, my son and I do struggle with our tempers. Despite the recent couple of minutes, I'm proud to say I've learned to control mine."

"I'm glad I wasn't standing in the room. You might have

punched me before you remembered you have learned to control your temper."

He chuckled, thinking he might like this woman after all. "What do you know about my son?"

"I'm sorry to be the one to have to tell you this, but Jonas is rotting away in a jail cell, sir, with two black eyes, probably a broken nose, and possibly a couple of broken ribs."

Daniel felt his emotions start to hurl out of control. What had Jonas gotten himself involved in? "Why was my son arrested?"

"Andy Carmichael was beaten senseless and left for dead the other night. Jonas figured the sheriff and his buddies did it, so he went to the courthouse and tore into Gabe. The sheriff messed him up pretty badly, I'm afraid."

Daniel groaned. He knew he shouldn't have allowed Jonas to go to Georgia to keep an eye on Andy. "How high has his bail been set?"

"The sheriff's denying bail. Says he'll keep Jonas in jail as long as he wants to. I thought maybe if you sent one of your lawyers down, that might intimidate the fat bumpkin into letting Jonas go and dropping the charges."

Helpless fury clutched at Daniel. His boys. Hurt, in danger. "What about Andy? How is he?"

"His eyes are swollen shut, and the doctor said he's been kicked around a lot. All of his fingers are broken."

Daniel heard tears in her throat, and his own eyes misted. "What hospital is he in?"

"He's at Penbrook House. The doctor patched him up. He said there's not much they could do for him at the hospital, and the less moving around he does, the better. Miss Delta is taking good care of him."

"Thank you for calling, Miss White."

GEORGIA 1949

The only thing Jonas remembered after he threw the first punch at Gabe was the sound of a woman's voice calling his name. Promising to get him out of there. Pain exploded in his head as he tried to sit up. His mouth was foul with the taste of blood. He stumbled to the corner, fell to his knees, and vomited. Then he passed out where he fell.

"Who's there?" Andy woke to blackness. He tried to open his eyes, but they were swollen shut. The telltale sound of turning pages alerted him to someone's presence in the room.

"I'm sorry I woke you. It's me, Shea White. Do you remember me?"

"My angel."

She gave a little laugh. He heard her walk close to the bed. "The doctor left some pills for the pain. Do you want a couple?"

Andy nodded. "Thanks."

His ears picked up the sound of pills sliding from a bottle, water pouring. "Here you go." He felt the pills touch his lips and took them in, followed by a sip of water. The girl set the glass on the table next to him and clicked her tongue. "Miss Delta is going to fuss at me something awful when she gets back. She gave express orders not to wake you up."

"I'll pretend to be asleep."

"Oh, would you? That would be ever so helpful."

Andy attempted to smile, but it hurt too much to stretch his swollen lips. Besides, he could just imagine how grotesque his smile must look. "Don't make me laugh. It hurts."

"Okay. How about if I sing you a song? That would make you cry."

"That bad?"

"Terrible. My parents used to spank me every time I tried to sing."

"Ouch! You made me laugh after you promised not to." Andy wished he could see her face. "Have you met Jonas yet?"

"I'm not sure how to tell you this, but Jonas is in jail."

Knee-jerk instinct pushed at his body as he tried to sit up.

"Easy there, Slick. What do you think you're going to do? Go break him out? You can't even use the bathroom without help."

Expelling a frustrated breath, Andy lowered himself back to the bed. "What happened to him?"

Andy listened to the details of Jonas's arrest.

"I should have known he'd do something stupid."

"We all let our hearts run away with our heads when someone we love is hurt."

She had a point. But her easy acceptance piqued Andy's curiosity. "You don't seem to think there's anything odd about a friendship between a black man and a white man."

"Oh, I know you were raised by Jonas's father. He's a little gruff at first, but he softens pretty quickly."

"You've met Uncle Daniel?"

"I talked to him on the telephone. Not sure what he intends to do, but I have a feeling Jonas won't be in jail nearly as long as the sheriff has planned."

"So, why are you watching over me? Where's Miss Delta?"

"She wanted to take a bath. Your sister was here earlier, but she went back to her brood. Don't worry. I won't tell anyone you have a white girl taking care of you if you don't."

Andy sobered. She didn't realize the ramifications of a white girl taking care of him. But ignorance wouldn't keep them from being harmed if the wrong people found out. "I think you'd best go sit back in the chair. Push it all the way to the far wall."

"My goodness. You're awfully proper for a sick man."

"You don't realize what could happen. I have a family in Chicago to think of."

"Of course. I'm sorry." The chair scraped across the floor and bumped against the wall. "I'll just go on with my reading if you don't mind. Those pills are going to knock you out any second anyway."

"What are you reading?"

"Oh, just some old diaries I found."

Andy drew a sharp breath. "What diaries?" Had he left any here after Miss Penbrook's death?

"I found them in the attic back home."

Relief flooded Andy, followed closely by curiosity. "Would you mind reading to me until I fall asleep?"

She hesitated. "I guess it would be all right."

GEORGIA 1847

"How could you behave like common trash?" The sound of his mother's heartbroken voice filled Mac with remorse.

"I'm sorry, Mother. The situation isn't exactly as Miss Blythe depicted."

Mr. Blythe's face turned a dangerous shade of red. "First you compromise my daughter, and then you insult her by calling her a liar."

"Sir, I do not mean to insult you or your lovely daughter. I do admit to being caught up in her charms for a few minutes. But I have certainly not ruined her for the true love of her life to marry her someday."

"My daughter claims you are the true love of her life."

His father pushed himself up from the leather chair. "My son will do the proper thing and marry your daughter."

Mac bristled. He wanted to fight against these two men. To refuse to marry the girl regardless of her erroneous claim that he'd compromised her. But without Celeste, what difference did it make whether he married Janette or not?

"See that he does, or I will be forced to call him out," the rotund little cotton baron snapped before waddling out of the room like a penguin.

"What have you to say for yourself?" His father turned on him in fury. "Are you going to do the right thing?"

"Excuse me, Father." Mac hurried after Mr. Blythe. "Sir, please wait."

The man turned around, his face beginning to lose its awful shade of red. "I have nothing more to say to you until you ask for my daughter's hand."

"I'm afraid Janette has misunderstood my intentions. If we marry she will not receive the life she hopes for with me."

His deepening color began to spread across his cheeks. "What are you talking about?" he bellowed.

"She wants to be mistress of Penbrook. And I'm afraid that's going to be impossible."

"There is nothing wrong with a woman wanting to care for her own home."

"I understand that, sir. And I agree that if I planned to become master of Penbrook, no other woman would be more suited to the purposes of running this household efficiently."

"Son, you are not making sense."

"The truth is, sir, that I do not intend to run Penbrook. I will be forfeiting the land in lieu of a cash inheritance. I want to be a teacher. I plan to go west someday soon and settle my own land, maybe start a school for boys."

The stodgy man peered closer with the ferocity of a wild boar. "You would take my little girl across the country to live in an uncivilized land?"

"If you insist upon a marriage between the two of us, then yes. As my wife, she will go where I go. And make no mistake, I am going west."

The man's cheeks puffed out and the veins showed like purple streaks of lightning beneath his stretched skin. "I will not allow this ploy to humiliate my family. You will marry and run this plantation."

"No, sir. I will marry Janette if I must to uphold our families' honor. But I will choose my own profession."

"You are the eldest son. It is your responsibility to carry on after your father's demise."

With a rueful smile, Mac inclined his head. "I assure you, my father has many years ahead of him."

Mr. Blythe stared at Mac. He gathered several breaths and blew them out. "I can see you've made up your mind."

Mac gave a short nod. "I have, sir."

"Then I shall leave the matter in my daughter's hands." He took a step closer, his double chin lifted so he might meet Mac's eyes. "But if she chooses to go with you, you will marry her."

Caught between his desire for Celeste and his family's honor, Mac reluctantly agreed. "If she chooses to come west with me, I will marry her."

"And when do you plan to go?"

"The next wagon train leaves in the spring. After traveling north to Missouri, it will meet up with a train coming from Independence."

"You seem to have it all worked out."

"Yes, sir."

"Very well, then. I shall relay the situation to my daughter. She had planned to go to Europe soon, but I cannot predict what she will choose to do in view of this new occurrence." He shook his head and mopped his brow with a white handkerchief. "I do not know how I will tell my wife."

If all went well, that wouldn't be necessary. Mac couldn't imagine Janette giving up a trip abroad in order to go west. The thought of her working alongside him, cutting out a new life in the wilderness, seemed ludicrous. A smile touched his lips as he imagined the simpering debutante up to her elbows in dirt.

"What is it that makes you smile today?"

Mac turned to greet Madeline, Henry's pretty young wife and mother to their young daughter, Camilla. She held out her two slender hands. Mac accepted the gesture and lifted first one and then the other to his lips. A pretty blush stole across her cheeks. "Now, don't try to distract me. I saw your smile. Are you actually happy about being forced to marry that woman?"

Mac lifted his brow in surprise at the disdain in her tone. "You dislike Janette?"

Maddy walked across the foyer. "Oh, I don't know her well enough to dislike her. But I can't believe she is good enough for my brother-in-law." She gave in to brief laughter. "Of course, I doubt anyone would be."

"I highly doubt Janette will agree to marriage when she hears my terms."

A frown creased her brow. "Jason McCourt Penbrook, do you mean to tell me that you are trying to get out of marrying that girl? It isn't like you to behave in a less than honorable manner."

"Maddy, I didn't compromise her. If anyone was compromised, it was me."

Clearly uncomfortable with the direction of the conversation, Maddy rubbed her hand over her slightly protruding belly. "That isn't the point. Once the accusation is made, a gentleman has no choice. Think about it, Jase. If you don't go through with the marriage, she'll either be ruined or called a liar. Either way, she'll never find another decent man to marry her."

"You're a kindhearted soul, Madeline Penbrook. But you've misunderstood me completely."

"How so?"

"I'm going west."

"To Alabama?"

Laughter rumbled in his chest, and he felt lighter than he had in days. "No. I mean the wide-open, wonderful west, where lush, open land stretches on for thousands of miles."

Maddy gasped and touched her fingertips to the brooch at her throat.

He took her by the shoulders. "I'm tired of living this fairy-tale existence that has no choice but to fail."

"Whatever do you mean?"

"You know. I know you do."

Maddy, a Missouri native, born of abolitionist parents, nodded gravely. "Yes, I know."

"We've built this utopian society where men of wealth set themselves up for others to serve. There weren't enough poor whites, so they stole the blood of thousands of Africans."

Tears welled in Maddy's eyes. "It breaks my heart, too."

Mac turned to her suddenly. If anyone would understand his plight, she would. "That's why I want to go west with the woman I love."

She stepped back, eyes wide as saucers. "Love?"

"I can't help myself. She has such beautiful hazel eyes, and skin so soft it feels like satin."

"Janette has blue eyes."

Mac suddenly realized what he'd almost done. If Father discovered he was still entertaining notions about Celeste, he'd follow through on his threat to sell her.

"Of course. You're right. Blue."

"Well, I'm not sure what brought about the sudden change in your feelings. But I suppose it's for the best."

"Thank you, Maddy." He leaned at the waist and brushed a kiss to her cheek.

"Have I reason to be jealous?" Henry's voice burst into the room like the grating sound of a squeaky wagon wheel.

"You know my heart belongs to only one man, dearest," Maddy said, smiling at her husband with unabashed love and devotion.

Henry slipped his arm around her waist and pulled her against him. "That's good news."

"Besides," Maddy said with a smile, "Jase has a love of his own."

"Does he now?" Henry's eyes turned to steel, but his lips smiled.

"I admit I wasn't too crazy about the idea of him marrying Janette, but listening to Jase speak of his love for her convinced me that she must be the right woman for him."

"Oh, she is most assuredly. Such a lovely young thing." He gave a mocking grin that was lost on Maddy. "And so eager to be a bride."

Maddy laughed. "All ladies are eager to be brides, dearest."

He glanced down at her, and Mac saw a look of genuine

affection pass over his features. If anyone could tame his wayward brother, Maddy was the woman to do it. He only prayed Henry didn't break her spirit before she broke his.

"You're looking well, Henry." Mac couldn't resist baiting his brother.

"Yes, I've recovered more quickly than the doctor predicted."

"Perhaps you should stay out of poker games if you can't keep from brawling."

"Your brother is right, dearest." Maddy's eyes held earnest concern. "I worry so much about you."

Henry pressed a kiss to Maddy's forehead. "Then I shall be more careful."

A rustling noise at the top of the stairs caught their attention, and they turned.

"Ah," Henry said. "Here's the lovely bride-to-be now."

Janette, radiant in a lavender gown of silk and lace, descended without taking her smiling gaze from Mac's. His heart sank to his stomach as he realized what that glowing countenance must mean. Janette planned to accept his ultimatum to travel west.

CHAPTER TEN
GEORGIA 1949

Shea stopped reading aloud when she noticed Andy's labored breathing. He slept, but he was fighting for every breath, gasping for air. She watched him as memories of Granddad drawing his last breaths slithered over her. Panic rose.

"Miss Delta!" Running down the hall, she continued yelling for the housekeeper until she showed herself at the foot of the stairs, wearing her nightgown and wrapper.

"Gal, what in blazes is wrong with you?"

"It's Andy. I think he's dying."

Horror shot to the old woman's eyes, and she ran up the remaining steps, her own breath so heavy by the time she reached the top, Shea thought she might keel over.

"Call for the ambulance," Miss Delta commanded.

Shea sprinted to the end of the hall and dialed the operator. "Get me the hospital. I need an ambulance at Penbrook House out on Old Millcreek Road."

When she was sure the ambulance was on its way, Shea ran out onto the porch to wait for it.

It seemed like an eternity before the vehicle arrived and two men in uniform shot out, one of them carrying a cot. She waved them to the door. "Hurry, hurry!"

They stopped when they reached the room. "Where's the patient?"

"What do you mean? He's right there on the bed. Are you blind?"

The stocky, middle-aged man gave her a disgusted grunt. "Lady, we can't take *him*."

"Why not?"

Delta placed her hand on Shea's arm. "Honey, you called the wrong hospital."

All at once it dawned on Shea. The white ambulance driver didn't accept black patients. But now that he was already here, surely he wouldn't turn his back on a man who obviously needed medical attention. "Then just take him to the right one."

The driver swallowed hard and shook his head. "Sorry, ma'am, but I'm not allowed. I'll lose my job if I do that."

The other man gave a disgusted shake of his head. "I ain't standing around here arguing with these folks. Let's go." He sauntered out of the room.

The driver started to follow, still carrying the cot, but Shea stepped in front of the door.

His eyes pleaded for her to understand. "I got eight kids to feed."

Shea was having none of it. If he let Andy die, he deserved to watch all eight of his ratty children starve to death one by one. "Are you telling me you'd let him die before driving him to the right hospital?"

"I ain't got a choice."

"Fine. Slide that cot under him."

"Ma'am, I just said—"

"The least you can do is help me get him to the car so I

can drive him to a hospital that *will* treat him. Listen to his breathing! This man's death will be on your conscience if you walk away as though his life is worthless just because he isn't the right color!"

He hesitated, casting a cautious glance at Miss Delta, obviously looking for some moral support.

"He can't put a black body on a white man's cot," Delta explained.

"Oh, what absolute rot!" Shea exploded. "Are you people so ignorant you think his skin will rub off on you?"

The driver shrugged. "I don't make the rules."

"Then at least help me carry him. You take his arms and I'll take his legs. And be careful."

The man started to protest, but Shea cut him off. "I have five dollars in my purse. It's yours if you don't kill him between here and the car." Her last five dollars. She'd have to look for some sort of job soon. For now, she had to make sure Andy didn't die. If God was sovereign and if He had entrusted this man's well-being to her care, she didn't want to risk angering the Almighty.

The driver's chest rose and fell as his face registered a determination that spoke of a decision. "We'll use the cot. But that's the best I can do."

They worked together and slid Andy onto the cot, strapped him in, and carefully made their way down the steps. The ambulance driver carried the bulk of Andy's weight.

To his credit, he refused the five dollars. "Wish I coulda done more to help, ma'am."

Shea thanked him but couldn't squelch the ache in her gut. What a tragedy things had to be this way.

Miss Delta and Shea followed the ambulance, past the

shiny white general hospital it had pulled into, then drove twenty more minutes before pulling into the Shady Avenue Hospital. How many black children had died for lack of immediate medical treatment? The thought made Shea shake with rage. She had been on the receiving end of prejudice all her life, and she was sick of it.

At the hospital, Shea noticed an orderly standing inside the glass doors with his back to the entrance. She honked the horn to get the orderly's attention. He and another young Negro man hurried outside, wheeling a gurney. They frowned when they saw her.

"Don't worry. The patient's black."

Shea and Miss Delta waited in a dingy room that smelled of sweat and dirt. Shea hoped the rest of the hospital was cleaner.

"It makes me so mad, Miss Delta. Andy could have been receiving care a full hour sooner if he could have gone to the other hospital. It doesn't make sense. I mean, fine, keep your schools separate if you must, keep your parks separate. But for the love of God, don't deny a man his chance to live."

Miss Delta fixed her with a stern frown. "Missy, if you start actin' like black folks is your cause, you is gonna get yo'self into trouble. And it ain't gonna do a lick of good, noways. So you might as well save your strength."

"I just get so frustrated."

"Well, keep it to yo'self. You think you feels worse than we do? You can walk into that hospital if you cut yo' finger. You can drink from that water fountain if you gets thirsty and yo' chillens can play in them parks without the sheriff taking a billy club to 'em. So you jus' mind yo' business and let us mind ours. They's gonna be a heap less trouble that way."

"I'm sorry, Miss Delta." Shea took the old woman's hand.

"I didn't mean to cause you any more pressure. I guess I just don't understand your ways yet."

"Our ways ain't hard to learn, gal. White folks don' mix with black folks, and everyone do jus' fine."

Shea fell silent, the only white woman in a roomful of black men, women, and children. Was Miss Delta hinting that she shouldn't be here? She debated leaving. But she couldn't. Let them glower and treat her like she didn't belong. That was nothing new for Shea. She wasn't going anywhere until she knew Andy's condition.

❧

Jonas couldn't bring himself to lift his body to the cot sitting against the jail cell wall. His legs refused to cooperate, and for the first time in his life, he felt helpless—locked up, lying in his own vomit, unable to care for himself. His arm throbbed with more pain than he'd ever experienced, and he'd be surprised if he didn't have a concussion. He felt himself sliding back into unconsciousness. The last thing he did, before blackness claimed him, was pray.

GEORGIA 1949

Daniel Riley wasn't prone to changing his mind once he had it set on something. As soon as he'd learned about Andy and Jonas, he'd called his attorney and made arrangements for the two of them to drive down to Oak Junction.

Andy's wife, Lexie, had begged to be allowed to come, too. Against his better judgment, Daniel had allowed it. She had left the baby with her mother and now sat in the backseat. She received stares from people who passed by—both pedestrians and those riding in cars—some curious, some outraged. But she didn't seem to care. She only wanted to be with her husband.

"We'll take you to Penbrook House," Daniel told her, "so you can be with Andy. Then we'll pop in on the judge and get my son out of jail."

"Thank you, Uncle Daniel."

Daniel's Mississippi-born attorney, Vic Chambers, cut him a sideways glance and shook his head.

Daniel cleared his throat. "Honey," he said, looking into the rearview mirror, "you'd better call me Mr. Riley while we're down here. No sense raising suspicions and making people mad."

She emitted a small sigh. "You're right. I'll be careful."

As they passed the courthouse, Daniel started at the sight of Jonas's car parked alongside the street. Had they let him out?

"What is it, Daniel?" Vic asked.

"My son's car." He pointed.

"Go ahead and stop, Unc—Mr. Riley. I don't mind."

"Are you sure?"

Lexie nodded.

Daniel pulled his car alongside Jonas's and turned to Vic. "Maybe you'd better stay in the car with Lexie for now. I don't want her to be left alone."

Vic gave a nod. "Don't worry. I'll keep her safe."

The courtroom was jammed with people, but Daniel didn't see Jonas anywhere. He walked the halls until he found a slightly built blond-haired clerk sitting behind a counter. "Excuse me, sir. I'm looking for my son. He's new in town. From Chicago. Tall, dark hair."

"The only fella fits that description started a fight with the sheriff the other day. He's been in jail ever since."

"But his car is out front."

The bespectacled young man shrugged. "I don't know what to tell you. Unless. . . There has been a young lady in town putting her nose into things. Could be she drove it here. Last time I saw her she was headed down to the records room."

Daniel suspected he knew who that young woman might be.

He followed the clerk's instructions down the steps and two doors to the right into a dingy old room piled with boxes of old files. Sitting in the middle of them all sat a young woman with strawberry blond hair.

"Excuse me."

She looked up and pressed her palm to her chest. "Jeepers, mister, you about scared me to death. Don't you know better than to sneak up on people?"

Yes, this was definitely the woman he'd spoken with on the phone. "I'm looking for my son."

"Well, he's not down here."

"I believe I spoke with you on the phone last night."

"Mr. Riley?"

"The same."

Her silky eyebrows lifted. "You must have driven all night."

"And most of the day."

She met his gaze and stood, dusting off a pair of men's trousers with her palms. He'd seen plenty of women wearing men's clothes during the war, but not so often lately. The sight never failed to disturb him a bit. There was something charming about the old days, when men went into the world to make a living and the wives took care of the home. But he supposed things were bound to change. That was just the nature of things.

The young woman reached out her hand and shook his. "Shea White. Nice to meet you. I'm driving Jonas's car. I hope you don't mind, but I picked it up yesterday. It's a long walk from Penbrook House."

"I'm sure it's fine. What about Jonas?"

"He's still in jail. But I know he'll be glad to see you."

"I brought my lawyer with me." He smiled. "And Andy's wife, Lexie."

She gathered a deep breath and lifted a box that seemed to strain every muscle in her neck and arms.

"Here," Daniel said, "give me that. You shouldn't be lifting heavy boxes."

"It didn't look that heavy," she said, handing it over. She nodded toward a corner. "Just set it down over there." She slapped her hands together to remove the dust, then looked at him with troubled eyes. "Sir, I don't know how to tell you this, but Andy had to be taken to the hospital last night."

A troubled wave passed over his heart. "Is he all right?"

She wiped sweat from her forehead, leaving a smudge that made her look more vulnerable. "The doctor said one of his broken ribs punctured a lung. He needs a few days in the hospital, but he should pull through."

"I'll go see him as soon as I get my son out of jail."

"I caution you to prepare yourself. He looks pretty bad."

"Have you seen him today?"

The young woman shook her head. "That sheriff told me if I come back he'll arrest me and put me in a cell with a murderer who's on trial for ordering the killings of a mixed-blood couple."

"I'm sure he was bluffing."

"I'm not willing to gamble my virtue on it."

Daniel felt heat rise to his cheeks. Young people these days certainly had less modesty than his generation.

"Sorry." She dropped her gaze as her face darkened in embarrassment. "My granddad wasn't much for mincing words. I guess I picked it up."

"Don't concern yourself about it." He sent her a wink. "Those outspoken ways might be part of your appeal."

She smiled, showing beautifully straight, white teeth. "I'm about finished up here. After you see your son, I can take you to see Andy if you'd like." She hesitated. "But if the sheriff releases Jonas, you're going to want to take him to the hospital, too. Do you know they have one for black folks and one for white folks?"

He shot her a rueful smile. "Yes, I am aware of that unfortunate reality. Perhaps I could impose upon you to drive Lexie to the hospital to see her husband."

"I'd be happy to. Just let me put these records away." She gathered up the rest of the files strewn across the floor and slipped them into the last box.

"Did you find what you were searching for?"

The young lady shook her head. "No. I'll have to come back. Although I don't know when I'll have time. I have to find a job. I'm running out of money, and I'm sure Miss Delta is tired of having me impose on her good nature."

Daniel's lips twitched. "My dear, Penbrook House is mine. And I don't throw pretty girls out into the street."

She gave him a sideways grin. "Well, I'm not one of the pretty ones, so I suppose I'd best pack my bag."

He lifted his brows in surprise. "What an odd thing to say."

"Just practical."

"Well, I think you sell yourself short, my dear."

Her cheeks bloomed and the blush went straight to his heart. "You may stay at Penbrook as long as you need to."

Her hazel eyes widened. "Do you mean it?"

"I never say anything I don't mean."

"Thank you, sir. That's a load off my mind."

Daniel followed the young woman back the way he'd come, down the hall, and up the steps. She was a walking contradiction. She stood with dignity and grace yet spoke with slang and an utter lack of social graces. Wouldn't his wife, Lois, love to get her hands on this girl and turn her out? He had a feeling Chicago society wouldn't know what hit them. He chuckled at the thought.

She turned. "Something funny?"

He shook his head but couldn't keep back a grin. Yes, she would make quite a splash. He wondered what Jonas thought of the girl.

Sam tossed on his cot, frustration rushing through him. Finally, he turned his head and stared out at the sheriff. "For God's sake, Gabe, clean out his stinking cell. I'm sick of breathing the stench of his puke."

Gabe didn't bother to look up from the meal he was consuming at his wooden desk. "Cleaning woman's coming in tomorrow."

"I can't take it another day."

"Well, I ain't cleaning it, so you got no choice."

How he hated that fat, freckled know-it-all. When he got out, he was going to put a bullet through him, just like he had his old man. Then he'd get out of town before anyone could catch him. Gabe smiled.

When the door creaked open, he sat up on his cot and looked toward the two men entering the sheriff's office. He'd never seen those fellows before. From the city, if he had to make a guess.

Gabe sat back and laced his fat fingers over a fatter gut, staring at the newcomers as if he were a king. "Can I help you?"

"Are you the sheriff?"

"I am. Who are you?"

"Vic Chambers. Attorney-at-law."

"That right?"

Sam gave a low chuckle at Gabe's discomfort. The guy was looking downright nervous. It was one thing to lock up a man. Another to beat him, throw him in a cell, and not give him medical attention for twenty-four hours. Now, that might be okay if the prisoner were a colored boy, but a city fella? That wouldn't hold up in court. And that attorney would have something to say about the condition of the other man's cell.

"I have been informed," the older man spoke up, "that you are holding my son and denying him bail."

"You talkin' about Jonas?"

Dumb Gabe. How he ever dressed himself in the morning, Sam had no idea.

"Yes," the older gentleman said through gritted teeth. "Jonas Riley."

Gabe leaned forward, shaking his head. "He started a fight with an officer of the law in a public courthouse. I had every right—even a duty to arrest him."

The attorney gave a curt nod. "Which is an offense. But that doesn't excuse the fact that his civil rights have been violated to the highest degree."

The older man shook with rage as he walked toward the cells and stopped in front of the one holding Jonas. "Get my son out of that stink hole this instant or I will file a civil suit as well as talk to the state's attorney about this sorry excuse for a law-enforcement office."

Gabe cleared his throat and jangled the keys. "All right. I think he's learned his lesson. I'm willing to drop the matter if you are."

Gabe's hands trembled so much he dropped the keys. He grunted when he bent over to retrieve them.

The old man yanked the keys out of his hands. "Go call an ambulance. My son needs immediate medical attention."

"Hey, how about tossing me those keys when you're done?" Sam called out.

The old man didn't even acknowledge that he'd spoken, but the attorney sneered at him. How dare they treat him with such disrespect? He'd make them pay, too.

Shea sat alone in the waiting room, allowing Andy and his wife some time to themselves. On a whim, she'd grabbed the diary this morning and stuffed it into her handbag. While she waited, she read. . .

GEORGIA 1847

"You did what?" Mac's heart felt as though it might beat right out of his chest. "How could you send her away like that?"

Mac's father rested his palms against his desk. "She is my property. I have the right to do with her as I choose."

"The way Henry had the right?"

His father scowled, pushing his gray eyebrows together. "If I choose."

"And have you chosen?" He wouldn't stand for it.

"If I had taken a liking to the girl, do you think I would have rented her services as kitchen help to Mr. Haverty?"

Relief shot through Mac but not enough to dull the ache at the knowledge that Celeste was gone. "Why would you rent Celeste out to another plantation? Don't you see how valuable she is around here?"

His father raised his brandy glass and swirled the contents. "I've seen the way you look at her, and it displeases me greatly. It's not natural for a cultured white man to fall in love with a darky. How do you think your future bride would feel if she discovered this abnormality?"

It was all Mac could do not to tell his father that Janette had told him he could have Celeste, as long as he was discreet and didn't claim any of the children born of the union.

"Father, the reason I requested this meeting was to ask you to release me from my responsibility as eldest son and make plans to leave Penbrook to Henry. I intend to leave for the west next spring."

His father gathered a full breath and released it. "I see. And why didn't you mention this before?"

Mac sent him a rueful grin. "I wanted to wait until absolutely necessary rather than endure months of Mother's weeping and your displeasure."

"I don't care for your tone, son."

"My apologies, Father. I understand if this decision means I will not have an inheritance, but it's a choice I'm willing to make."

"Is that so? And what will you subsist on while you carry out this plan of yours? How do you intend to provide for your new bride?"

Since he had anticipated the question, the answer spilled

from Mac's tongue without a pause. "I have enough savings from my years of teaching to outfit a trip west for two people. Once there, I'll homestead some land."

"And what makes you think you can care for yourself, let alone a woman?" The sneer curling his father's lips failed to elicit the same dread Mac had always felt in the face of that displeasure. Instead, boldness shot through him. He gave a curt bow. "If you've nothing else to say, Father. . ." He turned on his heel and walked toward the door.

"I forbid you to walk away from me."

Mac stopped and faced his father once more. "There is no point in arguing. I will go west, with or without your blessing, and with or without the inheritance."

Mac's father sized him up over the rim of his snifter. "Your mind is made up?"

"Yes."

"Then you are right. We have nothing more to discuss."

CHAPTER ELEVEN
GEORGIA 1949

The sky rumbled Andy awake, and it took a moment for him to get his bearings. He eyed his unfamiliar surroundings through narrow slits. The swelling in his eyelids had finally diminished, allowing a small amount of sight.

"Hey." The soft sound of Lexie's voice pushed a sigh from his chest. He must be dreaming.

"How you feeling?" The gentle touch of her fingers. . . How could that be?

"Lex?"

"It's me, honey."

"I thought I was dreaming."

"No. But you probably wish you were. Are you in much pain?"

Excruciating. "Not too bad." He squeezed his wife's hand, relishing the touch of comfort. "What are you doing here?"

"I came with Uncle Daniel as soon as we got word that you were in the hospital."

"Do you know what happened to me? All I remember is listening to Miss White reading, and the next thing I knew I woke up here."

A damp, cool cloth wiped across his brow. "A broken rib punctured your lung."

That would explain the difficultly breathing. But that wasn't Andy's first concern. "You shouldn't be here, honey. It's too dangerous right now with Sam Dane's trial going on."

"Shh." She pressed silky fingertips to his lips. "Nothing could have kept me from you. I'm just relieved Shea got you here in time."

Shea. The memory washed over Andy. He had a lot to think about. A lot to discuss with Uncle Daniel about that young woman. He had recognized Madeline Penbrook in the diary Shea had been reading that night. The diary had brought back memories of his own discovery of Madeline Penbrook's diaries last year. Maddy had mentioned Henry's brother but hadn't hinted of a love affair between Mac and a young slave girl. Maybe she hadn't known. The most pressing question for now was, what did Shea White want from them? Money? Or was there something more?

"They broke your fingers, Andy." Lexie's voice broke.

Fresh pain washed over him. "I know. The doctor set them as best he could."

"Will you be able to write?"

A rueful smile touched his lips, despite his desperate desire to weep. "I'll find a way."

Shea jolted awake as a blast of thunder shook Penbrook House. She lay still, willing her heart to slow to a steady rhythm. It was the third day in succession that storms had pounded the Georgia countryside. Pushing aside the covers, she swung her legs around the side of the bed.

What would today bring? She still hadn't found the birth certificates or death records she had been looking for when Daniel Riley located her three days earlier. But she no longer had access to an automobile. Mr. Riley's attorney had driven to Alabama to visit some relatives, so Mr. Riley had been using Jonas's Ford to attend court every day and to visit his son and Andy in their respective hospitals.

Jonas would be arriving home today. Shea couldn't make up her mind about that man. He was handsome in a brooding sort of way. Those types usually didn't appeal to her. She liked safe, gentle men, the kind who'd never hurt a woman. Not a man who thought he could wrap a woman around his little finger. Shea wasn't the sort of woman to allow herself to be wrapped.

But she had to admit, Jonas did something to her insides. Something that frightened and disturbed her. The verbal sparring energized her and made her feel alive in a way she hadn't felt since Jeremy had entered her life.

Shaking her head, she slung the bedspread across the mattress and attempted to smooth it out. She absolutely could not fall for this man. How foolish would it be? Fall in love with the man who at this moment lived in the house that should have been hers? The home she had every intention of claiming through the legal system very soon. In a few days, hopefully, she would have everything she needed to contact the attorney who handled Miss Penbrook's will. And then she would be at odds with the Rileys.

Regret passed over her heart as she thought of Daniel Riley. He was a good man, a kind man, and she didn't want him to think less of her. Still, she had no choice.

Willfully, she made a firm decision to close herself off from thoughts of friendship. This was about what rightfully should have come to her. Not because of love or relationship, but because of blood rights. The facts were simple: She was a Penbrook and Mr. Riley was not. The Penbrook land and this wonderful Penbrook House belonged in the family. And she had every intention of seeing that it legally ended up in her possession.

Jonas felt like slugging someone—a fat, redheaded sheriff, to be exact. Every muscle in his body screamed with pain. According to the doctor, it was a good thing he'd come to the hospital when he had or he might not have lived to see next week. Dehydrated and bleeding from a gash in the head that had left him feeling disoriented and dizzy, Jonas also had to deal with a broken nose and a broken arm. One entire side of his rib cage was bruised but not broken. A fact for which he supposed he should feel grateful.

His memory barely extended beyond the moment the first punch was thrown—and he believed he had actually been the one to throw that punch. But as the day wore on and the pain medication started wearing off, he was left with throbbing pain and flashes of memory of Shea White, promising to get him out of that "hellhole." And she had apparently been true to her word. Because here he was, safe and sound and recovering under a doctor's care.

But the little spitfire Shea hadn't come anywhere near the hospital. Jonas had expected a visit from her. Truthfully, he was sort of disappointed that she never showed up. He couldn't bring himself to ask if she was still at Penbrook but was a little surprised to discover the depth of his hope that she was.

His three-day stay in the hospital had done little for the pain, but the doctor had stitched him up, set his broken arm, and bandaged his broken nose. This morning the physician had pronounced Jonas ready to go home.

Home. Despite his father's insistence that he return to Chicago, Jonas had no intention of leaving Georgia until he saw Sam Dane get what he had coming to him. And if he had his way, he'd see the sheriff put behind bars, too, or at the very least, released from his duties. Bullies like that had no business in positions of authority. Power went to their heads and brought out the meanness in them.

Pops wouldn't be happy with the plan to stay. As a matter of fact, Jonas was already gearing up for the fight.

The pretty, rosy-cheeked day nurse entered with a bright, toothy smile. Jonas might have enjoyed a flirtation with the young woman in other circumstances, but now wasn't the place or time. He sent her only a cursory smile.

"I hear you're going to be leaving us today," she said in a soft Southern drawl.

"That's right. I'm just waiting for my father to pick me up."

She brushed his shoulder with her fingertips, leaving no doubt in Jonas's mind that she'd welcome his attention. Any other time, he'd have taken her phone number or made plans to take her out once his wounds allowed, but the only thing that touch did for him was conjure up a thought of the cute, freckled nose of someone else. The nurse didn't seem to notice his lack of interest. "Maybe you'll come back and see us once you get all better."

The sound of footsteps on the tiled floor spared him the necessity of answering the leading statement. Jonas looked up as Pops entered the room, filling the air with his big presence.

Jonas sent the girl what he hoped was an apologetic smile and lifted his shoulders in a shrug.

The young nurse's expression fell. "I'll call for an orderly to help you outside, Mr. Riley." She walked toward the door.

"Thank you, Nurse," Jonas's father said. He turned to Jonas. "She's a little young, don't you think?"

Jonas gave a chuckle. "Any woman who is trained to fix up a man's body is old enough to capture his heart."

Daniel's lips twitched with amusement. "I'd be willing to bet that one hasn't captured anything but your briefest admiration."

A rueful smile touched Jonas's mouth. "I'm not in any condition to give a woman the proper amount of attention."

"Just as well, since you won't be in Georgia much longer. How are you feeling? Your mother wants to know when you're coming home." He smiled. "She's already prepared your old room for you and has ordered all your favorite foods from the grocery."

At the thought of his mother, Jonas almost lost his resolve. But he caught sight of his father's keen eye, observing with that alert reporter's curiosity while trying to remain aloof. Mentioning his mother had been nothing more than a ploy to manipulate his emotions. And Jonas almost fell for it. He must be slipping.

"I'm not going back until this trial is over and Andy comes home with me, Pops."

Daniel hefted a sigh. "I don't know what you expect me to tell your mother."

"You could hide out down here with us for a while. That way you won't have to face her until you deliver Andy and me safely to her doorstep."

"Don't tempt me."

An orderly arrived, pushing a wheelchair. Jonas wanted to refuse the thing, but as he stood, his head spun mercilessly, and he knew he'd never make it out of the room on his own, let alone out to the car.

With Pops on one side, taking great care not to disturb his broken arm, and the orderly on the other, Jonas shifted to the chair, silently cursing his weakness.

The drive to Penbrook House drained whatever energy Jonas had. All he wanted was to take a dose of the pain medicine he'd been given and fall into a blissful sleep to silence the screaming in his head and muscles.

He expelled a sigh of relief as Pops halted the car in front of the palatial Penbrook House.

"Wait there," his father commanded. Not that Jonas would have been stubborn enough to try to climb those stairs alone. He let out a groan as his father helped him swing his legs around the seat and plant his wing tips on the red clay driveway.

"Let me help." The soft voice seemed to come from nowhere. Jonas glanced up at the sound. The sun shining behind her head acted like a halo, and Jonas wasn't certain if he was hallucinating from the pain or if Shea White was indeed an angel.

Shea needed five minutes alone to sort out her thoughts. He'd looked at her, with his blue eyes piercing through hers, as though he could read her thoughts. Discern her secrets.

She reached her room and shut the door without making a sound. Even beaten, bruised, and broken, Jonas was still the most handsome man she'd ever laid eyes on. Pressing her hand to her chest, she willed her heart to stop throbbing at twice its normal beat. Surely it was from the exertion of helping Mr. Riley walk Jonas up the steps and settling him into bed.

Flinging herself onto the soft bed, she sank into the fluffy feather mattress and buried her face in her hands. She was becoming too attached to these people. Miss Delta, Andy, Mr. Riley. . .Jonas. Especially Jonas. She had to stop allowing her heart to soften toward him. Otherwise, how would she ever have the strength to carry out her plan?

She had to find more evidence than the diaries to prove her case if she were to have a chance to win against a powerful man like Daniel Riley, who could afford an attorney to fight for him.

Maybe Mr. Riley would allow her to drive Jonas's car into town. She could make up a believable excuse.

Outside her window, a motor roared. She pushed up from the bed and walked across the room. Her heart sank as she pushed aside the lacy curtain and looked down from her second-story bedroom. Mr. Riley was driving away. *So much for that idea.*

Heaviness descended upon Shea. Time was running out. The distraction of Andy and Jonas being beaten had bought her some time, but if she didn't find evidence soon, she'd wear out her welcome, and without money or a job, she'd have nowhere to go. True, Mr. Riley had left her with an open invitation to stay, but how long could she honestly rely on his generosity?

She propped her pillows against the headboard and sat back on the bed, then reached for the diary on the nightstand. With the rumbling skies threatening another downpour at any moment, there was no point in attempting the five-mile hike into town.

GEORGIA 1847

A week had passed since Father sent Celeste to work for Mrs. Haverty, and Mac felt like he was losing his mind. Finally, under pretense of trying to discover if Mr. and Mrs. Haverty were satisfied with her skills, he had saddled his horse. He now sat in their parlor, drinking sweet tea with a touch of mint.

The rotund, middle-aged woman chose a butter cookie from a tray held out by a young female slave. "Would you care for one, Mr. Penbrook?" she asked, batting her pale, thin lashes as if she were the belle of the ball.

Mac molded his lips into his most engaging smile. "You spoil me, Mrs. Haverty." He took one of the revolting sweets and nibbled the edge, carefully ignoring the young servant.

Mrs. Haverty waved the girl away, speaking in a clipped, annoyed tone. "That will be all, Rose."

"As I was saying, Mrs. Haverty, we wanted to be sure you felt you were getting your money's worth out of Celeste," he said. "If the girl isn't to your liking, we'd be happy to substitute another young woman to help in the kitchen."

The woman gave a long-suffering sigh. "Oh, one is just as good as another, I suppose." She gave him a knowing glance. "I'm sure you know what I mean."

"Indeed I do, ma'am." Mac fought to keep his irritation in check.

"The darkies are a lazy race. We feed them, clothe them, provide them a place to sleep at night, and what thanks do we get in return?"

"Laziness?"

"Precisely."

"Mrs. Haverty, we make it a policy to check on our slaves when we rent them out to neighbors." He flashed what he hoped was a winning smile, a smile he was far from feeling. "I'm sure you understand."

The woman's eyes narrowed. "Are you implying we have somehow damaged your property, sir?"

"Please, my dear lady, you misunderstand. This is strictly to satisfy my father's curiosity as to how well she is working for you. As a matter of fact, if I could observe her without her knowing I'm here, she will be less likely to try to deceive me into thinking she's working harder than she might otherwise be."

"I see." The woman didn't sound convinced. But Mac could see she was struggling with propriety. She couldn't very well call him an out-and-out liar, despite the irregularity of this request.

"If you object, I will inform my father of your hesitance. I'm sure he will bear you no ill will."

The veiled threat seemed to hit its mark. Penbrook was the largest plantation in the county, and it never did one well socially to be at odds with Mac's father.

"Well, of course, I'd be delighted to take you to your girl, Mr. Penbrook. It's just that. . ."

"Yes?" Mac's ears began to roar as he pictured his darling in harm's way.

"Well, as it turned out, we didn't need her in the kitchen after all, so we've taken her to the fields."

Mac's stomach turned. He took a deep breath, fighting for composure. The thought of Celeste working in the kitchen had been bad enough. But the Havertys' overseer, Able Turner, was known as the meanest overseer in the county. If he'd touched one hair on her head. . .

Mac stood. "My father doesn't respond well when his slaves are not used in the manner for which they are requested. May

I ask if you've relegated Celeste's mother, Anna, to the fields, as well?"

Her face turned pink. "Yes. Oh, I feel just terrible, sir. I didn't realize this might upset your father."

Truth be told, it wouldn't. Father couldn't care less as long as his slaves weren't harmed in such a manner as to lower their value. But she didn't know that. Nor did she have any reason to doubt Mac's word.

The woman trembled in her tight-fitting, dark green gown of taffeta and lace.

"Not to worry, Mrs. Haverty. I'll just go check on Celeste and her mother so I can put my father's mind at ease. Then I'll be on my way."

Like a nervous bird, she twittered behind him as he strode to the doorway. "It could be that our overseer has become a bit heavy-handed. Mr. Haverty has on occasion had to strongly correct that man for his overbearing ways. We do our best to control him."

Her words pushed a ball of fear to Mac's throat. "Thank you, ma'am," he said with difficulty. "I'll be sure to inform my father."

He mounted his horse and sped toward the fields behind the main house. An oppressively hot wind whipped across his face as he forced the spirited stallion to a gallop.

GEORGIA 1949

A tap on her door drew Shea from the diaries. Impatience at the interruption made its way into her tone. "Yes?"

"Ain't no cause to be snippy with me."

Shea crossed the room and opened the door, confronted with Miss Delta's scowling face.

"I'm sorry. I didn't mean to speak that way. What can I do for you?"

"My brother done fell and hurt his leg, and he's too dadburn stubborn to go to the hospital. Buck's pickin' me up in a few minutes to drive me over there to talk some sense into that man."

"Oh, Miss Delta, I hope he's all right."

"He'll be fine once I convince him to go see the doctor. But I need you to look after Mr. Penbrook until his pa gets back from town." Delta peered closer. "Now, don't look so scared, gal. Them pills they give him for pain'll likely knock him out for the rest of the night. But you be listening for him just in case."

Shea nodded. "I will, Miss Delta."

"You'll be just fine." Delta gave her an affectionate pat on the arm and turned to go.

"Shall I prepare dinner?"

"Well, it ain't gonna fix itself, honey."

With one last glance at the diary, Shea gave a sigh and headed down to the kitchen.

OREGON 1949

Jackson Sable wasn't used to not getting his way. The old woman's stubborn refusal to disclose Miss Penbrook's whereabouts was certainly beginning to wear on his nerves. She sat on her porch, rocking back and forth in a rickety old chair, pretending not to have a care in the world. But Jackson knew the true state of her affairs. His connections at the bank had informed him this old woman was close to losing her own home.

He tried on his best cajoling tone. "Miss Nell, I'm prepared to up my offer for any information about her whereabouts."

"You're wastin' your breath, Jackson. I'm not tellin' you

anything, so you might as well stop comin' around here struttin' like some peacock and cluckin' like a chicken."

Fury ignited in his breast and he leaned over her, dropping his tone to a calculated threat. "You listen to me, old woman, I intend to have those acres. If you don't tell me where she is, I'll find another way to obtain what I want."

The old woman sized him up, unflinching. "Well, aren't you the big man when it comes to bullying women?" She gave a disgusted sniff. "You do what you think you can. But know this: I will never help the likes of you get to my Shea."

Jackson fought the wave of violence flooding him. He pushed back the image of his hands curling around her neck, squeezing the worthless life out of her.

GEORGIA 1949

It seemed to Andy that every time he woke up he discovered a new pain. This time the light shot through his eyes as soon as he opened them, sending sharp jabs clear back to his sockets. He closed them quickly.

"Easy, son. The doctor said your eyes will take some adjusting."

"Uncle Daniel?"

"That's right. How are you feeling?"

"Better." He slowly opened his eyes again, this time more cautiously. The pain still came, but not as suddenly nor as severely as before. "Where's Lex?"

"I sent her down to the café to get something to eat. She's been here round the clock for days."

Guilt seared Andy's heart. "Thank you for forcing her to take a break."

"She mentioned you wanted to discuss something with me."

Andy nodded, fighting to sit up.

Daniel took his arm and helped hoist him to a sitting position, then propped two pillows behind his back. "How's that?"

"Fine. Thank you."

Uncle Daniel perched himself at the end of Andy's bed. "What can I do for you, son?"

"What do you know about Miss White?"

"Shea?" Daniel frowned. "Not much. Only that you're one lucky man that she came along when she did."

Andy nodded. "You're right. But is anything about her setting off warning bells?"

"Other than the fact that she appears to have traveled to Oak Junction alone with no family to come to?" Uncle Daniel gave a rueful smile.

Andy grinned back. "I should have known you'd be on top of things. What do you plan to do?"

"So far she's come between us and disaster three times. First by finding you and bringing you home, next by getting you to the hospital, and then by phoning me in Chicago and informing me of Jonas's situation. I'd hate to think she has ulterior motives."

"She seems to be perfectly willing to accept your generosity in staying at Penbrook."

"She has nowhere else to go. And I feel it's the least we can do. Besides, I'd just as soon have her staying where I can keep an eye on her for now. Maybe discover what she's up to. If anything."

"I might have a clue. But I'm not sure how to connect the dots just yet."

Daniel raised his bushy brows and shifted on the bed. "What do you mean?"

"The night I came into the hospital, Miss White sat in my room reading to me."

"And?"

"The book she read from was an old diary she said she found in her family's attic. Now, unless I miss my guess, her accent comes from the Northwest."

"I concur."

"Before I drifted to sleep, I heard her read references to the Penbrooks."

"I suppose there could be other Penbrooks." Daniel stroked his chin. "It's quite a coincidence, though."

"Several references were made to Henry Penbrook and Madeline."

"Henry," Daniel said bitterly. "The man who forced himself on my mother. . .many times."

"She wasn't the first household slave Henry forced his attentions on. There was another girl first. Her name was Celeste."

"Too much to be coincidence, I suppose, that Miss White showed up on our doorstep?"

"Obviously she has discovered diaries that connect her to the Penbrook family. I believe her presence here is intentional."

"Do you think she's after something?"

Andy shrugged. "Possibly. There's one more thing."

"Yes?"

"The diary seems to have been written by Henry's brother, Jason Penbrook. Maddy called him Jase, but it appears the rest of the family called him Mac. According to the writings, Mac was in love with the slave girl, Celeste, and desperate to remove her from harm's way."

"And Miss White said she found the diary in her attic?"

"That's what she claims."

"Well, then. I suppose we'd best keep a close eye on the young lady until we can figure out just what her connection is."

CHAPTER TWELVE
GEORGIA 1949

The room was pitch black when Jonas opened his eyes. The pain medicine had worn off, and his arm and head throbbed. He was sure the entire household was asleep by now, and he hated to be a burden. But there was no way he could get up and take care of necessary things by himself.

Knowing his father's room was just beyond the wall behind him, Jonas lifted his good arm and gave as solid a knock as he could muster. He waited a minute and tried again, this time a little more firmly.

He expelled a relieved breath when he heard a rustling noise in the hall and the door creak open.

"Mr. Penbrook, are you awake?"

Jonas felt his heart skip a beat at the sound of Shea's voice. "Yes. Can you please awaken my father? I need his help."

"I'm afraid he isn't home."

"What time is it?"

"After midnight."

"Help me up. We have to go find him."

Shea was at his side in a flash, restraining his good shoulder with a firm hand. "Settle down, Jonas. He's all right. He brought Lexie here, but she wouldn't stay unless someone was with Andy. So he volunteered to sleep at the hospital."

Relief flooded him and he relaxed against the pillow. But the fact that Pops was safe at the hospital with Andy presented Jonas with another kind of problem.

"Now, what can I help you with?"

"Nothing. Get Miss Delta."

"She isn't here either."

"Where is she?" he growled.

"Her brother hurt himself and she went to take care of him. Or at least to make sure he gets looked after."

Heat seared Jonas's ears. He had two choices: suffer or ask her for help.

"There's nothing to be embarrassed about. I took care of my granddad for six months while he lay bedridden. Let me help you to the bathroom. I'll wait outside the door and then help you back to bed."

"Just help me stand up and maybe I can make it."

She pursed her lips but didn't argue with him.

Waves of dizziness swept over him, along with black spots and flashes of light as the blood rushed to his head. He sat down fast.

"Take it slow there, Ace," Shea admonished. "We'll try again when you get your bearings. You have a nasty gash on your head and a concussion."

"I know," he snapped, though he didn't mean for the words to come out quite so abruptly. He was on the verge of apologizing when she stepped back and planted her hands firmly on her hips.

"Look, do you want my help or not, Mr. High and Mighty? Because I have better things to do if you'd rather try to get there on your own."

"Far be it from me to keep you from your important work," he said, this time meaning every sarcastic syllable.

"Fine. Good-bye." She wheeled around and flounced to the door.

"Keep it open!" he called after her.

Without a word, she slipped through the doorway and disappeared down the hall.

Shea huffed to her room and flung the door open, then gasped and caught it just before it could shut with the intended *bang*. She'd forgotten about Lexie, who was next door. After three nights looking after Andy in that hospital, the woman needed a good night's sleep.

Jonas Penbrook was an ungrateful slug of a man. Did he honestly think she took pleasure in the task of helping him to the bathroom? He could just lie there and suffer for all she cared.

Of course, she had promised Miss Delta to take care of him. And what if Jonas squealed to his father, and Mr. Riley turned her out of Penbrook House before she found a job and earned enough money to move into a decent boardinghouse?

Caught by her own needs, Shea yanked open the door and stomped down the hall just as Jonas, pale and shaking, appeared at the door. Compassion flooded over her at the absence of color in his cheeks.

"Lean on me and I'll get you down the hall."

He nodded, and Shea knew by the look of pain in his eyes that it was the best he could do. It was enough.

A full thirty minutes elapsed before she got him tucked back into bed. "Can I fix you anything to eat, Mr. Penbrook?"

His eyes remained closed, but his lips twisted into a sardonic half smile. "I think we know each other well enough for you to call me Jonas."

"All right, Jonas. Are you hungry?"

He shook his head. "Could you get my pills and some water?"

Shea did as he asked.

"Thank you," he breathed after swallowing the medicine.

"You're welcome." She smoothed away a lock of hair that had fallen across his forehead. He sighed and she snatched her hand away.

"I never thanked you for your part in getting me out of that stink-hole jail."

"No thanks are necessary."

He opened a sleepy eye and stared at her. "Yes, they are. You put your neck on the line for a stranger. One, I might add, who hasn't always been very nice to you."

She gave him a teasing smile. "That's true enough."

"Well, thank you. You saved my life."

"I wouldn't say that."

He gripped her hand, and his blue eyes appeared focused and alert. "If you hadn't stepped in, I'd be dead, or close to it by now. So let me thank you."

Uncomfortable with being the object of anyone's gratitude, or for that matter, having any reason to be proud of herself, Shea tried to slip her hand away. But Jonas tightened his hold with amazing strength for someone in his condition. "Just accept the apology."

"All right. You're welcome then."

His grip and expression relaxed and he closed his eyes with a smile. "That's better, Slick."

Shea remained by his bedside and watched him while he drifted peacefully to sleep. What was it about this man that made her emotions run the gamut? Anger one minute, admiration the next.

Back in her room, sleep refused to come. Finally, she threw off the covers, switched on the lamp, and picked up Mac's diary.

GEORGIA 1847

Mac yanked on the reins, and his stallion skidded to a halt behind a gathering of slaves. He dismounted quickly and handed the reins to the nearest slave boy along with a coin. The unmistakable sound of a bullwhip zinging through the air tore at his heart as he made his way through the crowd.

A woman stood tethered to a pole in the middle of the group of wide-eyed Negroes. Mac's heart nearly stopped. Celeste? He'd kill that overseer!

"Stop!" His voice sounded guttural to his own ears. But he didn't care. He rushed forward.

"What is this?" the burly overseer demanded, breathing heavily from the whipping he'd been giving out. "Who in blazes are you?"

Without bothering to answer, Mac headed straight for the woman. He nearly passed out with relief. Not Celeste. He turned to the overseer and sneered. "You're wasting your time. She's unconscious. Cut her down."

The man's face mottled with anger. "You ain't go no right to interfere in this business."

"My name is Penbrook, and some of our slaves are being leased to Mr. Haverty." He stood over the man, using his six-foot-three-inch height to intimidate. "We don't whip our slaves."

Mac scanned the faces of the slaves in the crowd. Hopeful,

admiring, fearful. How could all three expressions mingle into those large, dark eyes? "Do any of you know Celeste?"

"I'm here, Mastuh."

The sound of her sweet voice sang like a mockingbird's song. He turned as she slipped through the crowd, fighting the urge to gather her into his arms and cover her face with kisses.

"All of you, back to work," the overseer growled.

Celeste tore her gaze from Mac's at the sound of her oppressor's voice. She turned to accompany the rest of the slaves as they headed for the fields.

"Wait. Celeste."

She turned. "Mastuh?"

"Get your things. You're coming home with me."

"I ain't got no things, suh."

"Then let's go." He took her by the arm and she winced. "What's wrong?"

"Nothin'."

"Something's wrong. Did you hurt your arm?"

She averted her gaze to her bare feet and shook her head. But he knew she was lying. "Let me see your arm."

"Look, Penbrook." The overseer stomped through the dust until he stood in front of Mac. "You can't take the girl away from here. We got a lease."

"I'll do as I please. And I strongly suggest you stay out of my way. Celeste, let me see that arm."

She rolled up her sleeve and revealed a slash that Mac instantly recognized as the bite of a whip. He could only imagine the state of her back. Fury thundered through him and he turned on the overseer. "Give me one good reason I shouldn't kill you with my bare hands, you filthy excuse for a human being."

Fear struck the overseer's eyes and he stepped back. "Well,

I suppose you'd have to suffer the consequences for your own illegal actions."

"Suh, what about my ma?" Celeste's voice penetrated Mac's anger and he looked down into her pleading eyes. "I can't go wifout her."

"Where is she?"

"In the sick cabin, suh."

"Sick, my foot," the overseer interjected with a sneer. "Lazy is more like it."

Mac silenced him with a warning glare and turned back to Celeste. "Take me to her."

The cabin stank of waste. The air smelled so foul, Mac was forced to grab a handkerchief from his pocket to cover his nose and mouth. Skeletal bodies lined the floor. "The sick cabin, huh?"

Celeste nodded, tears flooding her beautiful eyes. Mac slipped an arm about her shoulders, then dropped it when she winced. "We'll get your ma out of here, honey. Don't cry."

He relished the look of simple trust that came over her face. She walked ahead of him until they came to her mother. Fury rose in Mac at the sight of the poor woman. Once healthy and robust, she now appeared wasted, her face and body marred with scars and bruises.

Holding his breath, Mac handed the handkerchief to Celeste and reached for her mother. Lifting her gently, he carried her outside in full view of the overseer, who had been joined by Mr. Haverty.

The little man, as fat as his wife, waddled forward, outrage painted across his face. His cheeks puffed out with each breath he took. "What's the meaning of this?"

"I should be asking you the same question, sir." Keeping his tone filled with disdain, Mac maintained a steady gaze on the social climber.

Mr. Haverty shifted his eyes away from the emaciated woman in Mac's arms. "I'm sure I don't know what you mean. I had a business arrangement for the lease of these slaves."

"Does that agreement include killing them? We sent you a healthy woman with no marks on her. And this is what we are getting back? How long do you think it's going to be before she can work again? It's no wonder you are forced to lease slaves from your neighbors. You have no regard for property."

"I will not be spoken to in this insultin' manner."

"You have brought the insult on yourself with your deplorable treatment of my father's slaves." Mac peered closer. "I've half a mind to spread the word to the rest of the county not to lease slaves to you if they value their property at all."

"Surely you don't mean that!"

"If I hear of any more treatment of slaves in this manner, I will do just that. I suggest you move those sick people to clean quarters and call for a doctor."

"Yes, yes. Right away." He turned to his overseer. "Get it done!" he bellowed.

"I'm going to need to borrow a wagon," Mac said.

"Of course. Whatever you want."

The woman in his arms never stirred as he waited for the horse-drawn wagon to arrive. She didn't move when he laid her in the wagon bed nor when they reached Penbrook.

Celeste's weeping confirmed what he had feared: Her mother was dead.

GEORGIA 1949

Andy woke, fighting for breath. Pain exploded across his face as something pressed down hard, denying him life-sustaining air.

"You're gonna die this time, darky." The sinister whisper barely registered as the man pushed on the pillow, squashing Andy's face.

Andy felt himself losing consciousness as blackness slowly washed over him.

A pounding on the door downstairs awakened Shea. She fought to open her sleep-deprived eyes and slowly came awake.

The pounding became more insistent. Shea threw on the white flannel robe Jonas had given her the day she'd arrived. Had it been less than a week? "I'm coming," she called as she raced down the long stairway.

She unlocked the door and flung it open. "Andy! Mr. Riley! I had no idea you were coming this morning."

"Neither did we," Mr. Riley said.

Shea moved aside so the men could enter.

"Close the door," Mr. Riley said sharply.

Shea did as she was told. "Is everything all right?"

"Andy!" Lexie, clad in her nightgown and robe, came running down the stairs. She gripped Andy's arm. "Are you all right? Why aren't you still at the hospital?"

The older man scowled. "Someone attempted to smother him with a pillow during the night."

Shea and Lexie gasped as with one breath. "Did you catch him?"

"Thank God I woke up just in time and startled him." Mr. Riley stared at Lexie. "It was KKK. But he ran off before I could grab him."

A look of terror shot to Lexie's eyes. "Will Andy be safe here?"

Mr. Riley nodded. "Safer than in the hospital, where anyone can walk in."

"How could an intruder get past the nurses without someone calling out?" Shea asked.

"A white hood and a gun can silence any black person, man or woman." Andy spoke up for the first time since entering the house.

"Oh, Andy. . ." Lexie's groan shot straight to Shea's heart.

"Let's get him upstairs to bed," Mr. Riley suggested.

"Wait," Lexie spoke up. "If anyone finds out Andy's alive, he won't be safe from the Klan. Not even here at Penbrook."

Mr. Riley nodded soberly. "I'm afraid that's true."

"Then we have to agree right here and now. No one outside of this house, other than the doctor, can know Andy's alive." She turned her gaze on Shea.

"Of course," Shea immediately replied.

"All right," Mr. Riley said. "Then we're agreed."

Once Andy was settled in, Shea stopped at Jonas's room and stepped through the open door. Jonas sat up in bed, a deep frown marring his handsome features. "It's about time you came and let me in on all the commotion," he growled.

Shea's ire shot to the surface. So much for Mr. Nice Guy from last night. "Good morning to you, too."

"What's happened?"

"The Klan made an attempt on Andy's life in the hospital, so your father brought him home."

"Is he all right?"

"I think so. He's resting now. Lexie's taking care of him."

"And my father?"

"Here, son." Mr. Riley entered the room.

"Pops, you need to take Andy and Lex back to Chicago. The next time those hooded cowards try to kill him might be the one that gets the job done."

"Perhaps we should all go home," Mr. Riley suggested.

Shea fought back a smile at the boyish grin Jonas sent his father. His tousled hair and sleepy eyes added to the effect, making him look like an ornery boy. "Then who would cover the trial for the paper?"

Mr. Riley sent his son a scowl. "Certainly not you." He turned to Shea and she stepped back. "Miss Delta tells me you are seeking employment."

"That's right. I'll be out of your hair as soon as I earn enough for a room."

"Nonsense. You'll stay here. How would you like to be a reporter?"

"Pops, what are you doing?" Jonas's words were laced with amusement.

"I'm conducting an interview, and I'll thank you to stay out of it."

"She's not a reporter."

"How do you know?" Shea demanded, stinging a little from his tone.

"Are you?"

"No." She tossed him a haughty glare. "But it doesn't seem so difficult. Just sit in the courtroom and write what I see and hear."

"There you have it," Mr. Riley broke in before Jonas could argue further. "We need eyes and ears down at the courthouse every day while the trial is in process. What do you think?"

What did she think? Not only would she have a paying job, she could stay at Penbrook House while she continued to search for birth and death records that would prove she was the rightful heir to all this.

She turned a smile on the elderly gentleman. "Sounds like just the kind of job I'm looking for, sir."

"This is ridiculous." Jonas's objections fell on deaf ears.

Mr. Riley extended his hand. Shea shook it with gusto, feeling as though something was finally going her way.

Sam smirked through his bars as he watched the sheriff waddle toward the office door.

"You have ten minutes," Gabe said over his shoulder, trying bravado on for size, despite the fact that he'd just been ordered from the room by his own prisoner.

When Gabe was gone, Sam looked at his visitor. "Well?"

"It's done. That colored Yankee boy never even woke up."

"Good. Good." One less thing he would have to take care of after this mockery of a trial came to an end. The thought of Andy lying dead in his hospital bed sent waves of satisfaction over Sam. And satisfaction quickly morphed into euphoria. "Get me some paper and a pencil from the sheriff's desk."

Senator Dane was just settling down in the library with his nightly brandy and Charles Dickens's *A Tale of Two Cities* when he heard the sound of glass shattering and a *thud* in the front room. He jumped to his feet as the squeal of tires against the pavement signaled that the perpetrators hadn't stuck around to do more damage than throw something through his window.

He set down his book and hurried into the front room, where he found a rock with a note attached. "Couldn't they have just left their message in the mailbox?" he muttered as he surveyed the broken window and the gashed grandfather clock where the rock had landed. As he peeled the note from the rock, a lump formed in his throat and tears sprang to his eyes.

The abomination has been erased. Your soul is purged.

It could only mean one thing. The Klan had somehow gotten to Andy, and more than likely it had been Sam who ordered the killing.

Hurrying to his bedroom, the senator dressed and headed for the garage. It had been a long time since he'd driven himself anywhere, but tonight he had no choice. He cranked the engine and headed the car toward the hospital where Andy was a patient. He no longer cared about his reputation or his office. For now, he was a father who needed to be assured that his son was alive.

Fifteen minutes later, he parked the car and strode through the doors, feeling the stares of every pair of dark eyes in the place as he walked to the counter.

"I'm looking for Andy Carmichael. A reporter from Chicago. He was brought in a few nights ago."

"You the one who's been calling every day to check on him?"

"I am."

"He ain't here no more."

Icy fingers of fear trailed down the senator's spine. "Was he released?"

"I can't give out any information, sir. I'm sorry."

Samuel leaned across the counter and looked the young nurse in the eye. "Do you know who I am?"

She gave a mute nod.

"Then I insist you tell me where Mr. Carmichael has gone."

An older nurse appeared seemingly from nowhere. "He's dead," she said matter-of-factly. "Died today."

Samuel felt a tightening in his chest. He clutched his left arm as pain trailed down the limb. "Help—me."

Chapter Thirteen
Georgia 1949

The buzzing courtroom became deathly still as the judge banged his gavel and called the proceedings to order.

"Your Honor?" the portly defense attorney spoke up.

"What is it?"

Shea had a feeling the judge's patience was wearing thin.

"Your Honor, I request a recess until such a time as determined appropriate by the court."

"For what purpose?"

"The defendant's father, Senator Dane, has suffered a heart attack and is in the hospital fighting for life at this very minute."

"I'm sorry to hear that, Council, for the senator's sake. But how will it affect these proceedings for us to wait?"

"Your Honor, the defendant is understandably distraught and wishes to throw himself on the mercy of the court."

Shea observed the man on trial for murder. His expression was smug, his eyes glittered like glass. He certainly didn't look like a man who was worried about his father, nor did he appear to be begging for mercy.

The judge must have thought the same thing, for he looked over his spectacles at the attorney. "And what form does the defendant wish this mercy to take?"

"Mr. Dane asks the court to allow him to visit his father in the hospital, as it may be the last chance he has to see him alive."

Shea held her breath as the people crammed into the balcony began to murmur and shift, finally causing enough of a stir that the judge lowered his gavel to bring the courtroom back to order.

"I'd like to hear from the defendant before I decide whether or not to allow the request."

Sam Dane Jr. slowly rose to his feet. He cleared his throat. "Your Honor, my father and I are alone in the world. My mother died when I was young, and I never had any siblings. Now, I know this request is irregular, sir, but I ask you to allow me one last visit with the only family I have left."

An award-winning performance, as far as Shea was concerned.

Apparently the judge believed the cockamamy plea. "Sheriff, keep this man cuffed and escort him to the hospital to visit his father." He leveled his gaze at the attorney. "You will accompany your client and the sheriff and report back to me as to the senator's condition."

"Yes, Your Honor. We appreciate the leniency."

"Court is adjourned until Monday morning at 9:00 a.m."

Cries of outrage echoed from the balcony and Shea felt a moment of alarm. Would there be an uprising? Two deputies stood gripping rifles, eyeing the large group of black folk.

The judge once more banged his gavel, even though he had officially adjourned the proceedings for the day. All eyes turned to him. "I am instructing everyone to stay put until the sheriff and the defendant leave this courtroom. I won't stand for any vigilante nonsense in Oak Junction. Is that clear?"

Shea watched the faces, angry, outraged. Murderous. How

safe would Sam Dane Jr. be leaving the seclusion of the court-house and jail? Going out a side door, she walked to the back of the courthouse, where she had parked Jonas's car.

Someone slipped out the same door she had just exited. A black man. How had he gotten to the main floor and left unno-ticed? She crouched down so she wouldn't be seen and watched the man as he looked around, then ducked under a weeping willow tree. He was quickly hidden by the drooping branches. Her curiosity piqued, Shea kept her attention riveted on the tree. A minute later the man reappeared.

The flash of sunlight glinting off metal sent waves of anxiety through her. The man walked around the corner of the building. She tiptoed toward the side of the courthouse. What if Sam's life were in danger? At least a hundred people in the balcony would happily see him dead. But would someone take the deed upon himself? Not that he didn't deserve it, but she couldn't stand by and watch a man be murdered in cold blood and not try to stop it.

Cautiously, she peeked around the corner. Her heart rate picked up. There he was, crouched alongside the building, watching the front of the courthouse, a rifle clutched in his hand.

Shea gathered a shaky breath. She had two choices—three, really. She could go back around the courthouse, enter through the door she'd just exited, and alert the sheriff to the danger. She could sneak up behind the would-be assassin and try to disarm him. Or she could walk away and do nothing, and figure justice had been served. She was about to take the first option when she noticed the man wipe a tear from his cheek. She couldn't rat him out. No matter if it was the right thing to do or not.

Inching around the corner, she tiptoed toward the man,

keeping her eye on the back of his head. When she stepped on a loosened rock, her ankle twisted. She gasped as she grabbed for the steadying brick wall.

The man whipped around, the whites of his eyes flashing against his dark skin. Before she could call out to him, he raised his rifle. A shot rang out in the muggy Georgia air.

❧

"I don't like prying into her private things like this." Andy's wife's tone was stern, her brow creased with worry, as she held the book in her hand.

"I don't like it either. But Shea obviously isn't who she claims to be, and I plan to find out who she is before she tries to do any damage to this family," Andy replied.

Lexie settled into the chair next to him. "I don't know, honey. She might not be telling everything, but she doesn't seem like the type to cause trouble. Look at everything she's done so far to help Uncle Daniel and you. I just don't like the idea of taking a book off her nightstand and prying into her life without her being any the wiser."

"I know. And I hope I'm wrong. But something doesn't add up." He nodded toward the diary, unable to hold the book with his broken fingers. "Do you mind reading aloud?"

She stood and closed the door. "Just in case Shea comes back before we're finished."

GEORGIA 1847

Father's face stormed with rage and Mother remained pale and sullen as they sat in his office the morning after Mac returned to Penbrook with Celeste. "I hope you're happy," Father growled.

"The Blythes are gone and have no intention of allowing their daughter to marry such a fool."

Even Janette had agreed with her parents that Mac wasn't the right man for her. Finally.

"Fool, am I?" Mac shook his head and gave a humorless laugh.

"What else do you call a man who chases around the country-side after a Negress?"

"A man in love?"

His father pounded the desk. "I won't have it! I'll not have a son of mine make a laughingstock of this family. I've made arrangements to sell the girl to Haverty in the morning, and you will not interfere, or so help me I'll have you locked away until she's gone."

Mac shot to his feet and leaned across the desk, meeting his father's glare. "Are you mad? I will not stand by and let Haverty and that bully of an overseer kill Celeste the same way they killed her mother." Panic shot through his breast. "Didn't you see the wounds on her back and arms? Haverty's overseer whipped her without provocation just to break her from being an 'uppity house nigger.' "

Mother stood and slowly walked to her husband's side. "Jim, perhaps Celeste would be better off if we sold her elsewhere. After all, how can we send her to a man known for his cruelty to the darkies?"

Father's eyes snapped. "Don't question me, woman. Besides, it's too late. I've already contacted Haverty. He arrives in the morning to take the girl back."

With all the discipline he could muster, Mac slowly nodded. "Then I suppose there's nothing left to say." He turned on his heel and left the room without another word. The sound of his footsteps echoed off the marble floor as he stalked to the stairs and took them two at a time. Instead of stopping at his own room, he continued down the hall until he found himself in front of Maddy's doorway.

She greeted him with a smile. "What a lovely surprise." Turning, she beckoned her daughter. "Camilla, darling, come and give your uncle Jase a kiss and a hug."

The beautiful four-year-old with chestnut curls grinned shyly and wrapped her chubby little arms around his neck. Mac drank in the clean, fresh scent of her, knowing this might be the last time he held his niece in his arms.

"Can we speak?" he asked Madeline over the little girl's shoulder.

"Of course. Camilla, sweetheart, take your doll and go to your room."

Angry creases lined the child's brow. "I don't want to." She stomped. "I want Uncle Jase to give me a ride on his back."

"Camilla Penbrook," Maddy said firmly, "I insist you obey me at once or there will be no apple pie for you tonight."

The child stood ramrod straight for a minute, and Mac thought she might argue further. But in the end, her stomach won the argument, and Camilla skipped out of the room.

Maddy's lips tilted in a rueful smile. "That child grows more willful every day."

A chuckle rumbled in Mac's chest. He was just as guilty as anyone of spoiling Camilla. "Better a spirited child than one without spunk."

"If you say so." Maddy motioned toward a brown settee next to the window. "Please sit down and tell me what's on your mind."

"I need to make an unusual request of you. One that will

require your silence should anyone question you about it."

A frown marred her brow. "Silence from my husband?"

"I'm afraid so. You know I wouldn't even suggest it if I didn't feel it was necessary." Mac hesitated. She deserved to know more than he could tell her. But how could he explain why Henry would be vengeful over Mac's relationship with Celeste? To do so would implicate Henry in Celeste's rape—he couldn't do that to Maddy. She was blissfully unaware of her husband's tendencies and infidelity, and as much as Mac despised his brother, he couldn't put Maddy in that position. It was doubtful she'd believe him anyway.

"What do you think?" he asked. "Should I just walk away now without asking for your help? Or can you give me your word not to divulge my plan?"

Maddy's lower lip disappeared between her teeth and she averted her troubled gaze. Then she squared her shoulders and gave a decisive nod. "I'll help. Tell me what you need."

"Thank you." Mac squeezed his sister-in-law's delicate hand and smiled in relief. "I need two of your gowns. Nothing fancy. Just everyday gowns and all the. . ." How could he say this delicately? "All the garments that are necessary to complete a woman's wardrobe."

"You need my clothes?" Confusion clouded her pretty face. "I don't under—"

"I know. I don't want to tell you any more than necessary in case you decide you can't keep this secret from Henry or my father."

She sat up straighter and jerked her chin. "I've given you my word, Jason Penbrook. Are you saying I may be found to be less than honorable?"

"Of course not. I'm sorry if I've offended you."

He hesitated, knowing he had a strong need for an alibi but also knowing that once his plan was discovered, it would immediately cast suspicion on the Northern-born Madeline, who had made no secret of her dislike of the institution of slavery. The less she knew, the better off she would be. Still, she was most likely the only person he could trust right now, and he needed her help. "All right. I'm planning to take Celeste and leave for Missouri tonight."

"Celeste? But why?"

"There are a lot of things you don't know, Maddy. The most important of which is that Celeste nursed me when I was ill with yellow fever and I fell in love with her."

Madeline's face softened. "Oh, my poor Jase. No wonder your father has been so desperate to remove her from Penbrook."

"Yes. So you see, I have no choice but take her away from here."

"But I thought your father sold her to Mr. Haverty."

"So far the sale is only by verbal agreement. No money has exchanged hands."

"Are you sure you want to risk the legal ramifications?"

"Only my father can claim I've stolen his property, and I doubt he'd be willing to subject the family to public scandal."

Maddy pressed her finger to her bottom lip as though deep in thought. "You're probably right." She glanced at him, determination etched across her face. "How do you want to get the clothes without someone seeing and growing suspicious?"

"Instruct Cookie Mary to come up and gather them. Tell her to take them to the barn. I'll take over from there."

Maddy moved to the door, opened it an inch, then closed it again before turning to him. She hurried to her desk, where she pulled out a tablet and an inkwell.

"What are you doing?"

She turned to him, a deep frown creasing her brow, and placed a finger to her lips to silence him. A few moments later, she blew on the ink and handed the paper to Mac. He glanced down at a rough, quickly drawn map. "People along the way who will help. Just tell them you're a friend of a friend."

Where was she? Jonas paced in front of the window, watching for his car to drive up the oak-lined lane. Shea should have been back hours ago. The sun was beginning to descend on the western horizon, and concern nipped at his insides like an unruly pup. He waffled between worry that she had stolen the car and left for parts unknown to worry that something sinister had happened to her.

He walked to the door, each step sending fiery shoots of pain through his midsection. "Miss Delta!"

The housekeeper appeared in moments. "What are you yellin' about?"

"Any word from Shea?"

"Did you hear that phone ring since the last time you had me runnin' up them stairs to answer the same question?"

Jonas scowled. "No."

"Then what do you think the answer is?"

"You think she ran off with my car?"

"Is that all you're worried about?" She shook her head. "And I thought for sure you were starting to like her a little bit."

"I don't even know her. All I know about her is that she came from nowhere and disappeared again." No way was he going to admit to any feelings about the young woman until he was certain she was on the level. And certain she felt the same way. Besides, it hadn't been that long since they met. Love at first sight was the kind of thing that happened in sappy love stories. He felt like an idiot for falling prey to the situation.

But Miss Delta couldn't possibly know where his mind was wandering.

She scowled at him. "Shea came from Oregon. And you don't know if she disappeared or not. Maybe the trial ran late."

"Until seven o'clock? I don't think the judge is going to want to miss his evening meal."

"That's most likely a fact."

"So where can she be?"

Delta shrugged and headed toward the door. "I ain't God. How do I know where she is?" She glanced back, her expression softened. "Try to rest so you can get your strength back."

"Let me know if she returns, okay?"

Shea woke up lying on the ground next to the courthouse, her shoulder screaming in pain. When she tried to sit up, she realized her hands were tied in front of her with a coarse length of rope.

"Let me help you." Jerome assisted her to a sitting position against the concrete wall, then examined her wounded shoulder. In a flash, she remembered seeing the man aim his rifle at her. She wondered why no one had come running when the shot sounded.

Through the haze of pain and disorientation, Shea heard the distraught father—apologize to her over and over, both for shooting her and for tying her up. "I couldn't take a chance that you'd warn Sam," he explained.

The cold concrete felt hard against Shea's back and her legs grew numb.

"I'll wait here 'til morning if I have to. But one way or another, I'm gonna put a hole through Sam next time he shows up." He swiped a tear from his cheek. "That man killed my little girl."

"I know, Jerome." Shea held her breath. "But you have to let the court punish him. If you take things into your own hands, you'll end up in jail yourself. And then what will your wife do? How will she take care of the rest of your children all alone?"

He stared at her, his eyes vacant.

"Let me drive you home. Your wife is probably worried sick about you by now." The folks at Penbrook House would undoubtedly be wondering where Shea was, as well.

His eyes glazed over with anger. "But Sam killed our little girl," he repeated. "I ain't gonna let the jury set him free."

"You don't know that they will. Maybe he'll be convicted."

Jerome turned toward her, and Shea shrank back. "That judge let him off to visit his father. You think they would have let a black man out for the same reason? Ain't I a father, too? My girl can't visit me, can she?"

Shea gulped back a sob, her heart filled with compassion for this hurting man.

He picked up his rifle from the ground. "Thanks to you, I missed my chance when they let Sam out to go visit his pa. But I'm going on over to the hospital and wait for him to come out. The minute he shows his face, I'm gonna shoot him. I swear I will."

Concentrating on keeping a level tone, Shea spoke slowly. "It isn't fair the way your race is treated down here. But if you shoot Sam, he wins. Don't you see? He will have stolen not only your daughter from your family, but you, too."

Silence followed her impassioned discourse. After a few minutes, Shea ventured a peek at his face. His expression stoic, he stared at the rifle in his hands. "Okay."

Shea held her breath as he slowly rose to his feet. Her body protested the change of position as he helped her up, then snipped the rope with his pocketknife.

"My car is behind the courthouse," she offered.

He shook his head. "You can't drive me home."

"Why not?"

"Someone might see, and it could cause trouble."

There was no way Shea was going to leave him. For all she knew, Jerome might wait for her to drive off and then head over to the hospital after all. "The sun's already gone down, so maybe no one will notice."

Skepticism painted a grim picture on his dark face.

"If you'd rather," Shea suggested, "you can lie down in the backseat until we get outside of town."

A slow smile spread across his face. "That might work."

As she led him to her car, Shea looked down at her blood-soaked dress. *Great!* The one decent outfit she had, ruined. Jerome hadn't intended for the gun to go off, so she bore him no ill will about the situation. Still, she'd have to spend part of her new job money on a dress.

But she couldn't let herself get too frustrated with that. After all, she'd managed to stave off a killing, simply by being in the right place at the right time. Could this be another example of God's sovereign will?

If patience was a virtue, Sam figured there must be a special place for him in heaven. He'd been sitting at the old man's bed-side like the dutiful son all day, and the senator hadn't budged. He'd like nothing better than to take one of those pillows and put it over his father's face. But Gabe would never allow it. Be-sides, seemed like God was going to rid this world of his father's abomination without Sam having to lift a finger. First Andy, and now the senator. Things were going exactly right. Accord-ing to his attorney, the trial wouldn't last more than a few more days and then the jury would deliberate.

A smile crept slowly across his lips. He was as good as free.

CHAPTER FOURTEEN
GEORGIA 1949

From his open bedroom window, Andy heard a car pull up the drive. He nodded to Lexie. "Better get that diary back to Shea's room before she comes inside."

"My eyes are starting to shut anyway," Lexie said, standing and stretching. "Be right back."

Andy watched her go, still amazed that she had come back to him last year after their marriage had seemed all but doomed, and amazed that God had graciously given them a daughter and a new start in their life together.

As much as he wanted her to stay, he knew she had to return home when Uncle Daniel and Vic Chambers left for Chicago the next day. Talking her into it was going to be the challenge.

She breezed back into the room. "All put back. Shea will be none the wiser." Her lips pursed in disapproval. "I still don't like invading someone's privacy like that."

Andy drew a breath. "I know. But you must realize from reading those diaries that she's keeping something from us."

Lexie plopped down on the bed next to him and stretched out. "Maybe she has a good reason."

"Maybe." Andy wanted to slide his hand along the silky

skin of her bare arms, and so much more, but the ache in his fingers and ribs reminded him he'd better take it easy. "Lex, we need to talk."

Flipping onto her side, Lexie faced him, the sheer grace of her movement taking his breath away. He loved this woman with everything in him. Enough to understand why Mac Penbrook would risk so much for the slave woman he loved. Enough to understand why he would go after her, rescue her, leave everything behind to keep her safe.

Lexie observed him through half-closed lids. "I'm not going back, so don't even ask."

"I'm not asking."

"Good." Pulling herself up to rest on one elbow, Lexie leaned forward and kissed him softly on the mouth.

"Lex. . .I'm more than asking. I'm insisting you go home."

She pulled back an inch, her breath mingling with his. Tears welled up in her wonderful brown eyes. "I can't leave you here to the mercy of the Klan."

"I'm safe at Penbrook for now. Only one doctor at the hospital knows the truth. The rest of the staff thinks I died night before last. That's the word they'll be spreading."

"I don't care." She flopped back to her side of the bed, and Andy knew he was in for a fight.

"Please, Lexie. If you stay here, I'm going to be worried every second of every day that something will happen to you. Things are volatile around here. It wouldn't take much to provoke these crackers."

"Who's going to take care of you if I leave?" Her voice trembled with soft resignation and Andy nearly wept with relief.

"God will have to take on that job."

Worry quickly gave way to anger by the time Jonas saw Shea park his car and enter the house. He waited for her at the top of the stairs. "Where have you been?" he demanded, then noted the blood on her dress. His heart nearly stopped beating. "What happened?"

Her steps seemed heavy, and she leaned on the rail as she climbed the last three stairs. She stood facing him on the landing, panting from the effort. "Which question do you want answered first?"

Something in the weariness of her tone wrapped around Jonas's heart. He placed his hand at the small of her back and guided her to her room. She didn't protest. He opened her door and entered after her. "What happened?"

She sat heavily on her bed, her shoulders slumped, and buried her face in her hands. Her slight body trembled.

Panic welled up in Jonas. "Are you crying?"

Stupid! Of course she was crying. What else would a woman do who had obviously been through a terrible ordeal? Throwing propriety to the wind, Jonas sat next to her and gathered her close with his one good arm. She buried her face in his shoulder. He felt ten feet tall.

"What's this?"

Jonas glanced up to find Miss Delta scowling in the doorway. Why did he suddenly feel like a child caught with his hand in the cookie jar?

"She just got home."

"I can see that. What I want to know is what you're doing in her room." She waved her hand toward them. "This ain't right. Do you want folks to talk about Shea and give her a bad reputation?"

Shea straightened. She swiped the back of her hand across her face. "It's all right, Miss Delta. I started bawling. What else was he going to do but comfort me?"

"Honey!" Delta rushed forward and inspected Shea's bloody shoulder. "What happened to you?"

She gathered a trembling breath. "It's not as bad as it looks."

"You let me be the judge of that." Miss Delta turned on Jonas. Once again, he felt like a naughty eight-year-old. "You best be gettin' on out of here so I can tend to this poor girl."

"Not until I find out what happened to her."

Delta sent him a fierce scowl. "This ain't about what you want. If you want to be helpful, go fill the tub with a hot bath for her. Otherwise, go back and be useless in your own room. But one way or another, I'm going to take care of her, and you'll have to wait for your answers."

Heat burned the back of Jonas's neck at the admonishment. He stood and glared down at Miss Delta. "I'll go run her a bath."

Shea settled into her bed after a hot bath and Miss Delta's ministrations to her wound. The woman was sufficiently satisfied that Shea didn't need a doctor, just a good, long soak and a full night's sleep. Shea couldn't agree with her more.

She fought to keep her eyes open as the elderly woman went to the kitchen to prepare a meal to ease the ache in Shea's stomach. Too bad food wouldn't ease the ache in her heart, as well. Poor Jerome. She could only imagine the heartache he must be suffering. First to lose a child, then to discover the man responsible wouldn't pay for her murder. If the jury acquitted Sam Dane Jr., Shea seriously doubted that any amount of talking would keep the distraught father from following through with his mission.

"Feeling better?"

Shea looked up and her stomach dipped. Jonas leaned casually against the doorframe, one hand tucked into his pocket, his legs crossed at the ankle. He was movie-star handsome. Clark Gable had nothing on this man.

His eyebrows went up and she realized she had been staring. Clearing her throat, she mustered her dignity. "Yes, much better, thank you. Just tired."

"You can sleep in a little while. First I want to know what happened today." He walked into the room, his mouth pulled into a rueful grin. "And hurry up before your watchdog comes back and boots me out of here."

Shea couldn't help but smile at his sardonic wit.

He started to sit on the edge of her bed, then seemed to think better of it and reached for the chair in the corner of the room. He pulled it with one arm to her bedside. "Now. All proper. No reputation-ruining antics in this room."

To her utter embarrassment, a giggle found its way to her throat.

His smile spread, and for the first time since she'd met Jonas Penbrook, his eyes smiled, too. Her heart soared.

Captivated, Shea couldn't look away. She wanted nothing more than to make him laugh again. But he sobered almost as quickly as he'd shown his soft side. "Now, Miss White, I'm ready to hear answers to both of my questions."

"What questions?"

"Where were you? And what happened?"

❧

Sleep eluded Shea long after Jonas left her room, questions answered, and she'd wolfed down a meal of roast chicken and mashed potatoes. She tossed on the bed, replaying the scenes with Jerome in her mind over and over. It wasn't every day a woman got grazed by a stray bullet and talked a man out of murdering someone who clearly didn't deserve to live.

Or did he? Her mind had been replaying the idea of sovereignty all day. Had something bigger than herself caused Shea to be in the right place at the right time today? Had God orchestrated events so that she could stop Jerome from killing Sam on the courthouse steps? Or had her appearance stopped the sovereign plan? Maybe Jerome was supposed to have killed Sam. What if that was the only way justice would be served for Jerome's daughter, Ruthie?

Shea's mind twisted with thought after thought until finally she sat up and switched on the light. She reached for Mac Penbrook's diary on her bedside table and frowned. She had specifically placed the book at the top-left corner of the nightstand. But now it was in the center. Had someone been in her room?

Breathe, Shea. More than likely Delta had moved it accidentally while helping her into bed earlier, and Shea had been too weary to notice.

Living in this house had fueled her curiosity about her ancestors. The thought that one hundred years after the events in the diaries a white man and a black woman had been murdered for the same kind of love Mac had felt for Celeste amazed her. How could events repeat themselves generation after generation?

Would there ever come a time when race didn't play such a large role in dictating whom a person could choose to love?

Shea opened the diary and became caught up once more in Mac's determination to keep safe the woman he loved.

GEORGIA 1847
"Friend of a friend."

Mac repeated Maddy's words over and over in his mind until they became emblazoned in his memory. *"Look for the sign of the Big Dipper on doors and quilts hanging on the line with odd patterns that might be a warning symbol."* This was how he would identify people willing to help until he was clear of Georgia.

He tucked the map deep in an inside pocket, taking no chances that something might go wrong. The extent of Maddy's help had astonished Mac. Although he'd always suspected there was more to her character than social graces and loving support of her husband, he'd had no idea she was connected to the people who helped slaves run away from their masters.

Pride swelled in his breast as he thought of the three runaways from this plantation who'd escaped in the past two years. Maddy needed to be careful, though. If anyone connected the time of her arrival at Penbrook six years ago with the disappearance of more than a dozen slaves in the county, she would be hanged without a trial.

Grateful for a sky with no moon or stars, he made his way through the pitch-black night, praying with each step that Celeste had summoned the courage to meet him. His heart thrummed in his ears as he crept toward the barn.

After a furtive glance around to assure himself no one had followed, he opened the barn door and slipped inside. His eyes, already adjusted to the darkness, scanned the barn for any sign that another human was there.

"Celeste?" he whispered.

No response.

His heart sank. He walked across the hay-sweetened barn floor to the stall where Maddy had instructed Cookie Mary to bring the dresses for Celeste.

Dropping to his knees, he fished around in the hay, but found no trace of the clothes. What could have gone wrong? He sat back against the wooden stall and raked his fingers through his hair, attempting to make sense of the unexpected turn of events. Had his father somehow discovered his plan? If so, how? Maddy? He rejected that thought as quickly as it had appeared in his mind. She would never betray him. One of the slaves, perhaps? Not Cookie. But there were certain incentives for slaves who showed loyalty to their masters, even if it meant betraying another slave.

Just as he was about to return to the house, the barn door creaked open.

"Mastuh?"

"Oh, thank the Lord!" Relief poured over him in waves. He jumped to his feet and covered the ground between them in a split second. He took her in his arms and swung her around. "I was afraid something had happened to you."

"No, suh."

Sensing her discomfiture, he set her on the ground just as a rumble of thunder sounded in the distance. "Rain. That's a good sign. Let's hope it rains hard and long. It'll be uncomfortable, but will wash our tracks and scent in case Father sends the dogs after us."

Celeste nodded. "I won't mind the rain. But Mastuh—"

"Stop calling me that. I'm Mac now."

"Mac." She ducked her head, clearly uncomfortable. "Is— are you sho' you wanna do this thing?"

Swallowing around a lump in his throat, Mac took her sweet face between his fingers. "I'm sure." He bent forward and pressed a gentle kiss to her forehead. "Very sure."

She made a grab for his hand and turned her lips into his palm. "Thank you, suh. Thank you."

Mac wanted nothing more than to gather her in his arms and kiss her long and tenderly, but he knew they had to get going. He looked her over and realized for the first time that she was dressed in one of Maddy's gowns. "Good. Cookie Mary got the clothes to you."

She nodded. "Yes."

"You look beautiful."

And she did. Her hair was gathered in a chignon at the nape of her neck, and the gown of soft yellow cotton accented her curves perfectly. The short, puffed sleeves showed wonderfully rounded arms. Mac had to force his gaze away.

"Do you have the other dress and shoes?"

"You don' like this one?"

A smile touched his lips. "I love it. But I asked Maddy for two."

"It be here, suh. . .Mac." She walked to the edge of the barn and lifted a small bundle.

"Good. We'll walk for ten miles along the river until we reach our first stop. We'll stay in the barn of a friend until morning. Then he'll take us fifty miles northwest. We'll be on our own after that. If anyone stops us, you are Celeste Delacroix, a woman of French descent traveling from New Orleans. You mustn't speak, or you'll give us away. I'll do the talking and will tell people you only speak French."

"I don't much like lies, Mastuh."

"Better than death."

"The Good Book say liars will have dey'r part in a lake of fire."

"Well, you don't have to worry about it. Not one lie will flow from your sweet lips, because you aren't going to say a word." Unable to resist, he bent forward and pressed a soft kiss on her mouth. She stiffened and he pulled back immediately. "I'm sorry, my dear. That was forward of me. I won't kiss you again until you let me know you're ready."

"I owes it to ya, suh."

"Mac. And you don't owe me anything, least of all kisses. I'm taking you away because I want to. Is that clear? Once we are free of the South, you can choose to stay with me or to leave, but I will never force myself on you. Is that clear?"

Her eyes glistened in the lamplight. "You is a good man, Mac."

"But you're not in love with me."

"I didn't know I could."

The honesty of that simple statement filled him with hope. "You can. You don't have to. But if you fall in love with me, you'll make me the happiest man alive." He squeezed her callous hands and walked to the door, sparing her the necessity of a reply. "Come on."

She followed him into the rain-soaked night. They had to hurry. Cookie Mary could hide the fact that Celeste was gone until morning. By then, hopefully, they would be at their first stopping place. Safe and on their way north.

GEORGIA 1949

The sun was peeking over the eastern horizon by the time

Jonas made up his mind to tell Andy about the day Shea had yesterday. As far as Jonas knew, he was the only person besides Lexie who was aware of Andy's paternity. The senator was close to death, and even though Andy didn't have a sense of familial love for the man—or maybe he did, who knew?—Jonas felt he deserved to know.

He waited until he heard Lexie leave Andy's room, then he made his way down the hall and knocked.

"Come in," Andy beckoned. His eyebrows went up at the sight of Jonas standing in the doorway. "Everything okay?"

Jonas motioned toward the chair against the wall. "Do you mind?"

"Since when do you need to ask?"

"I have something to tell you."

"Yeah?"

"It's about Senator Dane."

A frowned shot between Andy's eyes. "What about him?"

"Yesterday, the trial was recessed so that Sam could go to the hospital and be with the senator before he died."

Concern shot across Andy's face. "Died? What happened?"

"His heart, apparently."

"I should go see him, I suppose."

"Don't even think about it."

"For better or worse, he's my father, Jonas."

"Yes, and he never did a thing for you."

"Except give me life and love my mother."

"Some love." Jonas didn't even try to keep the sarcasm out of his voice. He knew he was being harsh, but he was the one who had lain awake at night when they were children, listening to his friend cry when he thought Jonas was sleeping. A child had been ripped away from his mother, and that man might have made a difference if only he'd tried. But Andy couldn't seem to see that.

"She was married and so was he. Things were more compli-cated than it seems."

"I don't see how you can be so easygoing about it, Andy."

Andy smiled. "I forgive the senator for not being a father to me. He couldn't have. I'd like to have a chance to tell him that."

"Then write him a letter. If he's coherent, I'll give it to him."

Andy nodded. "Will you take it to him today?"

"Right after breakfast, as long as Miss White can drive me into town. I don't think I could shift gears with this arm."

"I'll have Lexie dictate as soon as she gets back."

"Any luck getting her to go back to Chicago?"

Andy's shoulders rose and fell. "She's leaving with your pop and Vic Chambers today. But she's not happy about it."

"Tell her it won't be long. The trial should be over soon. Un-less I miss my guess, the jury isn't going to take long to decide he's innocent."

Andy sighed. "I don't know how Jerome and Bessie will take that."

Jonas decided not to mention that Jerome had come close to killing Sam Dane Jr. Better to let Andy deal with one family crisis at a time.

CHAPTER FIFTEEN
GEORGIA 1949

Shea didn't like being told what to do. Stay in the car? Not likely. Certainly not while Jonas went into the hospital. As soon as he disappeared inside, she slipped out of the car and followed him, taking care not to be noticed. She knew he was going to visit the senator. But why?

An interview, perhaps? Mr. Riley wouldn't like that Jonas had left the house so soon after his ordeal, not even for a big story. And truth be told, he wasn't ready to be out of bed. But without Mr. Riley to insist he stay put, there had been no talking him out of driving to see the senator.

"Can I help you?"

Shea jumped as a portly nurse behind the counter looked her up and down.

"I'm here to see—um—my uncle. Senator Dane."

The woman raised her eyebrows. "No one is allowed to see him except immediate family."

She should have said she was his daughter. "I understand." Shea stepped away from the counter. How had Jonas been able to get past the sergeant major? Then it occurred to her. Mr. More-Handsome-than-Clark-Gable had flashed that heart-stopping smile of his, and the nurse had sent him right to the room. Well, Shea wasn't going to give up so easily.

She returned to the counter, where the portly woman was examining a medical chart. "Excuse me, Nurse?"

"What is it?" Her terse reply didn't fill Shea with hope that the situation would go well for her. But she had to try.

"A man came through here a couple of minutes ago, looking for the senator."

Recognition flashed in the nurse's eyes. "Yes?"

"He's my husband. I parked the car while he came inside. He's expecting me to come to my uncle's room."

A second of indecision lit her eyes. "I can't tell you where the senator's room is."

"Believe me, I understand. But if you could maybe go to the room and let my husband know you won't let me in, I'd appreciate it." Shea forced a tremor to slither through her body. "I don't want to give him any excuse to. . .be angry with me."

The nurse perked up at the insinuation. "Oh, my. Listen. You promise you won't tell anyone I told you where the room is?"

"You have my word."

"All right." She lowered her tone considerably, forcing Shea to lean forward to hear her. "Take the stairs to the second floor. His room is all the way at the end on the right."

Shea smiled broadly and gripped the nurse's hand for a second. "Thank you ever so much. I won't tell a soul."

She hurried up the steps, her heels clacking on the tiled floor. Once she reached the second floor, she slipped off her shoes and tiptoed down the hall. She stopped at the sound of voices.

"Senator," she heard Jonas say, "I assure you, Andy is alive. After the attempt was made on his life, the doctor agreed to concoct the story of his death so he could recover at Penbrook and make it safely home to Chicago after the trial."

"I'm so relieved. Thank you for delivering his letter." The man's voice was frail and weak, and Shea had to strain to hear the rest. "I'm touched that Andy wanted to check on me."

"How are you, sir?"

"Apparently, I'll live. For a little while longer anyway."

"I'm glad to hear it."

"Tell Andy I'd like to see him once more before he leaves for Chicago if that is possible."

"I'll tell him, sir."

"My son is lucky to have such a good friend."

"More than a friend. He's my brother."

Shea tried to wrap her mind around those two statements. She understood that Jonas and Andy loved each other like brothers. But could they truly be related? And was the senator really Andy's father?

Jonas's voice intruded on her thoughts. "I'm going to leave now, sir. You need your rest. I'll convey your concern to Andy."

Shea stepped back quickly as the senator mumbled his good-byes. Before she could make it to the stairs, a hand grabbed her arm and spun her about. "You little sneak. I told you to stay in the car."

Shea yanked her arm away from Jonas and geared up for a fight. "I'm not accustomed to being told what to do."

"That's obvious." He walked past her, leaving Shea no choice but to follow. "Did it ever occur to you that I might have had a good reason for asking you to not to come inside with me?"

"Not until two minutes ago." Her answer was meant to be flip, but Jonas whipped around, took her elbow in his hand, and led her down the steps and down the hall. The nurse at the counter looked up, alarm showing in her face. Shea gave her a reassuring nod. "It's okay," she said.

Jonas raised a quizzical eyebrow but didn't pursue the matter, which saved Shea the necessity of having to lie about it. She was already in enough trouble without letting him know she had implied Jonas was a wife beater.

In the parking lot, an unbidden smile touched her lips as Jonas turned to her.

"You think this is funny?"

"No. Not at all. I just think—"

"Get in the car."

His tone and words raised her ire. It was all she could do not to blurt out everything that came to mind right then and there. But she sensed Jonas's worry. That kept her quiet.

He opened the car door for her, his closeness sending a wave of longing over her. Longing for what, she wasn't sure, but Jonas had definitely gotten under her skin in a way no man ever had. Not even her former fiancé. Definitely not Colin Sable.

After he climbed into the car and started the engine, Jonas turned to her. "How much did you overhear?"

"Enough to put two and two together."

He remained guarded, clearly not giving up anything she hadn't already figured out. "Such as?"

"Andy's father is the white senator from Georgia."

His sharp gaze penetrated hers. "Do you understand why you can never say a word about this?"

"I'm assuming the senator would lose his seat."

"If that were the only reason, I wouldn't care."

"What, then?"

"In this part of the country, Andy's life would be in danger if anyone found out he had a white father—particularly if it were known who that father is. Bad enough Sam Dane Jr. knows the truth."

"Is that why someone tried to kill Andy the other night?"

"I think it's safe to assume Sam Jr. ordered the killing."

"Then why didn't Andy go home to Chicago with your father and Lexie?"

"Probably for the same reason you didn't stay in the car." He looked at her askance and his expression softened. "Stubbornness."

"You don't know me well enough to call me stubborn."

Shea held her breath as he reached forward and traced a line from her cheek to her chin. "Are you sure about that?"

"Yes." What did he really know about her? If he realized who she really was—a white trash girl from Oregon—he wouldn't want anything to do with her. Add to that her Negro blood, and, well. . .that pretty much clinched the fact that Shea was going to be alone for the rest of her life. "You don't know anything about me, Jonas. So don't pretend you do."

A short laugh left him and he straightened in his seat. "Then why don't you tell me all about yourself, Miss White? I'm anxious to discover who you are."

Shea gave an inward groan and cranked the engine. How had she given him such an opening? And how would she get out of it without his news-reporter nose sniffing out the truth?

Curiosity had always been Andy's weakness. He supposed that was why he made such a good reporter. He had to know more, dig deeper, even if it meant risking getting caught. Boredom had pulled him from his bed to Shea's room, where he intended to find the diary and pick up where he'd left off the day before.

Maddy's diaries hadn't begun until after Mac Penbrook left Georgia, so reading Mac's diaries made him feel like he was learning another branch of his own story.

A knock at the front door startled him. He tucked the diary under his robe and headed back to his room. He had just settled in when Miss Delta appeared, her face scrunched into a curious frown.

"What's wrong?" he asked her.

"Postman just delivered some mail."

"For me?"

"Nope. But I'm not sure what to think about the letter that came." Her shoulders rose and fell as she handed him an envelope. He stared at the address: *Shea Penbrook, Oak Junction, Georgia.*

"Shea Penbrook?"

"What do you make of that?" Miss Delta asked, hands on her hips.

"I don't know. But I have a feeling you've known for a while now that something didn't add up about Shea." Andy gave her back the envelope.

"I did know that White wasn't her real last name. I admit that. But she never told me what her real name is."

Andy gave a wry smile. "Apparently it's Penbrook."

"You think she's after Miss Cat's money?"

Andy shrugged. "She doesn't seem like the greedy sort. More lonely. She goes out of her way to help and hasn't asked for a dime in return. If she's here for anything, I'd guess it's more a sense of belonging. . .and maybe the house."

"Miss Cat would roll over in her grave if a stranger moved into Penbrook House!"

Andy couldn't hide a smile. "Remember, Miss Delta, Cat

was a former slave. She didn't have any blood right to the place, and all the Penbrooks were dead. If Shea is a descendant of another Penbrook, and she can prove it, she might have a pretty good case."

Delta stared at the letter. "What should I do with this?"

"Put it on the table by her bed. Let her find it and come to you. Then maybe we'll finally get a straight story."

"You're a smart boy, Andy."

Fondness for the old woman touched his heart as he watched her leave the room as gracefully as her arthritic knees would allow.

GEORGIA 1847

Mac heard dogs before he and Celeste had traveled two miles. "Run, sweetheart," he hissed. "They're already looking for us."

A soft gasp left her throat. "Hide, Mac. Don't let them catch you. All dey'll do is whup me and sell me off to Mastuh Haverty. Dey'll hang you for sho'."

"I'm not leaving you." He took her hand in his and ran, pulling her along with him.

The barking grew closer, closer. Finally he knew it was no use. He stopped and gathered Celeste into his arms. "I'm sorry. We can't possibly get away."

She pulled back slightly and touched his face. "You did yo' best, Mac. No need to be sorry."

He grabbed her hand and pressed it to his lips. "I wanted to give you a wonderful life. I would have asked you to marry me once we made it to the West."

"I knows." She smiled. "I woulda said yes."

Horses' hooves accompanied the barking now, and the shouts grew closer. It would only be a matter of seconds before the runaways were caught.

"I love you, Celeste."

"I loves you, too, Mac."

They stood, hands wound together, waiting, until Mac saw the furious face of his father glaring at him from atop his horse.

"A little rainy for a walk, isn't it, son?"

Mac recognized the controlled rage in his father's voice. "As it is for a ride."

Celeste shrank from the hounds as they circled the pair and barked menacingly.

"For God's sake, Father, call off the dogs."

He nodded to the patroller, who gave a short command. The dogs stopped barking and settled down. "Thank you all for your assistance," he called to the men on horseback. "You may return home now."

Mac wasn't sure what he'd expected, but certainly not to be left with Celeste still sheltered by his arm. . .and his father, alone, staring down at him.

The older man dismounted and walked his horse forward. He reached inside his pocket, retrieved an envelope, and pushed it toward Mac.

"What's this?" Mac asked.

"Enough money to get you a good start out West."

Never in a hundred years would Mac have predicted this. Relief flooded over him as questions overwhelmed his mind. "What was the point of sending the dogs out after us if you were just going to let us go?"

"I've suspected all day you intended to leave, but I didn't plan to do anything about it. Until your brother went off to find her." He pointed to Celeste. "When he discovered her missing, he went to your room and found several of your things gone. That's when he came to me. I had no choice but to try to find you before he did."

"I'm surprised Henry didn't ride with you."

"He wanted to, but he was extremely drunk, and I forbade him to get on a horse."

"I appreciate the gesture, Father. But what's going to stop him from searching after you get home?"

"That envelope contains more than money. It also has the girl's papers, setting her free."

A glad cry tore from Celeste's throat. "Oh, Mastuh, thank you. Thank you."

Mac's father didn't so much as suffer a glance in her direction.

"Yes, Father. Thank you."

"I've done all I intend to do for you. You're dead to me now." The older man mounted his horse. "Don't come back to Georgia. Ever." He whipped the horse around and galloped away, flinging mud in his wake.

Mac stared after him until he was out of sight, then turned to Celeste. He gathered her into his arms.

She surrendered to his embrace and returned it. "I can't believe I'm free."

"I know. But we have to keep moving forward. There are no inns along the way. The first stop we'll come to is the farmhouse where we had originally planned to hide until tomorrow. Can you make it in this rain?"

She nodded happily. "I can do anything. I'm free."

They trudged along, mile after muddy mile, until finally reaching the farmhouse. "Our instructions were to go directly to the barn and bed down in the loft. There should be blankets and food waiting for us. Now that we don't have to hide, I'll ask Mr. Gardner if he'll sell us a wagon and team to carry us to

Missouri. We'll sell the horses and buy a team of oxen before the train pulls out west in the spring."

As promised, the loft held soft quilts and bread and cheese. Celeste fell asleep with bread in her hand.

Mac stared at her long into the night. A disturbing thought had plagued his mind since receiving her freedom papers: Would she still choose to come west with him? Or would he lose her forever now that she was free?

GEORGIA 1949

Andy slipped out of bed and tiptoed into Shea's room. He set the diary on the nightstand next to the envelope addressed to Shea Penbrook.

"Who are you, Shea?" he whispered.

As soon as Shea and Jonas walked through the front door of Penbrook House, Miss Delta ushered them into the kitchen and sat them down at the table, insisting they eat a midday meal. "Neither one of you ate a bite of breakfast before hightailing it out of here this morning."

Jonas gave Shea a guilty look, as though he'd just realized some people might actually get hungry. "Sorry," he muttered.

"It's all right," she assured him. "I ate supper late enough last night, it was still with me this morning."

A light lunch of vegetable soup and fresh-made bread filled her up and energized her. Miss Delta sent Jonas up to rest, and Shea decided to check in with the diaries. Being a Saturday, the courthouse would be locked up tight. No point in trying to look through death records and birth certificates. Besides, she was starting to think that would be a lesson in futility anyway.

She walked into her room and slipped off her shoes, tossing her hat onto the dresser. Fingers of fear clutched her stomach as she noticed a white envelope next to the diary on the nightstand.

Black spots appeared before her eyes in dizzy waves. She picked it up. *Shea Penbrook.* From Oregon. It had to have been sent by Miss Nell.

All her hopes and dreams started to fade. Who had collected this envelope and placed it here? She couldn't say a word to anyone, because she wasn't sure who now knew her secret. Shea sat heavily on her bed. With weary fingers, she opened the envelope.

Dear Shea,

You have been gone for more than a week, so I gather you've had time to arrive in Oak Junction. I hope your name and the name of the city will be enough to get this letter to you.

I have bad news. Jackson Sable is trying to go to court, claiming you have abandoned your property. He wants to buy it from you by putting the money in your name at the bank. So far he hasn't been able to find a judge to hear his case, but I'm sure he eventually will.

I ache with loneliness for you, gal. Write and let me know you're safe and sound. I'm counting the days until you come home.

Miss Nell

Tears burned Shea's eyes. She had been so busy with everything going on at Penbrook, she hadn't even thought about what might be happening back home in her absence.

"Oh, Miss Nell," she whispered. What would she do if she lost her home there and Penbrook House, too?

The most horrible feeling she'd ever known wrapped itself around her insides. Knowing someone had information about her, but not knowing who that person was, left her feeling more vulnerable than she had since she was a little girl waiting for her father to come home from the roadhouse.

Shea curled up on her bed, and for the first time since she could remember, she prayed. "God," she whispered around a lump in her throat, "I think I'm in trouble. Can You help?"

Andy heard Shea go into her room, and waited. . .and waited. He could only imagine the fear working its way through the girl, and part of him felt sorry for her. Ulterior motives aside, he had her to thank for saving his life. And truthfully, if she was Mac Penbrook's descendant, she did have a rightful claim to the property and land. The problem was, old Miss Penbrook never had any real claim to the land. The old lady deserved a better legacy than to be remembered as a liar and a squatter.

Life and love had continued at Penbrook over the century. The War Between the States had come and gone, and Cat had single-handedly orchestrated the rebuilding of Penbrook. It was one of only a few plantations in the county that had survived with dignity. She had taken care of the last remaining Penbrook—Camilla—until the woman's death. At that time she had become, for all intents and purposes, the only rightful heir to the Penbrook estate. She might not have held any blood claim to the land, but to anyone with a sense of justice, she definitely had deserved to call it her own.

Andy wasn't sure what was right. All he knew was that he needed to speak with Shea. To discover her plan and decide whether he would help her or fight her.

A knock at his door pulled him from his thoughts. Jonas appeared at his beckon.

"How's the senator?" Andy asked.

"Much better. He's out of danger according to the doctors. At least for now. They plan to keep him a few more days and then let him go."

Andy's heart lifted at the news. "You gave him my letter?"

"Of course. He seemed extremely grateful to receive it. He also mentioned a desire to see you once more before you leave for Chicago."

Funny how relieved he felt at the knowledge the senator would be fine. Not that he'd want anyone to die, but the familial sense of relief surprised him.

"Shea came home with you?"

Jonas's eyebrows lifted. "She drove. Why?"

"Just wondering."

"I think she went to her room to take a nap. Did you need her for something?"

Andy shook his head. "Nothing that can't wait until later."

Part of him wanted to share his suspicions with Jonas, but knowing what a hothead his friend could be at times, Andy thought better of it. He wouldn't tell Jonas until he had no choice. And when that time would be was entirely up to Shea Penbrook.

CHAPTER SIXTEEN
GEORGIA 1949

Packing was a quick affair. The ruined dress could stay; the other she would be wearing. Other than a few personal items, all that remained were her diaries. She had no choice but to leave most of them behind, for now at least. But she would be back. No telling when, but eventually she'd return and finish what she started here.

She had the money Mr. Riley had paid her in advance to sit in on the trial and take notes. A touch of guilt almost forced her to change her mind, but it couldn't be helped. She'd find a way to repay him after she returned to Oregon and dealt with the Jackson Sable issue.

A quick call to the bus station had revealed that the next bus would be leaving at 5:00 a.m. Shea planned to be on that bus.

The pit of Jonas's gut warned him something wasn't right. Frustration clutched him as he paced the room, trying to get a grip on the problem. Sleep eluded him. Food held no appeal. What if whoever had tried to kill Andy discovered the doctor's deception and came after him here? What secrets was Shea keeping from them? What had Miss Delta been referring to last week when she mentioned his grandmother?

So many events had occurred in quick succession, his mind was having trouble keeping up. Andy's beating and the attempt on his life. Shea White showing up and saving Andy. Jonas's ordeal in jail. Learning who Andy's real father was.

A creaking noise caught his attention, pulling him from his musing. He flashed a glance to the ticking clock on his night-stand. Three o'clock. Who could be up at this hour?

He hoped the house hadn't been broken into. As unlikely as that seemed, he didn't want to take a chance on letting the Klan finish the job they'd tried to start with Andy. He strode across the room, opened the door, and stepped into the hall. A slim figure stole down the stairs.

"Shea?"

She turned, her face hidden in the shadows. "Jonas, you nearly scared the life out of me."

Out of *her*? "What are you doing sneaking around at this hour?"

"I didn't realize I wasn't allowed out of my room except for certain hours of the day."

Her sarcasm bit through Jonas, raising his defenses. "Don't be ridiculous. And don't turn my words around. You have to admit it's unusual for anyone to be walking around the house at three in the morning." He reached the bottom of the steps and stood face-to-face with her. "Especially carrying a suitcase. Do you want to tell me what's going on?"

"I'm going home." She leaned against the wall as though her strength had failed. "I'm leaving a trunk of books upstairs. Please don't dispose of them. If I don't come back, I'll send for them."

If she didn't come back? His stomach knotted. "Hold on. What's this about?"

In the soft glow of the moonlight shining through the foyer window next to the front door, Jonas noticed her lip tremble. He stepped closer and brushed her cheek with his fingertips. "Are you in some sort of trouble?"

Her eyes closed at his touch, then she opened them again, staring up at him. "I'm close to losing the last of my family's land. The only thing I can do is go home and try to get a fair price for it."

She seemed so small in the shadows, so alone. Jonas fought the urge to gather her in his arms and offer her his protection, his strength. "Aren't there other family members who can take care of that for you?"

She shook her head. "I'm the only one left in my family."

Alarm seized Jonas at the idea of Shea being utterly alone. Surely that couldn't be the case. "You have no one at all?"

"No relatives." She raised her chin as though resisting his compassion. "But I'm not alone. I have a good friend back home who is on my side. She'll help me."

"It's good to have friends," he said softly. "You've been a good friend to my family. Maybe there's something I can do to help you."

"I don't think so." She ducked away from him and reached for the door.

"I'd like to try."

Shea shook her head. "There's nothing you can do, and I won't be beholden to anyone." She looked toward the door like a caged animal seeking escape. "I have to go."

"Were you planning to leave without saying good-bye?"

"I left a note for Miss Delta in my room." She cleared her

throat. "I don't like good-byes."

"Apparently not."

"I'm sorry. I have no choice."

Her indifference gnawed at his pride, and he did the first thing that came to mind—matched her indifference with his own. "How do you plan to get to town?"

"I'm walking, of course."

"Don't be ridiculous. I'll drive you."

A smile touched her lips. "You can't drive with that broken arm."

She had a point. "Then take my car. Leave it at the bus station and I'll have someone pick it up later."

She hesitated for only a split second. Then she shook her head. "No, thanks. It's better this way. Believe me." She opened the door and stepped onto the porch.

"Please let me help you."

"I appreciate the offer, but I don't need your assistance."

Jonas stepped back, his gut tightening as though he'd received a punch in the stomach. Fine. If she didn't want his help, she wouldn't get it. "Be careful walking in the dark. You never know what's out there."

"I–I'll be fine."

"I'm sure you will be." He turned. "Well, so long. If you come back to Georgia, feel free to stay here at Penbrook House."

"That's kind of you." She cast a nervous glance toward the dark lane from the house to the road. "I guess I'll be seeing you."

Jonas fought back a smile. "Sure you won't change your mind about driving my car?"

Shea whipped around. "All right. Yes. I would like that. Thanks."

"Good decision." Jonas turned to get the keys.

All the way to town Shea's mind replayed her conversation with Jonas. Clearly the attraction between them went both ways. His presence made her go weak in the knees. And he'd shown blatant interest in her.

He was breaking through her defenses in the strangest way. And she couldn't allow that to happen. Not if she were going to carry out her goal of proving she was the rightful heir to Penbrook.

She parked the car in front of the bus station, then pulled her suitcase and handbag from the backseat. She'd brought several of the diaries. As many as she could fit in the suitcase, plus two in her bag. That should hold her for a couple of days until she reached the first stopover station, where she'd have to wait for a few hours before changing buses. That would also be her first chance to freshen up. She certainly didn't relish the idea of wearing the same dress day after day for the entire week it would take to get back home.

She'd pretty much made her decision about the land in Oregon. After selling it to Jackson, she'd come back to Oak Junction. Her original plan had been to make sure she could acquire Penbrook House first. As a matter of fact, she'd hoped to gain enough revenue to hold on to both properties—and to keep Ernie on permanently to oversee the homestead. After all, their faithful employee had been the only reason the farm had survived all these years under Granddad's poor management. But Miss Nell's letter had changed her plans. Sped up the process. She had to let the land in Oregon go. She hated to do it. But she had no choice.

The sun was beginning to peek over the eastern horizon as the bus arrived—thirty minutes late—to take her home. With a sense of dread, Shea boarded and found a seat next to a tired-looking middle-aged woman with a smattering of gray in her strawberry-blond hair. The woman seemed happy to rest her head against the window and sleep, which served Shea's purposes quite well.

She pulled out the dog-eared diary and picked up where she'd left off. She read about Mac's escape with Celeste, their first kiss, and Mr. Penbrook's offer of money. She wept when Celeste was given her freedom and rejoiced when they made it to Independence.

MISSOURI 1847

Mac didn't know how to break the news to Celeste. They would not be traveling west with a wagon train for several months. That meant they'd either have to stay in Independence for the winter or risk going west before the snows hit.

Celeste had been counting on a speedy departure. She was more than ready to get out of any state where slavery was allowed. Missouri was an odd split of free Negroes and whites who owned slaves. He understood her reluctance to stay. It was as though she feared any moment someone might steal her papers of freedom and enslave her again.

Such a thing had been known to happen, so Mac didn't begrudge her that worry. Still, he wanted to alleviate those fears if he could.

Just this morning he'd seen an advertisement from a band of impatient pioneers who would travel as far west as Fort Kearney before the snows forced a halt until spring. Mac intended to be part of that wagon train. If not for Celeste, nothing would have convinced him to take such hasty action, but if this were the only way to spare her mind from worry, he was willing to take the risk.

There was just one thing. . . .

He knocked on the door to her boardinghouse and was greeted by Mrs. Harrison, the dour-faced widow woman who owned the place. "Is Celeste here?"

"Come in and sit in the parlor. I'll see if Miss McCourt is receiving visitors."

A smile formed on Mac's lips at the woman's use of his middle name—his mother's maiden name. Celeste needed a surname. She couldn't use Penbrook—not yet. Posing as brother and sister certainly wasn't an option.

As he waited for her to appear, his hands trembled at the thought of what he had to ask Celeste. He knew she wasn't ready for this, but what was the alternative?

She appeared, wearing a deep green silk gown Maddy had given her. The color made the green in her hazel eyes stand out. She took his breath away.

"Leave the door open," Mrs. Harrison said before walking away, her brown taffeta dress swishing in her wake.

Waiting until the widow was out of sight, Mac smiled down at Celeste. "You look lovely."

Celeste ducked her head as pink tinged her cheeks. "No."

"Yes, you do."

The more Mac grew to know Celeste, the lovelier she had become to him until now she was the most beautiful woman in the world as far as he was concerned. He reached out his hand. His breath caught in his throat as she slipped her warm fingers into his palm and allowed him to lead her to the rose-printed settee.

"I have something to ask you."

She looked at him with wide, trusting eyes, encouraging him to go on.

"I met with a man named Robert Sable this morning. He and a small group of wagons are planning to leave for the West next week."

"A wagon train?"

"Not in the usual sense. No company is sponsoring the train. Nor is the government. Sable and his group have decided to go as far as Fort Kearney and camp there for the winter. After the spring thaw, we'll be that much closer to Oregon."

"Is dat whut you wants?"

"I think it would be best for you. It's only a matter of time before someone recognizes your speech patterns and realizes that you're a former slave."

She ducked her head in embarrassment. "I am sorry, Mac."

Mac squeezed her hands. "There's no need to be sorry, my dear. But if we want to leave Independence before spring, we'll need to go next week, when the rest of the wagons pull out."

"We can't go alone? Just us?"

Tenderness clutched Mac's heart. He understood her fears, but he couldn't allow his desire to please her to cloud his judgment. "It wouldn't be safe for a lone wagon to head out. Between thieves and Indians, we most likely wouldn't make it two hundred miles."

Celeste's sigh of acceptance shot straight through Mac. His palms dampened as he prepared to move the conversation to the next issue at hand. "There's something else."

"Whut?"

"In order for us to travel together, we need to be married."

Her eyes widened. "Married? We can't—"

Mac cupped her face between his hands, feeling the softness of her tan skin. "I'm asking you to be my wife."

Shooting to her feet, she stared at him through horrified eyes. "B–but dat's against the law. The sheriff—"

"Your skin is light enough to pass for a white woman of French descent. Not that I'm ashamed of who you are. But in order for us to be married, you would have to say nothing about your Negro blood. And we'll need to work on your speech patterns. Otherwise, you'll give us away every time you open your mouth."

"I don' know if I can do it. Might be best if you jus' leave me behind."

"That's not an option. If you stay, I stay."

"Whither thou goest, I will go," Celeste quoted with a far-away look in her eyes.

"That's right," Mac whispered around a lump in his throat. "I'm not leaving you. But I need to know if you'll marry me."

Though her eyes remained clouded with trouble and uncertainty, Celeste nodded. "Yes, Mac. If you is sho'."

If he were sure? His heart nearly beat from his chest. He wanted to toss his hat in the air and whoop with glee. Instead, he stepped forward and gathered her hands in his once more. Remembering his promise not to give her a lover's kiss again until she let him know she was willing, he pressed her hands to his lips rather than take her in his arms. "I'll make the arrangements. I may not be back for a couple of days, but I will return."

GEORGIA 1949

For two days the jury heard testimony from witness after witness, testifying to Sam's whereabouts on the night of Rafe's hanging.

Sam smiled inside with each lie. Several folks had come forward to provide his alibi; those who hadn't known better than to give a different story. Now, after only two hours of deliberation, the jury sent word that they had reached a verdict.

Sam felt confident of the outcome. Justice always prevailed. His was a righteous cause, and God in heaven wouldn't allow abomination to go unpunished. Nor would He stand for His instrument of justice to be sentenced.

The jury filed in, all but one man making eye contact with Sam.

When the verdict of "innocent" was read, a cry of despair rose from the balcony. Outrage, anger, a mishmash of jumbled rumblings melted into one word thundered over and over: "No, No, No, No." Feet clubbed the floor in time with the shouted cadence. "No. No. No. No."

Sam's heart picked up speed. While God wouldn't allow for a verdict of guilt, He might not be able stop a group of sub-humans from vigilante justice. The courtroom was thick with police presence, but that did nothing to give Sam peace about the situation. Twenty just-sworn-in deputies carrying shotguns were about as dangerous to innocent bystanders as they were to the ones who would potentially cause trouble.

The judge banged his gavel over and over, to no avail. Finally he gave up and nodded to the sheriff. The burly man raised his pistol and shot into the ceiling. Sam couldn't hold back a sneer. Why didn't they just give the order to start shoot-ing into the crowd? That would stop any retaliatory violence before it could start.

The noise died down and the judge banged his gavel once more to establish his authority and gain the attention of all in the room.

Sam's lawyer nudged him in the ribs, and Sam realized the judge was speaking to him. "Mr. Dane. You've been found innocent by a jury of your peers. You are free to go."

"Thank you, Your Honor," his attorney said on his behalf. The wiry man turned to him. "Let's get out of here by the side door before the deputies allow the balcony to clear."

Once outside, Sam pulled fresh air into his lungs. The first air of freedom he'd breathed in several months.

"So, what are you going to do now that you're a free man?" his attorney asked.

Sam didn't have to think about it. He had some business to take care of. "I think I'd like to stop by the hospital and share the good news with my father."

Jonas sat in stunned silence and watched a murderer walk out of the courtroom a free man. He would have plenty of editorial input into this article. That was for sure. *So much for justice.*

He glanced into the balcony and watched the grim black faces in the crowd. Their expressions spoke of their pain. Sam Dane had killed one of their own and a man who loved one of their own, and he would go free. Jonas felt like cursing. He couldn't wait to get out of this godforsaken place. He lingered in the courtroom until the crowd thinned, then headed outside.

Buck waited for him in his old Ford truck.

"You heard?" Jonas asked.

Nodding, Buck started the engine. "Didn't expect no other

outcome. And neither did anyone else."

"Then why'd all those folks sit in that stuffy balcony day after day?"

A shrug lifted the stocky shoulders of the black man behind the wheel. "To show support for our family, I guess."

"That's nice."

"Yeah."

There wasn't much else to say. Jonas felt the heaviness of defeat thicken the air inside the truck. He supposed a similar gloom would descend on every black home in Oak Junction for some time to come. He hated to have to be the one to tell Andy, although Jonas felt sure his foster brother had never expected any other outcome.

If Jonas knew his friend, Andy would want to be with Jerome and Betsy and the rest of his brothers and sisters tonight as they mourned the jury's decision. Jonas couldn't allow him to take that chance, not when Sam Dane was out of jail and fully capable of finishing the job his crony had started on Andy in the hospital.

Buck dropped him off in front of Penbrook House. Jonas trudged up the steps, not fully recovered from his ordeal in the jail. He still bore the bruises and aching ribs from the beatings. Still carried his arm in a sling. He couldn't wait to get Andy and go home to Chicago.

He passed the room that Shea had occupied only a few days before, and his stomach turned over. The only thing he regretted about his impending return to Chicago was that if and when Shea came back to Oak Junction, he would be gone.

Andy was sitting up reading when Jonas reached his room. "Look at this," he said, glancing up at Jonas with a grin. "I can turn pages with my thumbs."

"Congratulations." Jonas sat on the chair against the wall.

"What are you doing back from court so early?"

His hesitation brought Andy's full attention.

"Don't tell me it's over that fast."

"Just like that. Jury left and came back in a couple of hours."

"Sam's free?"

"Yep."

"Poor Betsy. She must be distraught."

Jonas braced himself for what he knew was the forthcoming request.

"I need to get to Buck and Lottie's. I'm sure the whole family will end up over there, and I need to be with them."

"You can't, my friend." Jonas tried to keep his voice calm, but alarm seized him when Andy swung his legs over the side of the bed and stood slowly to his feet. "You can't go anywhere. Most of your family think you were killed, remember?"

"All the more reason they need good news. Besides, now that the trial is over, there's no point in me sticking around this town. We should be leaving for home soon."

Jonas gave a snort and held up his broken arm, as much as the pain allowed. "Which of us do you think should drive? The one with the broken hands or the one with the broken arm?"

"Good point," Andy replied, his brow lifted with irony. "So we wait another week or two."

"Until you are safely out of town, you can't show your face. If Sam finds out you're alive, you're as good as dead. Again."

"No one in my family will tell Sam or any of his buddies that I'm alive." He walked across the room and grabbed a pair of trousers from the closet. "I need to let Betsy and Jerome know I'm alive."

Something akin to panic shot through Jonas. "I could go see

them for you. Let them know you're okay."

"Buck and Lottie have probably already spread the good news about me."

"Then why do this?" Jonas nearly shrieked.

"I stayed away from my family for twenty years after my mother sent me to live with your family. I just reconnected with them last year. I want them to know I care. That I share their anger about this verdict."

"Do you think they'd want you to risk your neck? They've already lost Ruthie. They won't want to lose you, too."

Andy expelled a breath. "I suppose you're right." He sighed again. "I'll just make a phone call to Buck and Lottie's."

"Good idea."

"Any word from Miss White since she left?"

Jonas felt a tug in his stomach at the mention of her name. "According to the bus station manager, the trip between here and Prudence, Oregon, takes a full week because of all the stops and sleepovers. She's not even halfway there by now."

"I wonder if she'll be back."

"Probably. She left a trunk filled with books in her room."

Andy snapped his gaze to Jonas. "I need to see them." He headed for the door.

"There's a whole library downstairs if you're looking for something to read," Jonas said, following Andy as he slipped into the hallway.

"Not like these books. If I'm not mistaken, the secrets to Miss White's identity and her motive for being in Oak Junction are in those diaries."

Jonas's defenses rose. "Why don't you think she's who she says she is?"

"I have my reasons."

"Is there something I should know that you haven't bothered to tell me?" Jonas asked.

"Not necessarily. Just a hunch."

They stopped at Shea's room. Andy scowled at the closed door. "Open that for me, will you?"

"I don't know if I like the idea of poking around in her private stuff like that."

"Don't, then. I'll do it alone."

Jonas opened the door and stood aside while Andy entered.

"I need you to open the trunk. And help me carry the diaries back to my room."

"I thought you just said you could do this alone."

"Once I get the books back to my room, you don't have to do a thing."

"Fine. Move aside and I'll grab as many as I can carry."

"Wait. We need to get them in order. I'll show you the ones to take first."

Feeling more than a little guilty and knowing full well Shea wouldn't be too happy with him, Jonas opened the trunk. He spent the better part of an hour helping Andy invade the privacy of a woman he was starting to care about more than he wanted to admit.

CHAPTER SEVENTEEN
MISSOURI 1949

By the third day of the trip, Shea's throat ached so badly she couldn't even swallow water. The woman she had been sharing a seat with left the bus after a day and a half, and Shea had been alone ever since. Miserably, she curled up on the sticky leather, trying to calm her raging head. She knew she was burning up with fever, but there was nothing she could do about it except try to sleep on the bumpy bus and hope the illness ran a speedy course.

She knew mothers were holding their children close and all others were staying as far away from her as possible. But she was too miserable to be humiliated.

The pain and cloudiness in her head prevented her from reading the diaries. It didn't take a genius to figure out that Robert Sable was likely Jackson's ancestor. Just when she was starting to get to the part of the story where she might be able to make sense of the reason the Sables had always wanted to get their hands on Penbrook land, she was too sick to read further.

Well after dark, the bus stopped and the driver called, "Everyone off. Next bus leaves for St. Louis first thing tomorrow morning."

With a moan, Shea hauled herself up from the seat and shuffled toward the bus door. Pain leaked into every pore and all her muscles felt limp. Her legs barely propelled her forward and she nearly fell face first into the dirt as she stepped off the bus. If not for a uniformed black man reaching out to steady her, she would have landed on the ground.

"Easy there, miss."

Shea mumbled her thanks. Her one thought was to make it inside and find a place to lie down, even if that place turned out to be a piece of the floor. She didn't care. All she knew was that she simply couldn't go on.

GEORGIA 1949

Jonas hadn't wanted to read the diaries. He wanted to believe Shea had stumbled upon the Penbrook family accidentally. But as he read the story of Mac Penbrook's life, he couldn't deny her agenda. Shea wanted his inheritance.

He felt like a fool. She'd looked up at him with those big hazel eyes and wrinkled that cute freckled nose of hers, and he'd melted like a flaming marshmallow on a stick. Anger smoldered below the surface. Still, he couldn't stop reading.

OREGON TRAIL 1847

Four weeks had gone by since Mac married Celeste and left Independence. But Robert Sable had made life miserable for them and the rest of the thirty men, women, and children in his party. The man simply wasn't smart. The week before he had shot too soon and scared off an entire family of deer, thus sentencing the travelers to beans and cornmeal cakes for the tenth day in a row. And now he wanted to cross a raging river, swollen after two days of rain.

"I tell you, we can make it."

Doc Turner shook his gray head with a vehemence unusual for the mild-mannered physician. "No. If we try to cross now, we will lose our possessions and perhaps even our lives. We must wait until the water recedes."

Sable's breath left him in a rush. "We will lose precious time. There's no telling how long it will take for the river to go down."

Mac moved in next to the doctor and took up the cause. "James is right. We can't take any chances with our families' lives."

Eyes glittering dangerously, Robert Sable turned to Mac. "Who is in charge here?"

"You are," he replied, keeping his voice calm, "But we can't follow you into an avoidable danger."

Murmurs of agreement came from the other six men in the group. Still visibly shaken by what he apparently considered betrayal, Robert gave a curt nod. "All right. I can see I'm outnumbered. We'll camp here until the river recedes." He stalked off toward the wagon he shared with his pregnant wife, Prudence.

James shook his head. "That fool will get us all killed if we don't elect a new leader."

"I agree," said Floyd Hiram, a burly blacksmith. "I say we settle it right now. Penbrook, I vote for you to be the new leader."

The other men all voiced their agreement. Doc clapped Mac on the shoulder. "Well, that settles it. Want me to go with you to break the news to Sable?"

Taken aback, Mac shook his head. He was no leader. Had no desire to be the man in charge. "Find someone else. I don't want trouble with Sable."

Indeed, Mac intended to lay low and take care of Celeste. She was the most important thing to him, and he didn't intend to draw negative attention to them.

"Look, Penbrook." Floyd moved forward, towering over Mac. "It's either you or Sable. Except for the doc here, we're all farmers and blacksmiths. None of us can lead the train west."

"I'm not qualified to lead the group, either," Mac insisted. "This is the farthest west I've ever been. I don't know the terrain or the native tribes. I'm not any more qualified than the rest of you."

Doc Turner leveled a gaze at Mac. "Walk with me, my friend."

Mac followed him away from the circle of wagons. "Now, see here, Mac. Those men are right. We need a strong leader who commands respect. By virtue of your station in life, you have risen to a place of respect in this group. You've worked harder than anyone and seem to be the only one who can make Sable listen to reason. You have to realize that you are the logical choice."

When he put it that way, Mac could see his point. Still, he had no desire to take on the role. "I didn't sign on for any kind of leadership, Doc. I just want to get my wife to Oregon Territory and begin a new life with her there. That's all. I have no desire for a position of authority."

"Which is perhaps your best qualification. Are you going to turn your back on this group and continue to allow Sable to lead us with his bad decisions?"

"All right. I'll do my best. But I can't promise to be a great leader. Or even a good one."

"Your best is all we ask." Doc's face broke into a smile. "Let's go break the news to Sable."

As Senator Dane lay in the hospital bed, he observed his son with a collage of feelings coursing through him. No father wanted his child to be convicted of murder. But at what point did Sam need to pay for his crimes against that poor girl and her white lover? And how much responsibility did he, as Sam's father, bear for the hatred his son felt toward black people, especially anyone who dared mix races?

As a child, Sam had heard his mother's accusations after she discovered Samuel's affair with Andy's mother. Senator Dane still remembered the sickened shock on the boy's face. He'd done his best to try to make it up to him over the years, but now he had to wonder if he'd done Sam any favors. Overindulged and undisciplined. That's the way he'd spent his entire life. Why should things be any different now?

"So, the jury found you innocent?"

"Are you disappointed?"

"Don't be ridiculous, son."

Sam walked close to the bed. "Son? Seems as though you toss that word around pretty easily, Father."

Caution played in Samuel's mind. Sam was obviously gearing up for a fight. And Samuel wasn't sure he was up for it, even though he'd felt much stronger lately. The doctor had assured him he could go home tomorrow.

Forcing himself to remain calm, Samuel returned his son's gaze. "I don't know what you're talking about, Sam. Is there something you want to say to me?"

The young man closed the distance between them in two steps. He leaned ominously over the bed and stared nose to nose with his father. "Let me tell you about the last moments of your other son's life."

Staring into eyes of hatred, Samuel knew beyond a doubt that he'd lost his namesake, the son of his marriage, to the vile monster of prejudice. "It was you?" he asked.

Sam pulled back, his mouth twisted into a sardonic half smile. "Well, I can't take all the credit, since I was locked away at the time. But let's just say my power in this county is far-reaching."

The young man was sickeningly proud of himself for ordering another man's death. Samuel's stomach turned over.

At least Andy wasn't really dead. But Samuel could never reveal that to anyone. That boy would have to get out of Georgia soon, before anyone found out he was still alive. Samuel had already lost one son. He would not lose the other.

MISSOURI 1949

Shea's head pounded and her body shuddered as she came to. "Easy, gal," came a soft female voice. "Don't try to get up just yet."

It took a minute for her to get her bearings. Then the memories came back to her. She had gotten sick on her way back to Oregon.

She sat up quickly, but the pounding in her head sent her back to the bench, where something had been placed under her head as a pillow. "Did I miss my bus?"

"Yes, but there's another one in the morning. My Sheldon is the janitor here. He asked me to come take care of you. You hungry?"

Shea opened her eyes. A smiling face greeted her. Black and kind, the epitome of generosity. "Your husband helped me carry my suitcase earlier."

"Shel's a good man. Always helping someone in need. Says the Lord sent us to you to get you through this sickness."

"What's your name?"

"Kara Mae Dougherty."

Fatigue swept over Shea and she couldn't keep her eyes open. "Thank you for your help."

"Now, honey, you stay awake for just a few minutes. Then you can come home with me and sleep in a real bed the rest of the day."

A second of hesitation pushed through Shea, but her defenses were too demolished from fever and body aches to worry about whether Kara Mae was dangerous or not. "I couldn't pay you."

"That won't be necessary. The Lord always repays when we offer ourselves as instruments for His use."

"I don't really think the Lord cares one way or another if I sleep on a bus station bench or in a nice soft bed."

"Oh, honey, Shel was right. God did send you to us. Come on, we'll catch the next city bus and get you home."

Shea remained fuzzy-headed and faded in and out of sleep as she sat on the bench waiting for the bus to arrive. Through her semiconscious mind, she heard Kara Mae raise a prayer on her behalf. "Lord, help this lost lamb find her way to You."

GEORGIA 1949

Jonas spent the better part of two days holed up with Andy, reading these confounded diaries. As if they were volumes of a fantastic novel, he'd devoured each page of Mac Penbrook's life. Jonas found it fascinating to read history from someone who had lived it.

They came across a tremendous gap in time where Shea must have taken several volumes. The last thing he read, Mac had just rescued Celeste from the Havertys. But this new diary was written many months later, after they had reached Fort Kearney and had been granted permission to pass the winter within the walls of the fort. The party of pioneers had wintered there for a few months before the fort moved to the Platte.

FORT KEARNEY 1847

Mac stood just outside the door of the sod house that Celeste and several other women called home these days. They would have to live there for the next three or four months, until the warmth of spring melted the snows over the mountains.

Celeste had changed so much, she looked nothing like the slave from Penbrook plantation. Her speech patterns had improved enough that she could pass for white. She had learned to read and write, and Mac had given her a diary of her own to practice in. She looked much healthier these days, too. And she seemed genuinely happy. She smiled often and even laughed on rare occasions.

But for the past three days, she had refused to leave her soddy. None of Mac's messages, sent through Sable's wife, Prudence, made a bit of difference. But he kept trying, every day.

Prudence appeared at the doorway. "I'm sorry, Mac. She says she wants you to go away."

Frustration edged through him. "Why?" He slapped his hat against his thigh. "Surely you must know. What have I done that my wife refuses to see me?"

A smile touched the corners of her lips but left as quickly as it had come. "That's between you and Celeste."

He turned to leave, but a rush of determination spun him back to face her. "Is there anyone in the cabin besides you and Celeste?"

Alarm rushed to her plain brown eyes. "Why?"

"Because I'm going in there."

"Now, Mac, you know the captain's orders. Men and women are not allowed in each other's soddies. You'll be in big trouble if you violate that rule."

"I don't care. I have to see my wife."

"I'm here, Mac."

Celeste appeared behind Prudence, wearing the yellow gown he loved so much and draped in a lacy shawl. Mac drew a breath at the sight of her. Her face was pale and her eyes and nose swollen, as though she were either suffering from illness or had been crying. He wasn't sure which scenario was preferable. "Honey, what's wrong? Are you ill?"

"Let's walk, Mac. I suppose I can't keep this from you forever."

She took his proffered arm and they walked away from Prudence and the cabin. A shudder rippled through her.

Mac stopped and took his wife by the shoulders, forcing her to meet his gaze. "All right. Tell me what's wrong."

Tears flooded her hazel eyes, and Mac felt like a cad. "I'm sorry, darling. I didn't mean to startle you."

Celeste threw herself into his arms, nearly knocking the breath from him. He relished the warmth of her body against him, but that was soon replaced with worry as sobs wracked her small frame.

Soldiers and civilians passed them, some on foot, others on horseback, all staring unabashedly. Mac looked about for a place with a little more privacy. "Come on." He pushed her gently from him and wrapped his arm around her shoulders, guiding her to a spot behind his own cabin. Once there, he produced a white handkerchief and gently dried the tears from her cheeks. He pressed the cloth into her trembling hands.

"Th–thank you."

Mac bent at the waist and gently kissed her forehead. "Now. What's all this about?"

"I—" She looked away, assaulted by a fresh onslaught of tears.

"What is it? Your hesitance is only making me imagine the worst."

Her eyes fixed on him, and her next words sent waves of warning through his stomach. "When you imagine the worst, what do you think of?"

What a question. Taken aback, Mac frowned. "I don't know. I guess the worst thing that could happen is for you to stop loving me."

Her expression softened and she shook her head. "It isn't that. I love you more every day. But—"

"But what?"

"You won't love me anymore when you find out what I have to tell you."

Nearly weak with relief, Mac took her hands in his and brought them to his lips. He pulled her close, pressing their clasped hands to his chest. "There is nothing you can do or say to make me stop loving you, Celeste. Don't you know that by now?"

"Mac, I'm with child."

Uncertain he'd heard her correctly, Mac stared mutely at his wife. She couldn't be. They'd never. . . She hadn't been ready when they first married, and then they were separated by the limited space available at the fort. "Are—are you sure?"

She nodded, misery etching her face as tears streamed down her cheeks afresh.

Nausea crammed at his gut. *Oh Lord, say it isn't so. It can't be.* After all she'd endured, now she was carrying her rapist's child?

"I saw Doc Turner three days ago. He says the babe should come sometime in early spring. I–I'm so sorry, Mac."

Mac couldn't move. He couldn't speak. He had to get away. To think. The woman he loved, the woman who had been so hurt that she couldn't share his bed, was now carrying his brother's child.

"I'll understand if you don't want me to come with you the rest of the way. I can stay here and take in washing, or travel back east when the troops switch out in the spring."

He saw the hurt in her eyes, but he couldn't comfort her. All he saw when he looked at his wife was the image of Henry brutalizing her because he hadn't been there to protect the woman he loved. And now, even though he'd done everything possible to get her to safety, it wasn't enough. She'd always have a reminder of that night. As would he. "Come. I'll walk you back to your cabin."

As they ambled across the field, Mac chastised himself for his feelings. What sort of man didn't want any part of the child growing inside his wife's body?

Chapter Eighteen
Georgia 1949

Andy stepped carefully from the library to the foyer to answer the knock at the door. He still moved cautiously but was glad to be out of the bedroom and able to navigate the stairs enough to allow himself a change of atmosphere. At least for the amount of time per day that Miss Delta allowed him while she cleaned and aired out his room.

Jonas had driven into town to peruse the local newspaper office and to wire his pop the story of Sam's trial. Delta was upstairs working. So when the bell rang, Andy was the only one available to answer. He reached the door and opened it just as the bell rang once more.

The senator's driver stood on the porch. Andy peeked over the man's shoulder but couldn't tell if anyone else was in the car. "What can I do for you?"

"Senator Dane wants to know if you are receiving visitors."

"He's here?"

"Yes."

"I suppose since we've both been at death's door lately," he said with a grin, "the least I can do is invite him in to swap all the scary details."

Without cracking a smile, the driver nodded. "I'll go tell him then."

Andy watched from the doorway as the driver opened the back door and a frail-looking Samuel Dane Sr. exited the car. He leaned heavily on his driver as he climbed the porch steps, then stopped. "Thank you, Karl. I'll be all right now."

"Yes, sir." Karl turned away without another word.

The senator's face expressed all the joy and relief of a man whose child was lost and has been found. Andy couldn't help but feel affection for his father. "Come in, sir."

"Thank you, my boy." He patted Andy's arm as he stepped over the threshold into Penbrook House. Andy led him into the library.

The senator took a seat in the leather wing chair, his face showing relief as he sat. He settled his fedora on the arm of the chair and looked at Andy, smiling as brightly as his fatigued features allowed. "It's wonderful to see you looking so well."

"Thank you, sir." Andy sat on a matching leather sofa across from his father.

"You can't really say the same about me, can you?" Senator Dane let out a low chuckle. "I'm afraid I'm on my last leg. And look every inch of it."

Andy frowned, surprised at how deeply the statement—and the senator's condition—affected him. "Don't say that. I'm sure you have many years ahead of you."

"If only I hadn't wasted the years I could have spent fathering you, Andy."

"We don't need to talk about that, do we?" No, they didn't. Andy couldn't. "I had a wonderful upbringing after my tenth year, when I went to live with the Rileys. My mother understood your life when she started a relationship with you. I don't blame you."

"You make the entire situation sound very cold and unfeeling. It wasn't that way between your mother and myself."

"I apologize. I don't know how it was." Nor did he care to know, but he had the feeling the senator was here for a reason. Perhaps to purge his conscience?

"I loved your mother, Andy. I knew the relationship was wrong—she and I both being married to other people. But we fell in love almost instantly and. . ." He hesitated. "You know the rest."

"Yes. My mother became pregnant, and her husband assumed I was his until my white features became so prominent. Then he figured out that Mother had been unfaithful."

"Which he was himself on many occasions. Not to mention the beatings your mother took."

"And I."

His face went ashen. "I didn't know about those until you were older. When I found out, I tried to get her to leave him, but she decided to send you away instead. She didn't think she could care for her other children without her husband."

"So I was the sacrificial lamb." Surprised at the bitterness of his own tone, Andy tried to stuff down those long-held feelings of rejection. "She couldn't give up my brothers and sisters, but I was expendable."

"No, son. Never think of it like that. Your mother agonized over the decision. That's why you took as many beatings as you did. She couldn't bear to see you go. She finally went to Miss Penbrook, who contacted Daniel Riley in Chicago."

"Yeah. I was shipped off to Chicago, you and Mother stopped your affair, and everyone lived happily ever after." Except the lonely black kid in a white man's world who had no idea why his mother had sent him away.

"I was miserable without her. I would have divorced my wife and run off with her if not for Sam. But my son needed me."

"I understand. And I'm sure my mother did, too."

"She wouldn't have left her husband and children for me any more than I could have for her. There were too many lives involved."

"The needs of the many outweigh the needs of the one," Andy said, quoting *A Tale of Two Cities*. But he heard the bitterness in his tone, felt the clamping of his heart.

"It was wrong of us, but we sincerely felt that was the best choice for your life. I couldn't take care of you, and staying in that house with an abusive stepfather was no option either."

Andy fought the rush of resentment, the words spilling into his mind. All the things he'd wanted to say ever since discovering that the senator was his father. He opened his mouth to speak, but before he could, the front door burst open.

Andy left the library, headed for the entry. He stopped short, fear gripping his insides, his heartbeat increasing at a furious pace. He prayed he wouldn't faint as four white-hooded men rushed toward him.

MISSOURI 1949

The bright sun shining in her eyes woke Shea from a sound sleep. Waking up in an unfamiliar bed threw her a little until she remembered where she was and why. Her throat still hurt, as did her head, but a quick hand pressed to her forehead confirmed her fever had broken. She sat up and looked around at what was obviously a child's room.

Her dress was laid carefully over a rocking chair in the corner. Shea's legs trembled as she crawled out of bed and walked over to her dress. The woman from last night—Sheldon's wife—must have laundered it, because it looked and smelled fresh. But how had she had time to do such a thing?

Determined to find an answer, Shea slipped her dress over her head and buttoned it up the back with some difficulty. She opened the door and walked into a small, cozy kitchen that smelled of cinnamon and fresh bread.

Shea was about to venture beyond the empty kitchen through the opposite doorway when her hostess bustled in and went straight to the oven. "Lands, girl. You shouldn't be out of bed. You're about as sick as anyone I've ever seen."

"My fever's gone."

"I wouldn't doubt it with all the sweatin' you done yesterday. Sleepin' and sweatin'. I wondered if you was ever going to do anything else."

"I'm sorry to have been a bother."

Kara Mae pulled a baking pan from the oven, set it on the stove, and turned, plunking her hands on rounded hips. "Now, who said anything about you bein' a bother? It was my pure joy to look after one of Jesus' lambs. We's just His hands and feet on this earth." She pointed to the kitchen table and chairs. "Sit on down and I'll fix you something to eat."

Shea was on the verge of refusing. She never wanted anyone to feel obligated to look after her. But her stomach grumbled loudly in response to the heavenly aroma wafting throughout the kitchen from the pan on the stove. Cinnamon rolls, unless Shea missed her guess. She moved to the scarred table and mismatched chairs and sat.

From the corner of her eye, Shea caught movement and turned. A child of no more than five stood in the doorway, holding a raggedy bear in one hand, a finger stuck partway into her mouth. The little girl stared with wide brown eyes.

"Pansy, honey, come in here and meet our guest."

Reluctance edged the child's feet forward, and she eyed Shea as though she feared she might jump out at her. She reached Kara Mae and clutched on to her mother. Kara Mae pulled her loose, bending forward. She looked up at Shea with an apologetic smile. "She's never seen a white woman in our house before."

"It's all right. Nice to meet you, Pansy."

The child grinned a perfectly beautiful smile and pressed her face into her mother's thighs.

"Child, Miss Shea ain't gonna bite you. Now, you stop holding on to me so tight or I ain't gonna be able to get nothin' done."

Pansy stayed close to Kara Mae as she moved about the kitchen, her steps encumbered by the child, but seeming not to mind.

Watching mother and daughter, Shea felt regret that she would never hold a child of her own in her arms. She would never have to step over child's clutter or know the joy of tiny arms clutching her tightly for courage.

Kara Mae set a steaming cup of coffee on the table in front of Shea.

"Thank you. Just what I need." She sipped, allowing the hot liquid to trickle down her raw throat and give her a measure of relief. Her eyes followed the woman as she set about loading bacon into a pan. "What time is the next bus toward Oregon?"

"Not until this evening. We got plenty of time. My Shel is sleeping right now, but he'll be up to walk you to the bus stop when it's time."

"It'll be nice to have someone to visit with on the way to the bus station."

Kara Mae gave her an incredulous half smile. "Honey, Shel can't sit on the same seat as you."

Of course. How could she have forgotten? "I'm sorry."

A sigh rushed from Kara Mae's lungs. "I probably shouldn't have even brought you home, if you want to know the truth, but I can't resist someone who looks so lost and alone. We don't have more than a few hours, so while you eat, I want to talk about where you stand with God."

Shea felt her cheeks flush. "I'm afraid I don't stand anywhere with Him."

The woman nodded, setting a plate of bacon, eggs, and a fluffy cinnamon roll in front of Shea. Then she walked back to the counter. "That's what I figured." She poured herself a cup of coffee, Pansy a glass of milk, and placed a roll for each of them on a plate. "Tell me how you feel about God, and we'll take it from there."

This was the last conversation Shea wanted to have. "Look, I truly appreciate that you stuck out your neck for me and brought me home to sleep off my fever. But I honestly don't think God is very interested in me."

"But you do believe in Him, right?"

A shrug lifted her shoulders. "I guess so." The food was delicious, helping to ease the ache in her belly within the first few bites.

"What makes a woman believe in God but not believe that He cares anything about her life?"

The answer came without thought. "Experience." Shea spoke around a bite of the light, delicately flavored roll.

"Then you haven't had the same experience with Him as I've had."

Something about the reverence in her tone caused Shea to

sit up a little straighter and pay attention. "That's a pretty safe assumption."

"Why do you think God brought you to Shel and me if He doesn't care about your life?"

"Why do you believe that God did it? Maybe it was coincidence." She tossed Kara a grin. "Or maybe you and Shel are angels unaware."

Bold laughter exploded from deep inside the woman. "Angels? Shel? Honey, if that man of mine is an angel, I'm Lana Turner."

"If you was Lana Turner, you wouldn't be waking me up with that belly wallerin'."

Shea jumped at the sound of the deep voice. Shel stood in the doorway, a sleepy frown creasing his brow. Kara Mae rose as easily as her bulk allowed, and for the first time, Shea realized the woman was pregnant. "I'm sorry, honey. I couldn't help myself. You go on back to bed. I promise I'll be quiet."

His features softened, and he opened his long arms and enclosed his wife in an embrace. "I'm up now. Who could sleep with cinnamon rolls baking right under my nose? How about giving me one of those and some of that coffee?"

Kara rose up on her toes and smacked a kiss to her husband's dark cheek. "Sit yourself down and I'll have you some food and coffee in a jiffy."

Pansy scooted from her chair and stood at her daddy's knee until he lifted her and settled her on his lap. "Look at how pretty my little girl is looking today."

The child beamed under her father's attention.

Shea's heart clenched as she watched the affection displayed between the members of this family. What wouldn't she give to have a man to love and children to raise?

Kara's question mocked her. Why had God brought her to this couple? Perhaps to show her what she was missing. The life she would never have. Other children had mothers, but her father had murdered hers in a drunken rage. Other young women fell in love and got married, but both of the men she had loved had been ripped from her life, and the one she could have loved would never be hers.

She thought of her childhood home. It wasn't much, but it belonged to her, and no one had the right to try to weasel her out of it. Maybe she had been going about her quest all wrong. Instead of trying to take Penbrook House from Jonas, she should fight for her own Penbrook House. After all, Mac had left Georgia when his father disowned him. He'd gone to find a place where he could be his own man and live the way he chose with the woman he loved.

"Lands, Shel, would you look at that girl?"

Startled from her reverie, Shea glanced up at Kara Mae.

The woman placed her hands on her hips. "Honey, you are grinnin' like the cat that ate the canary. What is so funny?"

Shea couldn't wipe the smile from her lips. "I think I know why God might have sent me to you. This is what life is about. Love and family and staying close to your loved ones. I'm going home. And I'm staying home."

GEORGIA 1949

Jonas had that feeling again. The feeling that something wasn't right. As he neared the long Penbrook drive, he knew for sure something was out of kilter. A pickup sat in the circle drive, along with the senator's car. Angry terror burned through him. If the senator had decided he couldn't have Andy around for fear that he'd ruin the man's political career and had brought

Sam and his cowardly cronies to harm Andy, Jonas would kill them all.

He punched the gas, then eased off just as suddenly. Only a fool would rush in where he was badly outnumbered by men who were most likely armed. And Jonas didn't have a single weapon in his car. He'd never liked guns. Now he regretted that he didn't at least have a hunting rifle handy.

The crack of gunfire split the air. Jonas's heart nearly stopped. He revved the motor once more and slid to a stop as close to the house as he could. He slammed the car into PARK and jumped out, taking the steps two at a time.

He detected movement in the library and crept cautiously in that direction. The first thing he saw were two men sitting stoically on the couch, clad in white robes, but without their hoods. Jonas recognized them as two of the sheriff's deputies.

His gaze fell across the room to the body of the man lying motionless on the floor. Andy knelt over his brother Sam. The senator knelt on the other side, tears streaking the man's face. A warm breeze swept into the room through a pair of French doors that were normally kept closed.

A barrage of questions flooded his mind. What was the Klan doing in this house? Why hadn't anyone gone after the person who had obviously shot Sam and run away? But the only thing that came out of his mouth was, "What happened?"

"Sam's dead," one of the deputies said as though in a daze. "Nigger just shot him and ran away."

"Why didn't anyone go after him?"

Andy stood. "Jerome said a group of his friends were waiting outside to shoot anyone who went out after him."

Jonas scowled at the two cowards sitting on the seat. "You so-called deputies should know that's the oldest ploy in the book. He was probably alone the whole time."

One of the deputies regained his voice. "Don't matter. We know who he is."

Bolstered by his companion's words, the other man shoved to his feet. "He'll pay for killing Sam. You mark my words. Before the day's over, that nigger's gonna pay."

Chapter Nineteen
Oregon 1949

The bus pulled into Prudence, Oregon, at 9:00 a.m., and Shea hauled her weary body down the steps. She planned on leaving her bag at the station and heading straight for the newspaper office. The idea she'd had brewing on the bus ride couldn't wait. And if she didn't go now, she'd lose her nerve.

Billy Creighton did pretty much everything for the weekly publication that came out every Tuesday—reporting, editing, and typesetting. He reported on births and deaths, local crime, and anything exciting that might happen in the sleepy little town. But Shea knew people were bored. And she had an idea for how to spice things up for the patriotic folks of her hometown. And the only way she could keep her home in Oregon was to find a way to support herself.

Her pulse quickened as she entered the office, which boasted a cluttered desk, a lamp, a chair, and a telephone. No one seemed to be minding the shop, so she walked through the dusty little area. "Hello?" she called as she stepped into a back room, where a press was set up.

"Hey, what are you doing in here?"

Shea whipped around to face Billy, who was standing in the

main entryway, holding a bag from the bakery. "Is that break-fast?" she asked, nodding toward the bag.

"For me it is. What do you want, toots? I'm a little busy."

"I know you are." Shea hurried back into the little foyer. "And I don't want to keep you. But I have a proposition for you."

Billy's bespectacled eyes narrowed. "What sort of proposi-tion?" He sat at his desk and dove into the bag, pulling out a Dan-ish. Grudgingly, he pushed the bag toward her. "Want one?"

Normally, Shea would have taken the hint written all over his face that the last thing he wanted to do was share his breakfast. But her money was running out fast, and she hadn't eaten since lunch yesterday. She wasn't about to turn down free food.

"Thanks." She reached into the bag and pulled out the other Danish.

"No problem, hon," he said, as she nibbled the sweet treat. "Now, what can I do for you? Just so you know, I'm not buying anything."

She swallowed her bite. "I'm not selling anything." Gather-ing a deep breath, she leveled her gaze at the man, who looked to be in his thirties. "Actually, that's not entirely true. I *would* like to sell you something."

"Like I said, not interested."

"But you haven't even heard what it is."

"It doesn't matter. I'm broke. I'm just about to pack it in and head back to Chicago."

"You're from Chicago?"

"You got good ears, lady."

"What if I told you I could give you an ongoing serial that people will clamor for? You'll have more subscribers than you know what to do with."

"Sure, sure. Believe me, it would take an awful lot of subscribers to stump me."

Shea could tell she had the newspaperman's attention. She proceeded cautiously. "All right. There are several families here who have been around for at least four generations. Since the first settlers came. People are proud of their heritage." Most people, anyway.

"What's that got to do with getting folks to buy my paper?"

Shea leaned over the desk. "My great-great-grandfather was from a rich planter's family in Georgia before the War Between the States. He came to Oregon in 1848. I am in possession of volumes and volumes of his diaries. I propose you let me work for you. I could write his story in increments. I'll give you four weeks' worth of stories, and just see if subscriptions go up. If they don't, you don't owe me a thing. But if they do, I'd expect you to give me a steady job."

He stroked his chin. "Hmm. A serial, huh? Something to keep folks coming back for the next installment. You might be on to something here. What did you say your name is?"

"Shea." She hesitated, then forged ahead as pride shot through her heart. "Shea Penbrook." For the first time in her life, she didn't feel ashamed of her name.

"Well, Miss Penbrook, let's see what you can do." Standing, he shoved out his hand. "Welcome to the newspaper business. On a trial basis, of course."

Ten minutes later she left the office with the understanding that her first installment would be due in three days' time.

GEORGIA 1949

Jonas stood next to Andy in the tiny sharecroppers' cabin, listening to Bessie wail. "I tole him and tole him, revenge belongs to the Lawd. But he jus' been grievin' so bad over his little girl."

"Do you have any idea where he might have gone?" Jonas stepped forward. "My father is prepared to help by providing an attorney for him, but if he doesn't turn himself in, things could get a lot worse."

Bessie's sobs instantly ceased. "Mister, do you think my Jerome gots a chance in that white man's court? He wouldn't even make it to trial. If he turned hisself in, he'd be dead the fust night. Naw, he be long gone by now. I's never gonna see him again. But den, neither will anyone else 'round here."

Andy pulled his sister-in-law into his arms. "Listen, honey. You pack up the kids and you can all go back to Chicago with Jonas and me. You can't stay here. You know what will happen if you do."

Her jaw quivered. "I been expectin' 'em to show up any time an' burn me outta here."

"I'll help you get your things together. You'll all come over to Penbrook House and wait while Jonas and I pack up. We'll leave before first light."

After quickly packing the most necessary items for travel, Jonas, Andy, Bessie, and her five children headed to Penbrook House. Andy drove Bessie and the luggage, while Jonas took the children in his car. Driving was a challenge for both of them, due to their injuries, but Jonas was becoming adept at one-handed navigating, and Andy had figured out how to palm the steering wheel and gearshift.

Miss Delta met them when they entered the house. "I got all your clothes packed up and ready to go." She looked at Jonas. "You plannin' on comin' back to these parts?"

"I don't know, Miss Delta. According to those diaries I've been reading, this place probably rightfully belongs to Shea."

"You keep readin', Mr. Riley. You might find out you belong more than you think you do."

Jonas smiled at the woman's cryptic response. "I already know Old Miss Penbrook was my grandmother."

She gave a sniff. "Maybe that ain't all you need to know."

"Then why don't you just tell me?" Honestly, the woman threw out more hints than a Humphrey Bogart movie.

"Some things ain't my place to tell. But there are things you should know."

"What makes you think I'll find what I'm looking for in the diaries?"

A slow grin spread across her face. " 'Cause you ain't the only one that's been readin' 'em."

That got his attention. He'd planned on leaving them here for Shea in case she came back. But if there were clues about his own life within the pages of those old journals, how could he not take them?

Turning to the two oldest boys, both close to their teen years, he grinned. "I need help loading a trunk of books. You two want to earn a dollar?"

"Each?"

"Boys!" Bessie's horrified tone stole the excitement from their eyes.

Jonas winked at Bessie. "These are good boys, ma'am. It wouldn't bother me at all to pay them what they earn for helping me carry that trunk. Believe me, two dollars is a bargain, as heavy as that thing is."

Her expression softened. The woman had just lost her husband and had lost her daughter not long before that. Hearing someone say her sons were "good boys" obviously touched a chord in her heart. She nodded. "I guess it'll be okay."

The lads followed Jonas up the steps and into the room where the books were stored. Their expressions showed their pride as they hefted the trunk between the two of them.

They stepped out onto the porch just as a dozen men on horseback rushed from the woods, carrying torches. The boys stopped short. Jonas could feel their fear. "It's okay," he said. "Set the trunk down on the porch and go inside. Bessie," he called, "take the children into the house."

"You wait right there!" Beneath a white hood, the hate-filled voice shot into the air. He stretched out his arm, the wings of his white robe waving in the breeze as he pointed to Bessie. "I need to talk to that woman."

Jonas stepped forward just as Bessie, clutching two of her children close, reached the top of the steps. He pushed her behind him. "You're on my land. If you want to talk to anyone, you can talk to me."

"We don't got anything to say to you, Yankee boy. She knows where her husband is, and she's gonna tell us."

One of the teenage boys rushed onto the porch, slamming the door behind him. "She ain't telling you nothin'. Why don't you take off that hood and fight like a man?"

Andy grabbed the boy's arm and shoved him back into the house.

"Why don't you fellas take off?" Jonas tried to keep his tone even. But he had to admit he felt more than a little anxious. "Bessie doesn't know where Jerome is. She hasn't even told us."

"We ain't takin' your word." He dismounted. The rest of the torch-carrying, rifle-toting cowards did the same. "If you won't tell us where he is, we'll search the place until we find him."

"You aren't setting foot inside my house," Jonas said. He had to acknowledge the futility of the statement. Apparently, however, Miss Delta didn't have the same reservations. She stepped out onto the porch, shotgun in hand. "There are two shells in this thing. I can't take you all, but I can get the first two who try to step foot in Miss Cat's house."

To Jonas's surprise and amusement, the threat seemed to work. The men retreated back to the yard.

But that wasn't enough for Miss Delta. "Get your white-hooded selves off this land. You ain't got no business here."

They remained planted where they stood. Miss Delta shifted the shotgun against her shoulder. "I said, get off this land. Every last one o' ya." She cocked the trigger.

That seemed to spur the men into action. "We'll go for now," the apparent leader of the group responded as the rest began their retreat. "But we'll be watching. Mark my words." He joined his friends as the horses trotted off the property.

A wave of relief seemed to wash over the group on the porch.

"We gots to get out o' here," Bessie said, her voice taut.

Andy took hold of her arm. "If we leave now, the house will be vulnerable to the Klan. We should stay for one more day, maybe two. Until they get tired of looking for Jerome."

As much as he hated to admit it, Jonas knew Andy had a point. One of the Klan's favorite tactics seemed to be stopping victims when they were driving. For now, they would be safer staying at Penbrook.

❧

After Jonas helped Andy get Bessie and the children settled into their rooms, he returned to the trunk of diaries, which had been left in the foyer after being carried back inside. No sense lugging it back up the steps and back down again when they decided it was safe to leave.

Intrigued by Miss Delta's words about discovering something about himself in these books, Jonas took the next volume to bed with him. He read far into the night while keeping vigil.

FORT KEARNEY 1848

Celeste needed Mac, and he felt completely helpless for the first time in his life. Their relationship had been strained over the past few months as her body grew with his brother's child. Though he knew it wasn't her fault, he had a hard time accepting it.

His love for her forced him to declare that he would raise this child as his own and try to love it. But as he stood outside her cabin, listening to the sound of her groans, he wondered if he could live up to his promise.

His heart nearly stopped when she cried out, long and loud. Doc Turner and Prudence were the only two allowed to stay with her while the child was being delivered. *Just as well,* Mac decided.

The afternoon sun receded into a dusky twilight, and night finally descended, but still the baby didn't appear. When a shadowy figure caught Mac's attention sometime after midnight, his eyes followed it as it headed into Doc's cabin. He hated to leave in case Celeste called for him, but what if someone needed the doc and didn't know he was busy with Celeste?

Mac walked to the doc's quarters and stepped inside. The figure jumped and whipped around, then made a dash for the window. In an instant Mac realized this was the thief who had been stealing money from the fort over the past few months.

Mac dove and caught the man about the ankles. Both men tumbled to the floor. They struggled. Finally Mac overpowered the thief. "All right," the man said, "you caught me."

Mac nearly went limp with shock when he recognized the voice. "Sable?"

A sneer twisted his lips below a black mustache. "Don't act so high and mighty. Some of us weren't born with a silver spoon in our mouths."

"Come on." He yanked Sable to his feet. "You're going to the stockade."

As they stepped into the night air, Mac saw Prudence standing on the threshold of the cabin, looking for him. "My wife is having her baby," he said to Robert Sable. "You're coming with me. And don't try to run away."

"Where am I going to go? Outside the fort?"

They walked together to the sod cabin where both of their wives were quartered. "How is she?" Mac asked Pru.

Noticing that her face was streaked with tears, he didn't bother to ask again. She stepped aside as Mac rushed into the cabin.

The doctor stood there, wiping blood from his hands. Mac's throat went dry. He couldn't bring himself to look at the bed. "Is my wife—?"

"She'll be fine."

Mac turned and saw Celeste lying on the bed, the babe in her arms. Relief threatened to overwhelm him. "Why was Pru crying?"

Celeste held the baby out to him. "He was stillborn." Tears brimmed her lovely eyes. Sorrow such as Mac had never experienced struck his core, and tears burned his eyes. He took the babe from Celeste's arms and looked down.

"I'm sorry, Penbrook."

Mac turned to find Sable standing close, holding a weeping Pru in his arms. Sable peered at the baby and frowned. "That looks like. . ." He looked from Mac to Celeste and back to the baby.

Alarm seized Mac.

"I knew she wasn't French. Your wife is a Negro!"

"Shut up, Sable," Mac warned. "If you know what's good for you, you won't say another word."

"Mac." Celeste's pitiful voice reached through his fear and anger. "Don't start a fight, please."

Mac stared incredulously at his wife. She'd just pretty much confirmed what this man had accused her of. There would be no way to cover this up now.

A sinister grin spread across Sable's features. "Well, now. It looks like we need to talk, Penbrook."

Mac looked down at the lifeless babe in his arms. No one could deny the child had African blood, despite the fact that his mother was only a quarter black and his father was a white man.

He turned his gaze to Celeste, and their eyes met in a long, pain-filled stare. How could God have been so cruel?

Shea stood in her driveway and stared at the pile of rubble that had once been her home. She had a job now, but no longer had a place to live. How could that man have demolished her home? The longer she gazed at the heap, the angrier she became.

No one had bothered to move Granddad's truck, so she slammed across the yard, yanked open the door, and fired up the motor after several tries. She spun her tires and flung dirt across four miles of back fields, broke through three fences, and skidded to a stop in front of the Sable mansion.

She ran up the stairs and burst into the place without bothering to ring the bell. "Sable!" she yelled. "Jackson Sable, where are you, you low-down skunk?"

"Shea?"

Gasping for breath, Shea whipped around at the sound of Colin's voice. He stood in the doorway, shock and amusement covering his features. "What are you doing here?"

"I'm here to see your cowardly, stinking father. Where is he?"

Mr. Sable strode down the winding staircase. "Really, Miss Penbrook. There's no call for a young lady to come into a man's house and insult him. Especially the likes of you."

"The likes of *me*? What's that supposed to mean?" She rushed on before he had a chance to answer. "You think because I don't have as much money as you do that I'm not as good as you? Well, let me tell you something, mister. I've learned a thing or two since I've been gone. Like that worth isn't measured in dollars and cents but in one's ability to look past those surface things and see a person's heart. You might have taken my land, but you'll never again shove me under your feet."

"Please, Miss Penbrook."

"That's right. I am a Penbrook. And I'm proud to have that name. My great-great-grandfather was an honorable man. He loved and lived and died with honor. But you! You are a sorry excuse for a human being. Enjoy those ten acres. You're welcome to them. But I'm staying right here. I'm going to make sure everyone knows the name of Penbrook. And I'm going to make something of the name."

"Well said, my dear."

Shea whipped around as Mrs. Sable entered the room to her right.

"Julia, please," Jackson whispered.

"Please what? Please tell the girl she isn't to be commended for being determined to rise above her station in life despite all odds?" She gave him a mocking grin. "Why, that's the American dream."

Shea wasn't entirely sure whether or not the woman was mocking her. She turned back to Mr. Sable. "You stole my land. Now, where's my money?"

"*Stole* is such a harsh word. Everything I did was legal."

"No judge had the legal right to give you that land, and if you didn't own the law around here, you wouldn't have gotten it."

"Well said again."

"Julia!" Mr. Sable's voice thundered across the room, causing Shea to jump.

The woman ignored him and turned to Colin. "You see, my son, this is the girl you should have married. Full of spunk. But then, maybe it isn't too late." She eyed Shea. "His wife ran off. Did you know that?"

Shea turned to face Colin. "I'm so sorry."

"She has asked me for a divorce, which I will gladly grant. It's the best thing she's ever done for me." He took Shea's hand. "Do you think there could be a second chance for us?"

The room began to spin. Was she really standing in the entryway of the Sable mansion, confronting Jackson Sable, being championed by Colin's mother, and being courted by Colin? Or was this some crazy dream?

"Don't be ridiculous, son," Mr. Sable's voice knifed the air, confirming that this was no dream.

"Father, I will not allow you to dictate my life anymore.

Mother's right. I should have married Shea to begin with. No matter what sort of family she comes from. I love her. I always have."

He pulled Shea close and pressed her hands against his chest. His eyes shone with undeniable passion. "What do you say? Will you be my wife?"

"I will not allow it!" Jackson Sable looked as though he might burst a few blood vessels in his head.

"Calm down." Shea pulled her hands away from Colin. "My answer is no anyway."

"What?" Colin frowned down at her.

"Colin, I got over you two months after you decided I wasn't good enough for you."

"I never thought that! It was my father. He would have disowned me."

"I understand. I truly do." Shea gave him a smile. "But if I ever marry, it will be to a man who would risk being disowned for me." The way Mac did for Celeste.

"But I love you."

"For the love of God, Colin," Mrs. Sable spoke up, "stop groveling." She smiled at Shea. "You are a brave young woman. Much braver than I ever was."

"Thank you, ma'am." Shea didn't want to know what the woman was referring to, but she could imagine the regret in her heart at being married to a man like Jackson Sable.

Mrs. Sable cocked her head and stared at her husband. "Well, since you've obviously destroyed this young woman's home, I trust you intend to compensate her amply."

Mr. Sable's lips curled into a sneer. "I have already deposited a fair price for the land in an account at the bank. That's all I intend to do."

"Oh, I know how much you deposited. And it isn't nearly enough to compensate for what you've taken from this family."

"Mrs. Sable," Shea interjected, "I don't want anything from him except a fair price. If he says he paid it, I believe him." She turned to him. "I'll have that bank account number, sir."

Jackson stared at her as if she were a complete stranger. And in a way, she was. Shea knew she bore little resemblance to the woman she was when he saw her last.

CHAPTER TWENTY
GEORGIA 1949

A heavy *thud* woke Jonas from a sound sleep. He shot up and swung his legs around, then noticed the diary had slipped off the bed. Just as he was about to lie back down, he heard screams.

✤

Andy's heart nearly stopped at the sound of Miss Delta's screams. He sprang from his bed and slid into his trousers, fastening them on the run. Heavy smoke greeted him when he opened his bedroom door. He covered his face. "Jonas!"

Jonas's door opened.

"Fire!"

Together they rousted Bessie and the children and made their way down the steps. Flames shot out from the kitchen. Andy's stomach sank. Penbrook House would not be saved.

They headed straight for the front door. Jonas stopped, taking one end of the trunk of diaries. "Help me, Lamont." The boy took hold of the other end and they carried the trunk out to the yard.

Moments later they stood on the grass, watching fire consume the antebellum mansion. Andy imagined Cat, Henry, Madeline, their young daughter Camilla. . .and Mac Penbrook and his beloved Celeste.

Bessie moved the children farther away from the building as heat from the fire filled the night air.

Tears coursed down Miss Delta's leathery cheeks, and a moan erupted from deep within her. Jonas slipped his arm around her. "I'm sorry, Miss Delta."

"I'm sorry, too, Mr. Riley. Your family heritage is goin' up in smoke. And there ain't no good reason for it."

"I know. I know."

"You don't know nothing, boy."

The gruffness of her tone startled Andy. He turned to find her pulling away from Jonas.

She gave Andy an accusatory glare. "You never even told him, did ya?"

"Told me what?" Jonas asked.

"About Miss Penbrook."

"I do know, Miss Delta," Jonas assured her. "I know she was my grandmother. I told you that."

Andy drew a deep breath. "I know what you must be feeling, Miss Delta," he said, trying to soothe her and at the same time silence her.

"Do you?" She turned back to Jonas. "He never told you that Miss Penbrook was his grandma, too."

"You must be confused," Jonas said, his patient tone surprising Andy. Jonas had mellowed considerably over the last few weeks.

"I ain't confused about nothing. Am I, Andy?"

The old lady wouldn't let up. Grief had loosened her

tongue, and Andy knew Jonas was about to be told the whole truth.

"Jonas," he said, "it's true. Cat was my great-grandmother. She had my grandfather out of wedlock when she was only fifteen years old. He was already an adult by the time your father was born."

A grin spread across Jonas's features. "Well, I can't think of anyone I'd rather have as part of my family than you. So, which one of your ancestors married a Negro?"

"My grandfather, Hank."

A strange laugh left Jonas. "Wouldn't the Klan have something to be appalled about if they knew about this? A white man and a black man related through the same white woman."

"Miss Cat wasn't white," Delta said. "Not entirely."

"I'm not following you."

"Her skin and her hair color were light brown. Her features were delicate. But she was a slave, bought by Madeline Penbrook when she was about four years old. She only had a small amount of Negro blood in her, but back then, that was enough. The one-eighth of her blood that was Negro qualified her for the auction block."

Jonas stared back at Andy. "All this time I thought. . ."

"What?"

Regret slid across Jonas's face. "So our grandmother wasn't the rightful heir to Penbrook?"

Andy shook his head. "Not by blood, anyway."

"She was, too." Delta's voice slammed across the open space between them. "Her blood was spilled over and over again for this land. First by that monster Henry Penbrook. And then when she fought to save this place after the war. She worked harder than anyone, and she deserved every inch of Penbrook."

"I agree," Andy said.

Jonas turned to him. "But legally, she was a squatter. No one ever officially gave her the house."

"I suppose you're right."

"Then Shea is the rightful heir. The land should go to her."

Daniel Riley stared at the letter on his desk. He'd read through it three times and knew he had to give it to Jonas. It had been two weeks since he and Andy had returned from Georgia. The house had been nearly leveled in the fire and would soon be torn down the rest of the way.

Jonas had discovered his true heritage. Being part Negro didn't seem to have any effect on him, but knowing that Shea Penbrook was the rightful owner did. He'd been trying to find her for weeks now, but even the diaries were no help in locating her. All they knew was that she was somewhere in Oregon.

Jonas appeared at the doorway of his office. "You sent for me, Pops?"

"I received a letter I think will interest you."

"Oh?"

Daniel picked up the page and handed it over.

Jonas glanced down and read aloud.

Dear Mr. Riley,

Please forgive the intrusion, but the letter I sent to Jonas at Penbrook House was returned to me. He agreed to send me my trunk of diaries in the event that I didn't come back to Georgia. I have decided not to return.

Please give Jonas my best and ask him to send the trunk at his earliest convenience.

Shea

P.S. I am enclosing the fifty dollars you paid me in advance for a job I didn't complete.

Daniel watched the emotions play out across his son's face. "It appears your Shea Penbrook has decided not to pursue the land after all. What do you think we should do?"

Jonas snatched up the envelope from the desk, turned it over, and read the return address. "Prudence, Oregon. I should have known." He jerked his head up, eyes blazing in a way Daniel had never seen in his son. "Will you get the document ready for me? I'm leaving in the morning."

OREGON 1949

Shea gave the paper a frustrated yank, pulling it free from the typewriter.

Billy chuckled. "You'll get the hang of it. Eventually."

"I hope so."

"By the way, we got two new letters to the editor this morning. Did you see them?"

Shea looked up, almost fearfully. "Good or bad?"

"One of each."

She breathed in relief. The paper's subscription numbers had doubled in the three weeks she'd been writing her serial. Billy was ecstatic and had already made her a permanent employee, without waiting the full four weeks.

He didn't seem to mind the negative responses. Some folks called it smut. Others praised Billy's and Shea's courage. But they were all buying the paper.

Some readers treated her column like a novel. She knew it would never be accepted in a Southern paper, but here in the North, it was a lovely, romantic story. And even if she was completely ostracized, she would never again be ashamed of being who she was. She was Shea Penbrook, and her great-great-grandmother had been one-quarter black. And she didn't care who knew about it.

She only wished Jonas would hurry up and send her the diaries so she could finish the story. She had plenty of material to last a few months from the diaries she'd already read. But those wouldn't last forever.

Jonas. Her heart always picked up a beat at the thought of him. Miss Nell had prodded her to go back and fight for the Penbrook land in Georgia, but Shea didn't want to take it away from Jonas. The idea of living on Penbrook land lost some of its magic when she thought of Jonas losing it.

With the money Jackson had paid her for the land, she had decided to pay off the remainder of the loan on Miss Nell's house, despite her old friend's protests. Then she rented a small apartment over the doctor's office on Main Street.

"I'm going to the diner to get a bite to eat," Billy said. "You coming?"

Shea shook her head. "I want to finish this week's story. Besides, Miss Nell has been feeling a bit poorly, so I told her I'd pick up some things for her at the store during my lunch break."

"Suit yourself."

An hour and ten ruined sheets of paper later, Shea finally finished just as the door opened.

"Shea. Someone's here to see you."

She glanced up and caught her breath. *Jonas?*

Billy grinned. "He a friend of yours?"

Unable to find her voice, Shea could only nod.

"I thought so. He was asking about you over at the diner. I offered to bring him to you if he bought my lunch."

"Billy!"

He grinned. "Don't go working yourself into an uproar, doll. I'm just kidding."

Shea gave him an exasperated huff.

"Pops got your letter," Jonas said.

"I figured as much, since you knew where to bring the diaries." She smiled. "What are you doing here?"

"I brought your diaries."

A squeal found its way to her throat. "Oh, Jonas, you didn't have to come all this way just to bring them to me. But thank you." She wanted to rush forward and throw herself into his arms.

He tossed his hat onto the desk and walked up to her. He held out his hand. "That's not the only reason I came."

She slipped her hand into his and allowed him to pull her to her feet. "It's not?"

He shook his head and sucked in a sharp breath. "I missed you."

"You did?"

"Yeah. You have a way of getting under my skin."

Billy walked across the room. "Don't I know the feeling!"

"Billy!" Shea nearly exploded. "Go away."

"Fine, fine. I'll be at the diner. Lock up when you lovebirds are done, will you?" He closed the door behind him.

An uncommon shyness fell over Shea and she felt her cheeks grow warm. "Sorry about him."

"Should I be jealous?"

She laughed. "Billy chases every skirt in town, but he's all talk. Everyone around here knows not to take him seriously."

Jonas slipped his arm around her waist and drew her close. He lowered his head.

At the first touch of his lips on hers, Shea understood the love Mac and Celeste shared. She understood why a man would give up his inheritance. This kind of love was consuming. She wanted to become completely lost in this feeling. Her arms slipped around his neck and he drew her closer, deepening his kiss.

When they pulled apart, Shea smiled. "So you had two reasons to come find me."

He chuckled and gave her a quick kiss on the nose. "Actually, there's one more."

"Oh?"

He reached into his pocket and pulled out a document, holding it out for her.

Shea took it. "What's this?"

"Read it."

She did, then stared back at him. "I don't understand. What does this mean?"

"It means, my dear, that you are the rightful heir to the Penbrook land in Oak Junction, Georgia."

A gasp tore at her throat. "You knew?"

"We figured it out."

"But how?"

"The diaries, mostly, but also the letter you got while you were there, addressed to Shea Penbrook. It didn't take Sam Spade to put two and two together."

"But I want you to have the property."

"The woman who willed it to us had every moral claim but no legal claim to the land."

"What do you mean?"

"Cat Penbrook wasn't related to the family by blood. She was a light-skinned slave. After the Penbrooks all died off, she was the only one left, so she sort of took over the place."

"Oh my."

"So you see—the land really is yours." He paused. "The old lady made a legitimate fortune for herself through her writings. She left the money to my father because he was her son," Jonas explained.

Something didn't seem right. But Shea shoved the niggling feeling aside. "So that beautiful home is mine?"

He flinched. "Actually. . .Penbrook House is gone, Shea."

Her stomach tightened. "What do you mean?"

"The Klan burned it after Jerome killed Sam Dane. They thought he was hiding out at Penbrook."

Her heart sank for all the misery that had been caused. "How did the senator take it?"

"Badly. He resigned his seat and is living in Chicago with Andy and Lexie. But his health is failing. I'm afraid he's not long for this earth."

"Oh, Jonas." Shea couldn't seem to tear her eyes off the document in her hands. "Your grandmother was a slave."

"And so was your great-great-grandmother." The corners of his lips tilted slightly. "I think that pretty much proves that we belong together. Don't you?"

"Definitely." Shea laughed.

"Only one more question remains, then." Jonas pulled her close. "Will you marry me?"

Shea heard the words as though a melody played in her heart. She wrapped her arms about his neck and looked deeply into his eyes. "Where have you been all my life?"

"Waiting for you." Bending his head, Jonas kissed her. When he pulled away, the look in his eyes left no doubt about the sovereignty of God.

This man had driven across the country to find her. He'd given up his claim to the Penbrook land for her. And he loved her with all of his heart.

Jonas smiled. "So, where are we going to live?"

"Wherever you want."

"Let's figure it out later. For now I just want to enjoy being with you. If you're willing, we could go to Chicago so you can meet my mother."

"Sounds wonderful."

"Would you mind having our wedding there?"

"Not at all. Only I have one problem."

He frowned. "What's that?"

Shea sent him a teasing grin. "How am I going to break the news to Billy?"

EPILOGUE
OREGON 1848

Mac and Celeste stood side by side at the site of their new home. The two-story farmhouse wasn't fancy by any means, but it had everything Mac needed to be happy: Celeste.

"Think Robert will keep his promise?" she asked.

"He will."

Only the four of them and the doctor knew about Celeste's past. And only the four of them and the doctor knew about Sable's thievery. It was a deal Mac was willing to make in order to keep Celeste safe.

Though Celeste had mourned the death of her baby, they had finally been able to put Henry behind them and truly become man and wife.

"Well, Mrs. Penbrook," he said, sweeping his bride into his arms, "are you ready to go inside your new home?"

Her skin darkened in a blush. "I am."

He carried her over the threshold and set her down in the living room. It was the first time Celeste had seen it fully built and furnished. Her eyes grew round. "A grandfather clock! Oh, Mac. I always loved the one in your mama's house."

"Every woman should have one in her home."

"And there's something every man should have." She looked up at him, her eyes shining with joy.

"What's that?"

"A child of his own."

Mac gulped hard. "Do you mean you're going to have a baby?"

She nodded. "Is that all right?"

"All right?" He lifted her and swung her around until they were both dizzy. When he set her down, they tumbled into each other's arms.

After several moments, her eyes clouded. "Mac, what if our baby looks like a Negro?"

"It's possible," he said. "But he or she will still be our child. And we'll deal with whatever comes."

"I love you, Mac Penbrook. And I'm proud to be your wife."

Mac's heart swelled with love for this woman. He pulled her close, cradling her in his arms. There were many things about the future that confused and concerned him. But one thing he knew: He would love this woman for the rest of his life.

CHICAGO 1951
"That's the last one."

Shea wiped away tears from her swollen face. She lay beside her husband and accepted the handkerchief he pressed into her hand. "I wonder why Mac didn't write any more after this."

"Maybe once you find what you're looking for, you're too busy living life to spend time writing about it."

"Could be. I'm glad Miss Nell was able to tell me the rest of the story. Like that my great-grandfather was born looking as white as you and I." Shea sighed and rolled onto her back. "I wonder if it would have made a difference if he had been unable to hide the black features."

"No. Mac moved heaven and earth to be with that woman. He would have moved heaven and earth to make sure his child was safe, too."

"I suppose you're right."

Jonas turned onto his side and placed his hand on Shea's belly. "Speaking of which, how's my baby doing?"

"I wish he'd come out and tell you himself." She'd been pregnant forever, it seemed.

"*Himself?* You think it'll be a boy?"

"How would I know? I'm not God."

Jonas chuckled and kissed her nose. "You little grouch."

"You'd be a grouch, too, if your belly was so big you couldn't see your toes."

"Why do you want to see your toes? They're too long and skinny anyway."

Shea laughed and tossed a pillow at him. He caught it easily and pulled her close.

"Do you know how much I love you?"

"I think so, but tell me anyway."

"I love you so much, if I ever lost you I'd travel across the country—no, the whole world—to find you and bring you back to me."

"Is that all?"

"Ungrateful."

"You'll have to do better than that," she teased.

"I love you so much, I'd give up houses and lands, family and friends for one hour in your arms."

Shea closed her eyes and released a slow, contented sigh. "Now, that's the kind of love I've always dreamed of."

TRACEY BATEMAN

Tracey Bateman has over a dozen stories in print. Her life is filled with chaos and fun due to comical kids and a supportive husband. When not writing, she spends time with family and friends, reads works by her favorite authors, and attends a rapidly growing contemporary church where the focus is on raising the standard for God. She has adopted this philosophy in her own life and strives for excellence in every area. She believes all things are possible and encourages everyone to dream big. Tracey lives with her husband and four children in Missouri. For more information, visit www.traceybateman.com.

The Penbrook Diaries

BOOK 1

FREEDOM of the SOUL

by Tracey Bateman

The year is 1948. When a young black reporter, Andy Carmichael, travels to segregated Georgia to cover the story that will make his career, he finds there is more at stake than an article. His marriage, his life, his very soul are on the line.

"*The Color of the Soul* kept me guessing to the very last page. Tracey Bateman does a masterful job of weaving between the decades, tying stories of past and present together in a way that points to God's redemptive nature."

~Deborah Raney, author of
A Vow to Cherish and *Remember to Forget*

"Gritty and powerful, this story will remain in your thoughts long after you've read the final page."

~Judith Miller, author of the Freedoms' Path series;
coauthor of the Bells of Lowell and Lights of Lowell series

"Bateman tunnels below skin-deep differences, past the qualifiers that set us apart, to common ground. This is one of those rare stories which has filled my thoughts long after I reached the end."

~Susan K. Downs, coauthor of the Heirs of Anton series

Available at bookstores everywhere.

Heirs of Anton

by Susan K. Downs and Susan May Warren

Heirs of Anton: Ekaterina

When an unusual package arrives in the mail, Ekaterina "Kat" Moore boards a plane to Russia, her ancestral home, to seek some answers—and perhaps find love.
ISBN 1-59310-161-9

Heirs of Anton: Nadia

Former CIA spy Nadia Moore is sneaking into Russia to save her husband from a gulag execution. But can she resurrect the love she thought had died?
ISBN 1-59310-163-5

Heirs of Anton: Marina

When Russia is invaded by Hitler, Marina finds herself alone and pregnant. If she does—or doesn't—fight for the motherland, what will be her child's future?
ISBN 1-59310-350-6

Heirs of Anton: Oksana

Oksana harbors a state secret so dangerous she dares not share it with the man she loves. Will Anton's fledgling courage destroy her future?
ISBN 1-59310-349-2

Also available from
BARBOUR PUBLISHING, INC.